ENTER THE ENCHANTING WORLDS OF

Anne Logston

Praise for her previous novels:

"The rising star of Anne Logston burns brightly."
—*Romantic Times*

"Bright, cheerful, and charming, hotly spiced with magic and intrigue."
—Simon R. Green, bestselling author of *Robin Hood: Prince of Thieves*

"A fun mix of magic, culture-clash, and fast-paced adventure that pushes all the right buttons."
—*Locus*

"Highly recommended. Playfulness and pathos blend to form an entertaining and thought-provoking story."
—*Starlog*

"Entertaining . . . plenty of magic, demons, and other dangers."
—*Science Fiction Chronicle*

"Rollicking good adventure."
—*Science Fiction Review*

Ace Books by Anne Logston

SHADOW
SHADOW HUNT
SHADOW DANCE
GREENDAUGHTER
DAGGER'S EDGE
DAGGER'S POINT
WILD BLOOD
GUARDIAN'S KEY
FIREWALK
WATERDANCE

WATERDANCE

Anne Logston

ACE BOOKS, NEW YORK

This book is an Ace original edition,
and has never been previously published.

WATERDANCE

An Ace Book / published by arrangement with
the author

PRINTING HISTORY
Ace edition / April 1999

The Penguin Putnam Inc. World Wide Web site address is
http://www.penguinputnam.com

Check out the ACE Science Fiction & Fantasy newsletter
and much more at Club PPI!

ISBN: 0-441-00613-2

ACE®
Ace Books are published
by The Berkley Publishing Group,
a member of Penguin Putnam Inc.,
375 Hudson Street, New York, New York 10014.
ACE and the "A" design are trademarks
belonging to Charter Communications, Inc.

PRINTED IN THE UNITED STATES OF AMERICA

10 9 8 7 6 5 4 3 2 1

To my husband Paul,
who puts up with my hours and my moods

—and to Jeff,
who trusted me with the truth and didn't laugh too hard
at my poetry.

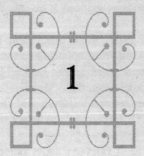

1

CROSSING THE BORDER OF AGROND, RIDING TO her doom, Peri thought wistfully that the Bregondish plains knew no shame.

The hot, harsh wind known as Mahdha, the Breath of Bregond, blew through the razorgrass, stirring it to a sibilant rustle and sucking away the sweat from Peri's neck. The hard-packed earth of the road still managed to raise puffs of dust at the horses' and wagons' passage. Somewhere to the south, a hawk cried in triumph that meant death for some other creature.

And that, Peri thought with a sigh, *says it all. No hills, no trees, no rivers. No secrets, no politics, no compromise; everything straightforward, just life and death and get on with your business. Mahdha, blow me away from here, let me ride with you at my back—*

She glanced over her shoulder at a familiar sound. Her cousin was hanging out the window of the carriage again. Vomit spattered into the dust.

"Uncle?" Peri called. "May we stop for the night? Kalendra's sick again."

Terralt, riding on the other side of the carriage, gave Peri a weary I-know-what-you're-up-to look, but turned his horse around, holding up his fist to signal a halt. He rode around the back of the carriage, glanced at his daughter's ashen face, and sighed.

"All right," he said. "We'll make camp here."

Peri fought to keep from bouncing in the saddle with joy. She touched her bow when Terralt glanced her way again.

"Uncle?" she asked eagerly. "May I—"

"Oh, go on, then, Perian," Terralt said crossly, waving her away negligently. He turned away to help Kalendra down from the carriage.

Peri hurriedly kneed Tajin to a gallop before her uncle could demand that she take a guard escort. This close to the Barrier garrisons, there couldn't possibly be any danger, but her uncle Terralt would never believe it.

The caravan's proximity to the garrisons and the Barrier had another effect, however—there was little game to be found. By the time Peri startled up a small herd of lopas, she'd nearly run out of patience—not to mention time—before her uncle, alarmed at her absence, sent guards out looking for her. Despite Peri's surprise when the lopas scattered into the grass, Tajin's speed and her skill with her bow were more than equal to the lopas' swiftness; her first arrow barely missed, but the second brought the plump buck down cleanly. Peri had time for another shot, but refrained. One buck was all they could use (and all Tajin could carry), and Bregond did not honor the greedy.

The buck was indeed large and plump, heavy enough that it would certainly slow Tajin significantly. Peri considered bleeding and gutting the animal, then shook her head. The blood, mixed with herbs and grain and the chopped liver, would boil in the lopa's stomach to a rich and hearty dish. Why, it was her betrothed's favorite meal—

Not her betrothed anymore. That thought took all the joy out of Peri's kill. By this time next month, her cousin Kalendra would be wed to Danber, and Peri—

"Well, it's your own fault," Estann had said sympathetically, sitting on Peri's bed while Peri packed. *"If you were determined to have a barn-loft tumble with Stevann's apprentice, you shouldn't have gotten caught."*

"We didn't get caught," *Peri said sullenly.*

"Didn't get caught with hay in your hair and your skirts up around your waist, you mean," her older brother said wryly. *"At least there's that, I suppose."*

"I didn't—" Peri bit her lip. It had happened in Loris's room, not in the barn loft, and they'd both taken their clothes off properly, but that was beside the point.

"I don't see what's so terrible," Peri said hotly. *"You were younger than me when you had your first lover."*

"That's different, and you know it." Estann had, in fact, celebrated his Awakening when he was thirteen, two years younger than Peri herself.

Isn't that just like my family, *Peri thought bitterly.* My older brother has his first tumble and Mother and Father throw a festival. I have my first tumble and my life is ruined.

"Anyway," Estann said triumphantly, *"what would Danber think?"*

"Nothing at all," Peri retorted. It was true, too. Her best friend and betrothed had actually suggested that she—ah—acquire some experience on her own, since his own interests lay—well—elsewhere.

Of course, Estann didn't know that; nobody did, which was the point. Lord Danber would be utterly disgraced in Bregond if it became known that he was a lover of men. He'd trusted

*Peri with his secret when they were much younger, and to-
gether they'd planned their betrothal. It had worked admira-
bly. The High Lord and Lady of Agrond were more than
delighted to pledge their daughter to the boy who would be
lord of the largest horse clan in Bregond. Lord Danber would
have his respectable marriage. And Peri would have the horse
clans, the plains of Bregond, discreet lovers if she wanted
them, the companionship of her best friend, and time and opportunity to refine her swordsmanship to perfection.*

Tajin knelt on Peri's command, and she wrestled the lopa up,
pulling the tie straps taut with a little more violence than necessary. A month ago she'd had everything to look forward to.
Now what did she have? A miserable hint of magical talent
awakened by her one and only tumble, far too little magic to
do anything useful with, but more than enough to swallow all
of Peri's plans and spit her back out into High Lady Kairi's
neat, orderly, and utterly stifling castle. *That's* what she had.

Oh, and the memory of one awkward and rather disappoint-
ing night with Loris, of course.

Tajin struggled to his feet, and grunted under the added
weight when Peri mounted; she made no effort to press him
beyond an easy walk. Despite her uncle's inevitable lecture,
she was in no hurry to return to camp.

*"My sister has never named her heir, and her advisers are
pressing her to do so,"* High Lady Kayli said with that unshakable calm Peri always found so infuriating. *"Your aunt
Laalen has never been strong enough for such duties, and
Danine—she has never been whole in spirit since the war.
Kairi can train your water sensitivity while she prepares you
to rule Bregond."*

*"I thought mages had to be trained while they were still
virgins,"* Peri had said sullenly. *"Besides, Aunt Kairi can't*

school me in healing, so what are you going to do about that?''

"Kairi keeps a healer at the castle to attend your aunts Laalen and Danine, and that healer will assist in your education," Kayli said implacably. "Yes, it's true that training traditionally begins well before you are Awakened. But because of the minor extent of your abilities and the nature of your talents, there should be no danger."

"In other words, what you're saying is that I don't have enough magic to be of any practical use either," Peri retorted. "If I weren't the High Lady's daughter, the best I could hope for would be work as a dowser or a midwife. But if there's no danger, then there's no reason I shouldn't just go ahead and marry Lord Danber, is there?''

"There is only one," Kayli said sternly. "And it is this: You have an obligation to use your gifts and abilities, no matter how minor, in the service of your country. Water magic is rare in Bregond, and your water sensitivity gives you an affinity with your aunt. This is the manner in which you can best serve Agrond and Bregond.''

Kayli took Peri's hand in both her own, and Peri couldn't help wincing when she saw the old burn scars dappling her mother's hands. Kayli had earned her scars with no less effort than that by which Peri had earned the sword calluses on her own fingers or the hard, wiry muscles in her shoulders and upper back.

"I was glad to see you make an advantageous marriage of your own choosing," Kayli said gently. "I was overjoyed that it was to be with your friend, and in Bregond. I know you have a vocation for the sword, and I know that in Bregond it's easier for a woman to pursue those studies than it is here. I wanted you to have more choice than I did. But Kairi must have an heir, and the opportunity to give her one of my children, of mixed Bregondish and Agrondish blood, is too good *to pass by. Your father and I thought it would take several generations to bind the two countries together, but with Estann on the throne here and you in Bregond, it could well happen during your reign. The people of Bregond will accept you because of the years you've fostered in the horse clans, and they'll see the Awakening of your water sensitivity as a sign. Even half of Agrondish blood, even born in Agrond, they'll accept you as Heir.''*

Peri made a sour face, her fingers clenching in Tajin's mane. If she worked hard enough at it, she might one day actually manage the most elementary water scryings. Her healing ability likely would amount to even less. If only she had kept her foolish mouth shut when she'd felt the rainstorm approaching from the east, or when her chambermaid, Arese, had mistaken indigestion for pregnancy.

But she was mage enough to feel an instinctive awareness of the Barrier not far to the north, like an itch she could not quite reach to scratch. If she stood in the saddle and squinted hard, she could see the faint shimmer of the strange magical wall that had guarded the border of Sarkond, allowing no magic to pass between the two countries, since not long after the war. She knew her uncle could feel it, too, as they rode west, parallel to the Barrier, and since his own mage-gift was every bit as uncontrolled as her own, albeit probably much stronger, he doubtless found it just as irritating. Small wonder he'd been in such a foul mood lately.

And, as Peri learned when she made it back to camp, his mood had undergone no improvement in her absence.

"There you are!" Terralt said angrily. "I was just about to send the guards out to look for you."

"I'm sorry, Uncle," Peri said with as much repentance as she could muster. "Tajin was tired and heavy loaded."

"So I see." Terralt examined the buck, then gave Peri a

smile of reluctant approval. "He's a beauty." He waved to one of the guards, who reached for Tajin's reins.

Peri clung to them stubbornly.

"I'll take him over to Cook," she suggested. "Then I've got to rub Tajin down."

"No, you've got to wash up and help Kalendra settle in," Terralt said implacably.

"Sparring after dinner?" Peri bargained.

Terralt sighed.

"Perian, I've been riding all day," he said patiently. "I'm too tired for swordplay. Why don't you wear out Captain Dorran instead?"

"Captain Dorran's not nearly as good as you," Peri said disappointedly. That wasn't true, not exactly, but Captain Dorran invariably pulled his strokes with her, and besides, flattery almost always won her uncle over. "What about first thing in the morning, while everybody's striking camp?"

Terralt gave her an impatient glance, then shook his head at last, chuckling.

"All right. First thing. Now go take care of Kalendra, and make sure she eats a good dinner. The Bright Ones know her breakfast will be all over the road within an hour after we leave tomorrow."

Peri found Kalendra huddled on her pallet, surrounded by maids—one fanning her, one waving a vial of scent under her nose, one chafing her wrists, and two more just generally fussing.

"Go on, go on," Peri said irritably, waving the maids away. "Get me a cold wet cloth, a hot wet cloth, and the ginger-mint tea Cook will have ready for you. Kala, sit up. I told you a hundred times, it's worse if you lie down. And I *told* you to keep your bodice loose if you—"

"Bright Ones, Peri, I'm dying," Kalendra moaned. "Don't be cross with me, please."

Peri took Kalendra's hands and pulled her upright, then sighed. It was impossible to stay angry in the face of Kalendra's misery.

"All right, then," Peri relented. "Lean your head forward."

By the time the maids returned, Peri had loosened Kalendra's laces and was rubbing the base of her skull just below and behind her ears. She took the steaming-hot cloth and draped it abruptly over the back of Kalendra's neck, eliciting a startled yelp; as soon as the cloth started to cool, Peri whisked it away, replacing it with the cold cloth, and Kalendra jumped again, then subsided.

"Oh, Peri, warn me next time," she said, shivering.

"Better?" Peri asked.

"Better," Kalendra admitted, accepting the cup of tea and sipping it. "Thank you, Peri. It always works, though the Bright Ones alone know why. If I'd known traveling would do this to me, I'd have asked Stevann for some real medicine."

Behind Kalendra's back, Peri made a face. *Real* medicine. She'd never be a *real* mage like Stevann. Just enough of one to ruin all her plans.

"Now, tomorrow, don't lace up tight like that," Peri said patiently. "Nobody's going to see you anyway. And when you start feeling sick, hum."

"Hum?" Kalendra laughed. "Really, Peri! What has music got to do with road sickness?"

Peri sighed and stood up. She couldn't explain to her cousin how it was that she knew that Kala's nausea came not from her stomach, but from someplace deep down in her ears; moreover, Kala would never believe her anyway, even though Peri's suggestions gave her relief. Yet Kala would unhesitatingly drink whatever potion Stevann might have given her, never asking what herbs it contained.

Leaving Kala to her maids' tender mercies, Peri gratefully

joined her uncle at the guards' fire. She and Terralt had argued about that briefly the first night; in the horse clans everyone sat as equals around the fires, but among the landed nobility of Agrond and Bregond alike, it was scandalous for an unmarried girl of noble birth to sit at the fire with men, much less common guardsmen. But since Kalendra and her maids preferred to keep to their tent, it was ridiculous to kindle a separate fire for Peri alone, as Peri had patiently pointed out. Besides, before this journey Peri had spent much of her free time with these same guardsmen, sparring with them or just sitting around companionably tending their weapons. Terralt, who disliked the company of commoners, was probably far less comfortable (and, if the guards admitted the truth, less welcome) at their fire than Peri herself.

"Ah, welcome, Per—ah, Lady Perian," Captain Dorran said, glancing apologetically at Terralt. "That lopa's a good fat one. Cook's got the liver for y . . ." Then his voice trailed off again confusedly, and Peri grimaced.

Captain Dorran was Bregondish, and Bregondish custom dictated that the liver of a kill went to women of childbearing age. But Peri, soon to begin training in magic under High Lady Kairi, wouldn't be bearing children for many years, most likely. So the choicest part of Peri's kill, like her betrothed, now went to Kalendra instead. As if Kalendra was likely to appreciate either one!

Peri grimaced. Suddenly the prospect of a jovial evening around a campfire seemed less appealing. She forced a friendly smile.

"I'll get some later," she said, shrugging nonchalantly. "Right now I think I'll have a look at Pechata's hooves. I thought she was favoring her near hind."

Pechata's hooves were fine and nobody was fooled, but Captain Dorran gave her a sheepish smile and a hasty,

"Thanks, Lady," as Peri retreated to her tent and her pallet and, eventually, to sleep.

Peri was up well before dawn, enjoying one of her few quiet practice moments in a small cleared area behind the camp. She'd already inspected her sword carefully, slid the practice guard over the blade, and meticulously performed the lunges and stretches to limber her muscles and the meditation exercises to focus her concentration. Now she worked her way slowly through the defensive qivashim. The Deep Roots qiva and the Bending Willow qiva, those were the ones she'd have the most trouble with, but if—

"I see you got an early start on me," Terralt said. He was squatting at the edge of the area Peri had cleared, his guarded sword across his knees. To Peri's relief, he looked more amiable this morning. "What is that you're doing?"

Peri scuffed her boot in the dirt self-consciously.

"I'm trying to invent a new qiva, an offensive qiva," she said, flushing slightly. It *was* presumptuous and she knew it. Only two new qivashim had been invented in Peri's lifetime, and those by seasoned adepts. "But there are a couple of the defensive qivas which might counter too easily. I don't know, maybe if I lead in with something else, Leaping Flame or Summer Lightning . . ." she shook her head. "I don't know. Maybe it just won't work."

"Mmmm." Terralt stayed where he was, his eyes narrowed. "Unfortunately what I know of Bregondish-style swordplay I observed at the wrong end of my sword, Peri. But you have the steel in your blood, and if you think you've found something new, I'd like to see it. Show me what you've got."

Peri flushed again, this time with pride at her uncle's praise. Taking a deep breath, she began the initial steps of the Waterdance qiva, her confidence growing as the movements became more natural; then abruptly she disgraced herself by stumbling and nearly falling in the dirt, barely avoiding the utter humiliation of dropping her sword.

To her utter relief, Terralt only nodded thoughtfully, standing and walking over to join her.

"I can see what you're working at," he said slowly. "You want to break your opponent's rhythm and throw him off balance at the same time. Problem is, I think you're too daring in your footwork, and you're throwing your own balance off at the same time. Come on, let's see what we can do with it."

Nodding, Peri settled herself in readiness, taking a deep breath, then danced forward to meet Terralt's attack. They were practicing, not fighting, making no effort at a quick kill, only testing each other's strengths and worrying at each other's weaknesses. When they were both adequately loosened up, Terralt gave Peri a nod and fell into a defensive pattern, letting her take the offensive. Although Terralt had never studied the Ithuara and knew only Agrondish-style swordplay, he settled into a well-balanced stance surprisingly similar to Deep Roots—exactly what Peri needed. She fell almost effortlessly into the smooth rhythm of Waterdance, flowing easily around his pattern of defensive strokes, and—

—found herself abruptly on her back, the guarded point of Terralt's sword at her throat.

Terralt withdrew the sword and held out his hand.

"Not bad," he conceded. "Your blade work's almost faultless, although I saw an opening or two you'll probably close with practice. But your feet are still getting you in trouble."

Peri took the proffered hand and pulled herself to her feet, brushing dust out of her face.

"All right," she panted. "Again."

Waterdance failed twice more, and when Peri grew too frustrated, they switched postures, Terralt taking the offensive. Defensive qivashim were Peri's weakness, even against the Agrondish propensity to favor an unsubtle attack very like the

Charging Boar qiva, but she held forth grimly, varying her defenses so Terralt could not find a pattern to break. Tall Grass against Charging Boar was too easy, he'd see right through that, but maybe Thorny Thicket—

"Uhhhh!" Peri grunted, all the breath driven out of her on a wave of pain as Terralt's sword slammed into her side just at the bottom of her rib cage. She went down to one knee, still grimly holding on to her sword, and Terralt broke off the attack immediately.

"You think too much," Terralt panted. "A first-year guardsman could've got through that. Too much theory and not enough drive, that's your problem. Are you all right?"

Peri nodded, momentarily unable to speak. Carefully *not* clutching her injured side, she forced herself back up to her feet, raising her sword.

"Again," she gasped.

Terralt sighed and sheathed his sword, stepping in front of Peri and pushing her own sword aside. He pressed gently against Peri's ribs, muttering an oath when Peri could not suppress a hiss of pain.

"We should've been wearing practice armor," he said, shaking his head. "I didn't expect you to let me hit you that hard. You're bruised right down to the bone. You're lucky if I didn't crack a rib."

"They're not cracked," Peri muttered embarrassedly. "A wrapping and a poultice and I'll be fine."

Terralt firmly pried the sword hilt out of Peri's hand.

"Well, you won't be sitting in a saddle today," he said. "Just as well. Kalendra can use the company."

"Oh, no," Peri said hastily. "I don't need—"

"You will ride in the carriage," Terralt said implacably, hefting her sword, "if you want this back." Then he relented slightly. "If you're doing well this evening, you can still go hunting."

Peri ground her teeth, but there was nothing she could do but join Kalendra and her tiresome, fussy maids in the stuffy— "Oh, shutter the windows, Peri! All that wind and dust!"— carriage. Kalendra, however, was overjoyed at the company.

"You've had so little time to talk to me since we left Tarkesh," Kalendra said, her eyes sparkling. "And our conversation will make the hours pass quickly."

Peri thought miserably that, on the contrary, the journey by carriage and the maids' prattle would make the hours drag on interminably, and she was right. Within less than two hours Kalendra had gone from pink-cheeked to pale to ashen to greenish, and Peri knew she would soon be hanging out the window again.

"Tell me about Lord Danber," Kalendra said determinedly, burying her nose in a scented hankerchief. "Is he handsome?"

Peri scowled. The last thing in the world she wanted was to talk about Danber. No, correction—the last thing in the world she wanted was to have to keep riding in this carriage, to become Aunt Kairi's wretched Heir, *and* to have to talk about Danber. She sighed.

"All right," Peri said. "I'll tell you about him. If we ride outside."

Kalendra protested, but Peri held out firmly, and at last the transfer was accomplished. The ride seemed less bumpy up on top of the carriage, although the swaying was worse, and Peri could at least enjoy the sun and wind she loved so much; some of the color returned to Kalendra's cheeks, too, and under considerable pressure from Peri, Kalendra admitted that the nausea was less.

"So tell me," Kalendra persisted. "Is Lord Danber handsome?"

Her mood somewhat mellowed by the change in seats, Peri leaned back against the trunks and bags tied to the top of the carriage.

"Handsome?" Peri shrugged. "I never really thought about it. I suppose so."

"You never thought about it?" Kalendra said disbelievingly. "You *suppose* so? Peri, you've fostered with the man most of your life. By the Bright Ones, you were *betrothed* to him!"

Peri grimaced.

"Kala, you're right, I fostered with him. He's more like—like a brother." *More of a brother than Estann's been.*

"Well, surely you've—" Kalendra raised her eyebrows. "You know."

Peri shook her head, fighting down a giggle.

"Never," she said.

Kalendra scowled.

"You mean to tell me," she said slowly, "that you tumbled a common-born apprentice mage, but not your own betrothed?"

"It's different in Bregond," Peri said vaguely. "Nobles—even if they're betrothed—don't lie together before they're wed."

Kalendra shook her head.

"And on your wedding night," she said impatiently, "how were you going to explain your misplaced virginity to your husband?"

"Danber knew customs were different in Agrond," Peri said truthfully. "We had an—understanding about it." *Although not the kind you'd think.*

"Well, surely you've at least kissed him," Kalendra protested. Then she smiled conspiratorially. "And perhaps just a little more?"

Peri grinned.

"Well—maybe a little more," she said, chuckling.

* * *

Danber leaned back, smiling.

"That was—rather nice," he said softly. "I've never kissed a woman before."

"Well, we're almost even, then." Peri chuckled a little nervously, leaning back on the softness of the cloak. "I've never kissed anybody before. Not like that, anyway." She'd liked it, too, although Danber's mustache tickled. Danber's chest had felt strong and hard against hers, his arms firm around her, the whole combination filling her with a shivery warmth that left her wanting more.

Gingerly Danber touched the laces of her tunic.

"May I—may I look at you?" he asked slowly.

Peri swallowed, but nodded, shrugging out of her tunic when Danber slowly unlaced it. She didn't protest that Danber had seen her already dozens of times in the sweat tent or when the water holes were large enough to make bathing practical; this was different and they both knew it.

Thankfully Danber made no indication of parting either of them from their trousers, and some of Peri's nervousness faded to curiosity as Danber laid his own tunic aside. In Agrondish terms, Danber was rather short—half a handsbreadth shorter than Peri herself—and strongly muscled, darkly golden-skinned and hairy. But Peri, who had spent much of her life here with the horse clans, looked at him with Bregondish eyes, the same eyes that saw Agrondish men as pale and sickly looking, and saw Danber as strong and full of life.

"You don't look like an Agrond," Danber said suddenly, startling Peri out of her reflections. "Except for the green in your eyes and that sort of red shine to your hair."

"Is that good?" Peri asked, a little awkwardly. She'd always thought of herself as boyish and ungraceful, especially next to Kalendra and Erisa, her uncle Terralt's daughters. Even Peri's Bregondish mother, from whom Peri had inherited

*her black hair and dark gold skin and strong features, was
softer and more graceful and seemed somehow more womanly.*

"I think it's good," Danber said, grinning a little. "Agrondish ladies always looked—well—"

"Sickly?" Peri guessed.

"Well, yes," Danber admitted. "I never could imagine how
any man could expect them to survive childbirth, much less
bear healthy children, ride with the clan, help manage the
herds and do their share of the hunting—" He paused, gazing
at Peri seriously. "But you're not like that. You look healthy
and strong. I'm glad." He touched Peri's braids, and Peri
smiled. Her mother had twisted her hair into the thirty-nine
braids, symbolizing mastery of the thirty-nine skills of a mar-
riageable Bregondish woman, only a few months earlier, on
her fifteenth birthday.

"Peri—" Danber hesitated. "May I touch you?"

Peri bit her lip. Eight years old, Danber teaching her to
ride bareback. Ten years old, their first real kill together—a
fine buck lopa, fat and strong, its blood warm and salty in her
mouth as they shared the heart. Fourteen years old, Danber
handing her the sword he'd commissioned for her, perfectly
balanced to her hand—he'd traded three of his best mares for
it, a small fortune.

"All right," Peri said shyly. She closed her eyes. Warm
callused fingers traced gently over her collarbone, down her
sternum, over her stomach, up her side to gently cup her
breast. Peri shivered.

"You're so soft," Danber said, marveling. "Your skin is so
smooth here."

Peri opened her eyes again and slid her hands up Danber's
chest, running her fingers over hard muscle, through thick,
coarse black hair.

"Danber—" She hesitated, swallowing hard. "Are—are
we going to—"

Danber met her eyes squarely.

"I don't think I could," he admitted.

Peri sighed with relief.

"Me either," she confessed.

Danber gazed at her a moment longer, then abruptly laughed, and Peri joined him.

"Yes," Peri said, smiling. "Maybe just a little more."

"Ah, then he's a virile man," Kalendra said contentedly.

Peri chuckled.

"I suppose so," she said.

Oh, Kalendra, are you ever going to be surprised. And I doubt it's going to be a pleasant surprise. On the other hand, when Danber finds out he's going to be wed to a frail, pale Agrondish lady with soft hands and perfumed hair, whose idea of riding is puking out the window of her carriage, who's never hunted anything but a lost earring in her jewel box, I doubt he's going to find it a pleasant surprise, either. I'd love to see their faces after the wedding night. The thought gave her a certain amount of spiteful satisfaction, then a flash of guilt. Kalendra had done nothing to earn Peri's spite, and Danber, if anything, deserved her sympathy.

Peri grimaced.

Sorry, Danber. Sympathy's a bit too much to ask of me just now.

"What?" she said, suddenly aware that Kalendra had said something to her.

"I said," Kalendra said patiently, "what does he like to do? Does he like dancing, jousts—"

Peri glanced sideways at her lovely cousin.

"It's not like that with the horse clans," she said gently. "There's a few simple festivals, mostly at trade gatherings, like at foaling time and when the herds are culled. There's no castle, just a winter holding at the center of the grazing territory; the clan moves with the herd through the grazing grounds except in the dead of winter. Sometimes merchants pass through, and once or maybe twice a year Danber visits the capital and takes the clan's tithes to court. Most of the rest of the time it's riding and herding and—''

Peri stopped. Kalendra had gone almost white, her eyes wide and shocked.

''F-Father told me there'd be a grand court,'' she whispered. ''He told me I'd hardly know I wasn't home.''

''Likely he didn't know himself,'' Peri said diplomatically, swallowing her shock. ''I don't think Uncle Terralt's ever dealt much with the horse or ikada clans. He never goes to Bregond if he can help it, and when he does, it's to Aunt Kairi's castle and the court. You know how he hates the company of commoners.''

It was a lie and she knew it. She'd had many a good talk with her uncle over sparring, or resting between matches, and Terralt had always been interested in hearing her experiences in Danber's clan. He'd deliberately lied to his daughter so she wouldn't make a fuss over her betrothal. Unwillingly Peri felt a pang of sympathy. At least nobody had lied to *her.*

''Anyway, Danber's very kind and understanding,'' Peri said awkwardly. That was true enough. ''He'll do his best to make you comfortable and happy. Maybe you can stay at the winter holding most of the time, or maybe you can represent the clan at court instead of Danber.''

Kalendra did not look up; her hands were shaking. At last she forced a faint smile.

''Yes,'' she said softly. ''Lord Danber must be kind, to have such an—an understanding with you.''

Now Peri felt *really* awful. There was nothing she could say to comfort Kalendra without causing trouble, and nothing she could say about Danber without betraying his secret. Inwardly she groaned. Courtly conversation was supposedly one of the thirty-nine arts she'd mastered, but dancing around her frightened cousin with polite lies seemed an altogether different matter.

To her relief, she noticed that the sun was sinking, and it was not long before Terralt signaled a halt for the evening, apparently irritated at their lack of progress.

"I'd hoped we'd reach the garrison before sunset," he said with a sigh, "and sleep in proper beds for at least one night. But there's a storm coming, if this rising wind is any indication, and the road is so rutted I don't dare continue after dark. Well, never mind."

Peri jumped on the opportunity.

"Uncle, why don't I ride ahead?" she said quickly. "If the garrison's only a short distance, then you and I can get Kalendra there and spend the night indoors and the guards can meet us there in the morning." Actually she had no desire whatsoever to spend the night in the garrison, but she knew how dearly her uncle preferred sleeping inside solid walls; if granted his preference, he'd be so pleased that possibly Peri could coax him into letting her stay in camp with the guards, unseemly or not. And even if it gained her nothing else, the simple opportunity to get back into Tajin's saddle was worth the effort.

Terralt gave Peri a look that said more plainly than words that she wasn't fooling him, but he nodded resignedly.

"All right, then, Perian," he said. "We're far enough inside the borders that you should be safe. But either take two guards with you, or turn around and be back here before sunset." He gave her a warning glance. "I mean it, Perian."

"All right, all right," Peri said hurriedly. She saddled Tajin as fast as she could, before her uncle changed his mind, then turned back to him. "My sword?"

"You don't need your sword," Terralt said patiently, "to ride a short distance to the garrison."

"Mother says there's a word for folk who take even a step outside their front door unarmed," Peri said, grinning. " 'Corpse.' "

Terralt grimaced.

"Of course," he said sourly. "High Lady Kayli, font of all wisdom. Here, take your sword, then, and your bow, too, if you like. But don't stop to hunt, Perian. There's not time."

"Yes, Uncle," Peri said obediently, scrambling into the saddle and firmly securing her scabbard in its slot.

She rode swiftly away from camp, letting Tajin have his head, laughing into the wind despite the hard ache in her ribs at every jolt. Storm indeed! It was only Mahdha, stirred up from her nest in a bad mood, hot and angry and dry as dust. But Mahdha was Peri's friend tonight, buying her a short delay, one more ride on Tajin's back, one more night out on the plains before walls closed around her.

Tajin was as grateful as Peri for the wind in his face, the wide plains before him; his hooves thundered along the hard-packed earth to the side of the wagon ruts and Peri could feel his heart beating fierce and strong inside his chest.

The road topped a gentle rise and Peri reluctantly pulled Tajin to a halt, both of them breathing hard. There was the garrison, the evening fires already lit—it looked so close, but Peri was not fooled. Distances on the plains confused the ignorant. No, the garrison was at least an hour's ride farther even for her, and slowed to a pace Kalendra could manage—no, there'd be no soft bed for her uncle and cousin tonight.

Peri grinned and turned Tajin back toward camp, then frowned, squinting through the dimming light. There were carrion birds circling to the north—not scavenger birds but the great plains vultures that came only to a large kill. What in the world could have died? Hunters from the garrison would have taken their kill back, and no predator large enough to bring down a sizable animal should be hunting so near a human settlement.

Then Peri frowned. The birds were circling near a wash containing a small water hole. Could someone have poisoned the water hole? If so, that was a serious matter indeed. And even if some animal had come there to drink and simply dropped dead, fouling the spring, that was no matter to dismiss lightly. The soldiers at the garrison would definitely have to be told.

Peri shook her head, grinning to herself. She was only looking for an excuse to justify delaying her return to camp a little longer. Well, so be it—no Bregond in her right mind, much less one gifted with a water sensitivity, would fail to investigate the possibility of a fouled spring.

There, Mother! NOW lecture me on my duty.

Tajin turned, obedient to Peri's signal, and left the road, his head slightly lowered so the plains grasses did not flip across his face, his thick, coarse coat fending off the sharp-edged swordgrass and barbed hookthorns as easily as the sturdy leather jaffs protecting Peri's legs. Peri let him set his own pace, an easy canter that allowed him to avoid any treacherous footing, thorny thickets, or more active hazards, while she, from her higher vantage point, nudged him occasionally with her knees to correct his course. She slowed him further before they reached their destination. Whatever had made the kill that attracted the carrion birds, better she surprise it than it surprise her.

When Peri pulled Tajin to a halt, however, it was only to scowl down in puzzlement at the corpse of the shaggy-coated mare crumpled on the ground. The spring was still a good distance ahead; it was not fouled water that had brought this good beast down.

The rest, however, remained a mystery. The mare couldn't have been there long; the carrion birds had hardly done more than taken the eyes and tongue, but there were other punctures in the hide that could have been inflicted by birds or possibly arrows. The mare's tack had been stripped off, but Peri's learned eye found plenty of clues nonetheless. The mare was a sound beast but no prize of the herd, only a few steps above a cull, but she was well shod for hard riding over bad ground. Who would buy such a poor beast and then shoe her so well? Who would have been riding out here, away from the road? She was certainly no soldier's mount. And what manner of fool left riderless on Bregond's plains would have stripped no meat from the carcass, not even the prized heart and liver, yet bothered to carry the heavy tack away?

Then again, perhaps the rider had walked to the garrison. It would be sensible for a stranded rider to carry his weapons and supplies with him for that journey. But again, why carry the heavy tack? Thievery couldn't possibly be a concern, not when the nearest human beings were the soldiers at the garrison.

Then Peri's eyes swept over the scene again. Scattered droplets of blood and crushed grass bespoke a struggle, and the tracks of at least four more horses led into the grass, toward the spring rather than the garrison. Peri's heart pounded as fiercely as Tajin's had.

Someone fought hard and lost. Someone was carried away.

Without thought, Peri bent low in Tajin's saddle and urged her mount slowly forward along the trail, her ears straining, her nose sifting through the scents Mahdha brought her. When her instincts told her to dismount, she did, sliding from the saddle and giving Tajin the three pats to signal him to stand. Her sword, well oiled, slid silently from its scabbard and she almost absently tested the draw of her knives.

There was a camp by the spring, a tiny, smokeless peat fire, carefully screened. The five figures around the fire did not speak, wore simple cloaks that concealed their clothing; but the movement as one of them reached for the pot over the fire exposed a swarthy hand and wrist and the sleeve of a black leather tunic studded with bone beads, and the sight of that tunic and hand told Peri all she needed to know. A shock ran through her.

Sarkonds!

Sheer amazement almost startled a gasp out of Peri. Since the alliance between Agrond and Bregond, the Sarkonds to the north were Bregond's only enemy—and since the war, since the Barrier, even *they* had ceased to be a threat. Raids by the vicious nomads that swept down from the Sarkondish steppes to steal horses and supplies were rare now, partly because the Barrier foiled any attempts to scry out Bregondish patrols or rich targets, partly because of the border garrisons maintained by Agrond and Bregond alike, and partly, it was hoped, because Sarkond had taken such a beating in the war that they no longer dared attack.

But here were Sarkonds in Bregond again.

Bright Ones, what in the world are they doing here? Not a raid, not with just five of them. And there's nothing out here but the garrison, nothing to raid, anyway. Are they spies? Saboteurs? Assassins?

A low moan drew Peri's attention to a sixth figure she hadn't noticed before, huddled on the ground a few feet away. The moan sounded male, but it was impossible to tell—the figure was almost completely swathed in cloth and bound in a tight web of ropes, one of the ropes connected to a stake driven deep into the ground.

Abductors!

Peri's breath shortened. Whoever had been riding the mare, despite his pitiful mount, he was apparently important enough to rate *five* Sarkondish soldiers to hunt him down—five Sarkondish soldiers willing to ride within sight of a Bregondish garrison. The Sarkonds had bound their victim tightly in time to keep him from suicide so far; possibly they could prevent it long enough for him to fulfill whatever purpose had made them seek him out in the first place—certainly long enough to subject him to the tortures for which Sarkonds were renowned. But if he could be rescued . . .

A great warrior could do it. Someone MEANT to be a warrior, destined to follow the sword. Anybody would have to admit that. Even High Lords and Ladies.

Peri touched her knives again, her fingers twitching. She could get at least one of them, maybe two with luck. Or maybe none—she really couldn't tell what kind of armor the Sarkonds wore under those cloaks. If she crept back and fetched her bow, she could still do no better, not in the fading light.

Right. Leaving me on foot facing at least three experienced Sarkondish soldiers, all half again my size and weight, armed as well as me and likely armored much better. Uh-UH. Not THIS great warrior.

Peri took a deep breath, forcing her muscles to relax, forcing her mind to calm.

A wise warrior doesn't pit her strength against her enemy's, she thought. Danber had taught her that, and it was true. *A wise warrior pits strength against weakness.*

Peri strained her ears, sniffing the air. The Sarkonds were eerily silent.

Tell me, Mahdha. Tell me their secrets.

No more Sarkonds patrolling around the camp—just the five of them. And the horses—ah, there!

They think they're smart, tying their horses downwind of the camp. They think the scent, the sound of the horses will keep others from hearing or smelling THEM. Oh, yes, it will, too. But that sword, Sarkondish scum, has two edges.

Peri crept backward ever so slowly, soundlessly, until she met Tajin back along her own trail. She toyed with the idea of muffling Tajin's hooves, rejected it. Coming from downwind, that sound would not betray her.

Visato root grew wild all over the plains; it was no effort to dig enough, little trouble to wrap them in sweetgrass so the horses would eat them. She'd done it a dozen times with Danber and his clan.

He always said I was talented tending wounded and sick horses. I'd be REALLY good now, wouldn't I? Of course, can't waste my talent somewhere where it might actually do some good—not now, Peri, not now!

Peri worked her way slowly around the perimeter until the five tethered horses stood between her and the camp. She stayed close to Tajin as she worked her way painstakingly forward. The horses would smell Tajin, just another horse.

Two things I know, Peri thought grimly. *Swords and horses.*

Silently she tied one horse's reins to Tajin's saddle; she fed the grass-wrapped roots to the others.

All right, she thought, her heart pounding. *Now it's got to be fast.*

She swung into Tajin's saddle, a movement as easy for her as breathing, and urged Tajin forward—

—and the time for thought was over.

Whinnies of the horses as they startled. Thunder of Tajin's hooves. Darkness, then firelight to dazzle her. Sarkondish eyes widening. Cloaks flung back from black leather. Hiss of swords drawn from their scabbards.

Peri hooked her knee around the high pommel of her saddle, her other foot into the bracing loop, and leaned down, drawing her knife. The blade cut through the rope smoothly and she dropped the knife immediately, winding her fingers through the web of rope confining the Sarkonds' captive as firmly as she could. Tajin was already moving again, fast, dodging swords.

Peri groaned, every muscle and her bruised ribs screaming

as she dragged the deadweight of her burden—try as she might, she couldn't heft the captive high enough to hook his ropes over one of the saddle clips. There was nothing to do but hold on and hope whoever she'd just rescued didn't wind up under Tajin's hooves.

"I'm going to stop in a minute," she grunted out between gasps. "I've got to get you up in the saddle, and you've got to help me. Understand?"

There was no reply but a hollow groan, and Peri doubted she'd been heard, much less understood; when Tajin slowed, however, the captive made a weak attempt to gather his legs under him, pushing upward as Peri wrestled him over Tajin's back. Then they were moving again, as quickly as Tajin could run under the doubled load and with the other horse in tow, but in addition to the shouts behind her, Peri now heard hoofbeats.

All right, she thought grimly. *Just see how far you get.*

Her passenger groaned weakly at every jar, and Peri remembered the blood on the trampled grass and realized she had no idea how badly he might be hurt. For all she knew, he might be dying.

No. If he's that important to the Sarkonds, they wouldn't have just left him lying there untended in that bad of shape. They wanted him alive. NEEDED him alive, to go to so much trouble when it would've been easy enough to put an arrow through his heart.

Then a crossbow bolt whistled past her, driving all other thoughts out of her mind.

Oh, Bright Ones—I never thought they'd have Agrondish crossbows. With Bregondish horses, I thought they'd have Bregondish saddle bows or longbows, that I could stay out of range—

She bent down as low in the saddle as the high pommel would allow, relying on the equally high cantle to protect her, just as it had protected generations of Bregondish warriors. A bolt thunked solidly into the cantle and Peri blessed the saddle, the hours she'd spent in it, the craftsmen who had made it, the ikada whose leather covered it—

Then the horse beside her screamed and faltered, dragging against the tow rope. Peri glanced over and groaned in dismay as she saw the bolt solidly embedded in its right rear leg.

Have to be cut out, she thought automatically. *A few stitches and a blackthorn ash poultice and—never mind that!*

Grimly Peri drew her knife and cut the lead rope. No longer held back by the second horse, Tajin leaped forward with new energy. A quick glance over her shoulder, however, gave Peri no encouragement—the four horses behind her had spread out, cutting her off. She couldn't turn back; the only possible route was north, toward the Barrier.

All right, then, she thought grimly. *The Barrier it is. But those roots had better take effect soon.*

By the time she neared the Barrier, Tajin was beginning to strain under the hard pace and the double load, although he maintained his speed—if she asked it of him, he'd run till he dropped. Peri could still hear the other horses behind her, but despite Tajin's heavier load they had drawn no closer; Peri hoped that meant the horses were starting to feel the effects of the soporific roots and beginning to slow, but she dared not count on it. She lowered her head, bracing herself, gripped her rope-bound burden more tightly, and rode directly at the shimmering wall.

A tangible shock ran through Peri as she struck the Barrier, exacerbated as Tajin shied instinctively, then stumbled hard, nearly falling; Peri's long-trained riding skill was all that kept her and her rescued captive in the saddle as Tajin gathered his feet under him again. Peri cried out from the shock and from the pain in her bruised ribs as she jolted in the saddle. The bound man in front of her cried out, too, and went completely limp—unconscious, Peri hoped, not dead.

Then they were through the Barrier, and Peri glanced around frantically for cover, straining her eyes in the starlight.

There was no cover to be seen. Tajin stood on what had once been plains not unlike those in Bregond, but here there was not even the concealment of tall grass, of thorny thickets. The ground was scorched and blackened, blasted bare of any life not only by fire but magic as well during the wars, and doubtless tainted, too, by the continuing magical presence of the Barrier. Peri shivered and reluctantly urged Tajin to continue north. She'd fare no better following the Barrier east or west, and who knew where the Sarkonds might come through? Her best chance was to get away from the Barrier, find some kind of hiding place, let her pursuers pass her, and then double back later.

She rode on miserably. In many places sandy soil had been fused by fire and magic into shiny rock-glass that could easily lame Tajin despite his stout shoes; in other places drifts of ash could conceal holes deep enough to snap a horse's leg. Peri dared not push Tajin beyond a slow, careful walk, although she shook in the saddle with impatience and fear. She could not hear any horses behind her, but that was no help; clouds had covered the stars and there was no light to guide her, no wind to carry scent and sound to her. For all she knew, the Sarkonds were already through the Barrier and closing on her.

By the time Peri and Tajin literally stumbled into a cluster of low foothills, woman and horse were equally exhausted. But Peri was provisionally encouraged; where there were foothills, there was probably cover of one sort or another. It was hard searching in unfamiliar countryside in almost pitch darkness, but at last Peri spotted a gulley deep enough to hide Tajin; the footing, however, was so bad that she had to dismount to lead him down into it. She felt a twinge of guilt as she signaled Tajin to kneel and the panting animal obeyed; Tajin needed walking, rubbing down, brushing, water—

The bundled man groaned loudly, and Peri hurriedly rolled him out of the saddle.

"Shhhh," Peri murmured. "I think we've lost them, but you'd better keep quiet. For all I know, they'll be here any moment. Keep still. I'll have you loose in a minute."

She drew her knife and carefully cut through the ropes binding the captive. To her surprise, the cloaked figure under the ropes was bound yet again with thongs at hands and feet, and gagged as well, his hood pulled down over his face and tied there as a kind of blindfold. Curious, Peri cut the gag and pulled up the hood—

—and her jaw dropped as wide pale gray Sarkondish eyes met her own.

"Free my hands," he said in heavily accented but understandable Bregondish.

"What the—" Peri hesitated, clutching her knife more tightly.

Sarkond. Enemy.

The gray eyes burned into hers.

"Either free my hands," he said, "or kill me. But whichever you choose, do it quickly if you wish to live."

Peri's hand clenched tightly around the hilt of her knife. This was a Sarkond, an enemy, fit only to kill on sight. Everything she'd ever been taught in both Agrond and Bregond told her that.

But he was a captive, unarmed and injured and bound. Peri had never killed a human being in her life, and she could no more make this helpless man her first than she could cook a baby and eat it. She hesitated only a moment longer, then silently slit the thongs binding the Sarkond's wrists and ankles.

He sat up slowly, painfully, never taking his eyes from Peri as he gingerly rubbed circulation back into hands that were probably long since numb. At last he flexed his fingers, grimacing, and touched the scabbard at his belt; of course it was empty, and he held out one hand.

"Your knife," he said.

"Other than blade first," Peri said grimly, "you'll get my knife the day the sun rises in the west."

The man muttered something in Sarkondish, probably an oath—Peri's lessons in Sarkondish hadn't included obscenities—and turned away, scrabbling at the ground. In a moment he apparently found what he wanted, and Peri saw a meager beam of starlight reflect off a sharp shard of rock-glass. She tensed, her hand clenching on the hilt of her dagger, but to her amazement the man turned the shard and slashed his own palm.

The man dropped the shard and pushed himself up to his knees. He tried to stand, only to fall down again, groaning.

"Help me up," he gasped.

Once again Peri hesitated, but at last she sheathed her knife and went to him, grimacing as she grabbed his upper arm and hauled him to his feet, shivering at the contact.

This is a Sarkond. I'm touching a Sarkond. HELPING a Sarkond.

As soon as the man could stand on his own, Peri snatched her hand away, but the man appeared not to notice. He squeezed his hand into a fist, droplets of blood trickling slowly down to fall on the earth. He walked in a shaky circle around Tajin and Peri, trailing drops of blood; when the circle was complete he collapsed back to his knees inside it. He raised his uninjured hand and chanted slowly; if his words were Sarkondish, they, too, were words Peri had never learned.

Peri gasped at a sudden sparkling of light from the ground; to her amazement, she realized that the drops of blood were glowing, shining like fireflies. Almost immediately the glow disappeared, and the man slumped back to the ground limply, as if utterly exhausted.

Peri squatted beside the man, gazing at him confusedly. He was not quite unconscious, but nearly so. She contemplated tying him again, then discarded the idea. He was a mage; that much was obvious from the spell he'd cast. Unless she was prepared to bind him as thoroughly as the Sarkondish soldiers had, she couldn't assure her own safety from his spells, and if she did that, as he'd said, she might as well kill him. If he'd wanted to use hostile magic on her, he could have done it already, and whatever spell he *had* cast—Peri suspected it concealed them somehow from their pursuers—might need tending later.

Now that Peri's eyes had adjusted to the faint light, she could see her prisoner more clearly, and what she saw surprised her. Even knowing Sarkonds were only humans like anybody, she'd somehow thought they'd be hideous. But this one—

He was taller than most Bregondish men, shorter than most Agrondish. His skin was darker than Peri's, but not the Bregondish dark gold, more dusky. His hair, twisted into a tail at the nape of his neck, was straight and black like a Bregond's, but the pale gray of his eyes was startling. He was completely clean-shaven, and his lack of an Agrondish beard or Bregondish mustache made him seem boyish; His features were sharp and narrow, exotic but surprisingly comely—

Peri flushed, biting her lip.

Mahdha, I'm addle-witted from weariness! she thought. *He's not handsome. He's a SARKOND.*

Almost as an afterthought, Peri pulled out her bandanna and wrapped the man's bleeding hand loosely. He moved slightly, and Peri glanced up, startled, to see him watching her.

"Thank you," he said in that strange accent.

Peri hurriedly released his hand. It troubled her that he

spoke Bregondish. He'd probably learned it for the same reason most noble Bregonds paid merchants to teach their children Sarkondish—knowing an enemy's language was always an advantage.

"Your hand needs cleaning," Peri said awkwardly in Bregondish. "But—"

"I know." The man shook his head. "No water."

"I have water," Peri said, scowling. What Bregond in her right mind would saddle her horse without tying at least a couple of waterskins on? "Not a lot, but some. Problem is, I don't have any clean cloths to wash it with. You're just as well off letting it bleed clean. I'll wrap it better when it's had time to bleed the grit out."

The man tilted his head, gazing at her measuringly.

"Atheris," he said at last, extending his uninjured hand.

Peri ignored the hand and turned back to Tajin, pulling out one of the waterskins.

"Perian," she said shortly, then grimaced. "Peri." Nobody ever called her by her full name except when telling her something she didn't want to hear. And it was a common enough name in Bregond; however short her stay in Sarkond, best nobody knew her noble birth. She dribbled a little water into her cupped hand and let Tajin lick it up bit by bit.

When she'd given Tajin a few handfuls of water—thank Mahdha his breed, like Bregonds themselves, could manage on no food and little water for a long time—she took a small sip herself and then, reluctantly, turned back to hand the skin to Atheris. His hand was still out; Peri wondered with annoyance if he'd sat like that the whole time.

"Atheris," he repeated, gazing into her eyes.

"Fine. Atheris." Peri fought down the instinct to take his outstretched hand and pushed the waterskin into it instead. "Go easy on the water. Two skins are all I have. All the springs near the Barrier in Bregond are fouled or dried up, so

I assume it's no better here." She made that last statement almost a question.

Atheris took a sip from the skin, shuddering and obviously thirsty, but after another small sip he handed the skin back, saying nothing.

Peri sat back on her heels, scowling.

"All right," she said, in Sarkondish this time. "I'll try it this way. *Is* there drinkable water anywhere nearby?"

Atheris looked startled—but whether by the question or by the realization that Peri spoke Sarkondish, Peri couldn't tell.

"I do not know," he said. "I have never been near the Veil."

Peri took a deep breath, forcing down her exasperation. Right now she needed whatever this man could tell her. She was trapped with an enemy in enemy lands, but there was nothing gained by letting him see her desperation.

"Okay," she said. "Who were those soldiers and why do we need magic to hide us? I assume that's what you did, at least."

Once again Atheris stared at her blankly, as if amazed that she had to ask. Then he closed his eyes and a shudder ran through him.

"Bone Hunters," he said. "Assassin priests." He shook his head. "My spell will hide us so long as we stay within the circle, but they will feel us—me—as soon as we leave it." He opened his eyes, glancing at Peri. "I cannot imagine how we have gotten this far. But I cannot feel them, which means they are still beyond the Veil."

"The Barrier?" Peri shrugged. "They won't be able to follow very fast on foot."

Atheris raised his eyebrows and sat up, grimacing with pain.

"Their horses?" he asked.

"Visato root," Peri said, shrugging again. "We—the horse clans—call it Mare's Sleep because it's used on mares when we have to cut out a foal. It's too strong to use on people. Their horses won't wake till midmorning tomorrow, at a guess, and won't be worth much for hours after that.'' She glanced at Atheris. ''Unless your Bone Hunters know some spell to wake them.''

Atheris shook his head, his eyes widening with surprise.

''Such a spell would be beyond them,'' he said. ''That is life magic. Women's magic,'' he added at Peri's uncomprehending look.

Women's magic? Peri had never heard of any such thing, but this was Sarkond, and who knew how they'd warped and twisted the systems of magic.

Anyway, what did it matter?

She caught sight of a dark stain on Atheris's tunic low on his left side as he shifted and grimaced again.

''Better let me look at that,'' she said unwillingly. She didn't want to touch him, much less help him, but the stain looked fresh. And while she was in Sarkond, in danger from these Bone Hunters, she needed his magic and his knowledge of the country. And she needed him able to ride.

Atheris gave her another of those measuring looks, but pulled up his tunic, leaning to one side to expose the wound. Peri frowned at the puncture low on his waist, near his hip; leaning around she saw the exit wound on his back.

''Crossbow bolt,'' she said. ''Any chance it was poisoned?''

Atheris shook his head.

''They wanted me alive,'' he said almost absently. ''It was an accident I was hit at all. They were aiming for my horse.''

Somehow it surprised Peri that he had plain red blood like anyone else, although it appeared almost black in the dim light. Taking a deep breath, she examined the wounds carefully—Atheris's skin was warm but not feverishly so, neither as hairy as Danber's nor as smooth as Loris's but—Atheris's slight hiss of pain startled her out of her woolgathering. Peri knew, without knowing precisely how she knew, that the bolt hadn't pierced anything vital, but dirt and threads were caked to the wounds and there were splinters of wood in deeper. The wound had bled, but not enough to weaken Atheris, and not enough to clean the puncture. Infection was the greatest danger now.

"This needs work," Peri said. "But I need things I don't have, including a fire." She pulled off her wool tunic, started to raise her linen undertunic, then stopped. "Turn around."

Atheris obeyed without the slightest hint of ridicule or impatience; Danber would have laughed at her modesty, but this was no clan member. Peri pulled off her undertunic and hurriedly put her tunic back on. She tore her undertunic into strips and made a hasty dressing, tying it in place.

"There's nothing else I can do right now," she said. "As soon as Tajin's rested, we'll head back across the Barrier, and come daylight I can clean this properly."

To her surprise, Atheris shook his head.

"We cannot cross back," he said. "Not now, at least."

"I think you're wrong," Peri said. "Now's the best time, before their horses come around. Even with Tajin carrying double, we can easily outdistance them while they're on foot."

Atheris shook his head.

"You assume too much," he said. "If the Bone Hunters have not crossed the Veil, they have stayed for a reason— most likely to trap us when we cross again. Remember that while their feet may be slowed, their magic remains unhindered except by the Veil. If we cross the Veil, they and their magic will find us."

"Oh yeah?" Peri challenged. "And what if I just leave you here?"

Atheris returned her gaze steadily, as if unsurprised by the question.

"The Bone Hunters want me badly," he said slowly, "but now they will also want you. You took me from them. That will anger them greatly, but their priority will be to take you for questioning, to learn how you took me, and why. And they will scent you by the magic in your blood even as they scent me. Have you defenses against the magical attack they will surely mount against us?"

"No." Peri grimaced. *Not enough magic to do me any good; just enough to get me in trouble.* She forced herself to consider Atheris's words although instinct told her to distrust anything a Sarkond told her. Still, what he said made sense.

All right, she thought grimly. *Play our strength against their weakness. Use our assets—all of our assets.*

"The Barrier works to our advantage, then," Peri said slowly. "As long as the Bone Hunters are on the other side, they can't find us, can't use magic to track or attack us. And if they're slowed and on foot, they'll probably stay in Bregond, because *their* best chance of catching us is to wait for us to cross back over and then use their magic—they know we'll have to do it sooner or later. Our best option, then, is to keep going west on this side of the Barrier, put as much distance between them and us as we can, before their horses would have time to recover, and *then* cross back and hope we're out of range or can outride them. Even if they anticipate what we're doing, the farther west *they* go, the more likely it is that they'll run into Bregondish garrisons or patrols." Peri hated her own strategy, hated the idea of staying even a moment longer in Sarkond—her every instinct insisted that she cross the Barrier and ride for the nearest garrison as fast as Tajin could carry her—but just about anything was better than riding into a Sarkondish magical ambush, she had to admit.

Atheris was silent for a moment, as if weighing her words carefully; then he nodded.

"Yes," he said. "That is a wise plan."

And by the time we cross the Barrier, Peri thought grimly, *I'm going to know whether it's worth my while to keep you alive, or whether I'd be better off leaving you for them and riding for the nearest garrison as fast as I can go.*

By the time Tajin had regained his wind, it was near midnight, and the cloud cover had thinned. At the slow pace Tajin could maintain over the uneven footing, there was little profit in burdening him with double weight, so Peri led the warhorse, waving aside Atheris's protests. He had open wounds, one possibly serious, and was exhausted from his spellcasting as well. Walking, he'd only slow them further. Riding, at least he could watch the footing ahead while he marshaled his strength.

Nearly two hours later Peri had her first bit of good luck—she stumbled almost literally across what appeared to be a road, heavily rutted but still in good enough condition to indicate recent use, and the better footing would allow Tajin a faster pace now, even with two riders. Atheris would have slid back behind her, but she shook her head silently, settling herself behind him instead. If Atheris grew too exhausted to ride, she could simply strap him into the saddle; but her main reason was more simple. She did not want a Sarkond, even unarmed, at her back.

A recently used road, Peri thought grimly. *This near the border it can be used only for two things—Sarkondish raiders heading into Bregond, or outlaw merchants who trade across the borders. Aunt Kairi should know about this.*

Then she chuckled humorlessly.

I'm the Heir—or probably will be. I guess I need to know about it, too.

Tajin quickly found his stride on the trade road, and Peri was relieved by their speed. Finally they were gaining ground on their pursuers, and the more distance they gained, the sooner they could leave this blasted and barren land and return to Bregond's wholesome plains.

Less than an hour later, however, their luck changed again.

"I don't believe it," Peri said, craning her neck to peer around Atheris. "A wagon caravan here? Now?"

"And a large one, too," Atheris said, shaking his head. "Outlaw merchants, I would guess, trading across the border. Bregondish goods sell dearly here."

Peri grimaced. She'd always known that some merchants in Bregond, and Agrond, too, traded illegally across the Barrier—known it intellectually. Why, she and Estann had learned Sarkondish from such merchants, just as, before the alliance between Bregond and Agrond, her mother had learned Agrondish. Even Danber's clan sold some of its culls to dubious dealers headed north, not asking too many questions about where the horses might end up. But she'd never really thought—

Then Atheris stiffened and gasped.

"What?" Peri said, reflexively glancing around them.

"At least one of the Bone Hunters has passed the Veil," he said. "Perhaps more, but not all of them."

"They can't be very close, not traveling on foot," Peri said, shaking her head. "Their horses must still be asleep."

"If I am close enough to feel their presence, then they are close enough to feel mine," Atheris said practically. "Perhaps they found new mounts or some other mode of travel."

"But why would they cross at all now, much less split up?" Peri said slowly. She didn't like to think how the Bone Hunters might have acquired new horses, not with her uncle's camp so near the place where she'd rescued Atheris. "They can't even communicate with each other through the Barrier."

"In their place I might do the same," Atheris said after a moment's thought. "Some of their number would remain in Bregond in case we crossed over; others would cross themselves to track us here, all staying near the Veil so that one could quickly cross the Veil to fetch the others in Bregond if there was a need. Such a division lessens their power, but—''

"But makes sure they always know where you are, at least unless we can get out of range of their detection," Peri said grimly. "And supposing that they're east of us and traveling west, too, the only way we could do that is either by crossing south and hoping we can dodge whatever they throw at us, making really good speed west, or turning farther north into Sarkond—''

"—or hiding ourselves," Atheris said suddenly, "and letting them pass us by."

Peri gazed around them in the starlight. They were past the rocky hills. The land here was as flat as the Bregondish plains.

"Can't," she said shortly. "No shelter."

"There is shelter," Atheris said simply, pointing to the caravan fires ahead of them in the darkness.

"That's ridiculous," Peri said irritably. "You think they'd hide us? I don't have so much as a copper for a bribe, and what makes you think they'd shelter a Bregond anyway? And even if they did, that'd be the first place your Bone Hunters would search. Besides, even if you could hide us with your magic, the Bone Hunters have to know we came this way, and if they lost our track suddenly, it wouldn't be too hard to figure where we've gone."

"Not," Atheris said softly, "if I give them something else to follow."

It took Peri a moment to realize what he meant; then she set her jaw firmly.

"No," she said flatly. "Absolutely not. Not Tajin."

"I can cast a blood spell," Atheris said insistently. "We can send the horse south into Bregond, meanwhile concealing ourselves in the caravan. The horse will seek to return home and the Bone Hunters will follow it—''

''It doesn't gain us anything but a little time,'' Peri said, grinding her teeth. ''And it puts us on foot, and when the Bone Hunters' horses wake, then *they'll* have the advantage of speed—assuming they don't just send some kind of magical bolt down on Tajin, that is, in which case they'll be after us that much faster when they don't find any bodies with the horse. I don't see that the idea does us any good at all.''

''Why are the merchants here?'' Atheris said suddenly, and fell silent.

Peri fell silent, too, thinking. Merchants here meant other merchants, Bregondish merchants, on the other side of the Barrier. The two groups would meet to trade sooner or later. If Peri could sneak into the Bregondish caravan, or hide and contact them later, they could be bribed, coaxed, threatened, at least to get her safely to the nearest village or, better yet, herding clan. It was true that Tajin would head for home— and to him, ''home'' would most likely mean Danber's clan deep in the south of Bregond. And magic or not, he'd lead those Bone Hunters on their culls a merry chase indeed. And if Peri *really* wanted to confuse the back trail, she could leave Atheris with the Sarkondish merchants. Let the Bone Hunters divide their attention between *two* false trails.

''How are you going to talk the merchants into taking us in?'' Peri asked after a moment's thought. ''I mean, they'll see I'm not Sarkondish. Even in the dark, even if I don't say a word, my clothes are different. Won't they be more likely to just turn both of us over to the Bone Hunters instead?''

''I did not propose to ask them,'' Atheris said rather abashedly. ''What they do not know, they cannot tell.''

Again Peri fell silent. It was a large caravan and surely well guarded, but a good mage could bypass their safeguards, at least long enough to find a hiding place in a wagon full of trade goods. They'd ride cramped and quiet and nervous but . . .

Peri slid off Tajin's back, trying not to feel the familiar warmth of his solid muscles, the familiar roughness of his thick coat.

"All right," she said grimly. "Let's do it."

Atheris slid from the saddle more slowly and awkwardly, and Peri, to her disgust, had to steady him on his feet. She pulled the waterskins, her weapons, her emergency pack from the saddle. As an afterthought she scratched her name and Danber's clan sign—safer than revealing her royal connections—onto the saddle skirt along with three symbols—"safe/ hiding/returning." Any Bregond could read that message or would know someone who could; any Bregond would see the message sent and the horse returned to Danber. And Danber would see that a message reached either Aunt Kairi or Peri's parents, or possibly both.

"Your knife," Atheris said, and this time Peri silently handed it over; there were no convenient shards of rock-glass here. Atheris chanted as he unwrapped his cut hand; Peri could not help wincing as he deliberately set the cut to bleeding again, letting the blood drip on the saddle. He wrapped the cut again, then glanced at Peri and held out his hand, still chanting softly.

Peri swallowed hard at the idea of participating in Sarkondish magic, of extending the slightest trust to a Sarkond holding a knife, but she pushed up her left sleeve and held her arm over the saddle. *What kind of fool cuts his hand? Hardest place in the world to keep clean and covered, hurts you worst in a fight*—clenching her fist, Peri pointed sternly to the fatty part where she wanted him to cut. To Atheris's credit he did it more carefully than when he'd cut himself before.

This time there was no glow from the droplets of blood, but Peri felt an odd dizziness, like a brief instant of double perception in which she seemed at the same time to be sitting in Tajin's saddle and standing beside the horse.

"All right," Peri said when Atheris had finished his chant, knotting her sleeve tight around the cut for lack of a better bandage. "We'd better get closer to the caravan before I send Tajin off."

"Yes," Atheris panted, not elaborating. He was noticeably unsteady on his feet now, so tired that he was shaking.

He'd better have enough juice left to get us into that caravan, Peri thought grimly, *and to hide us once we're there, or we'll be a lot worse off than when we started—no horse, no hiding place, and no mage, just a couple of exhausted and nearly defenseless fugitives.*

Atheris refused Peri's offer to lead him on Tajin again—he said it might ruin the blood spell—but he kept one hand on the mounting loop and leaned heavily on Tajin as he walked. At last they were close enough that Peri began to worry about the danger of caravan guards spotting them even in the meager starlight, and she left Atheris with Tajin to scout ahead more carefully.

Peri was concerned to find the guards rather sparse, and she hastily halted her approach. For a caravan this size and in this dangerous territory to have so few guards could mean only one thing—that they used mages and wards instead, and Peri was certainly not mage enough either to detect or to bypass such wards. She prayed Atheris was.

"You are half-right," Atheris said soberly when Peri returned and told him what she'd seen. "Mages, possibly; wards, no. No reliable wards of any strength could be sustained this close to the power of the Veil. Instead they will rely on smaller and more localized magics—trap spells on their most valuable cargo, alarm spells on the horses and such—to protect the goods, and a few guards to patrol the camp. At this point on the road that is more than sufficient.

This area is too poor and open to sustain Sarkondish bandits and raiders, so patrols rarely come this far south, and no one from Bregond could know they are here except those with whom they have made arrangements to meet. They are relatively safe here, and when they return north into the more populated lands, their more powerful magics will become reliable again.''

That made some sense. Peri gathered her belongings into the best bundle she could manage under the circumstances; when she could not put it off any longer, she turned to Tajin, patting his neck and scratching behind his ears. Her heart broke when he snorted in that familiar way, butting his nose against her shoulder. Clenching her teeth hard, Peri forced herself to release Tajin's head.

"*Neycha,* Tajin," she murmured in his ear. "Home." She slapped his rump sharply, turning away so she would not have to watch him turn obediently south, heading straight for the Barrier. He was trained to carry a message in an emergency; he'd head south as fast as he could.

"He will soon pass through," Atheris said a moment later. "We must hide ourselves now."

"And let's see how you plan to do that," Peri muttered to herself. There were guards and protection spells—however minor—to sneak past, and Atheris looked pretty exhausted to her.

To Peri's surprise, Atheris's chant seemed short, almost cursory, but there was no doubt he'd done *something;* she felt a strange prickling, itching sensation that seemed to crawl over her skin so that she had to fight hard not to fidget and scratch.

Atheris walked slowly but without any real stealth toward the caravan, beckoning to Peri to follow. She took a deep breath and gave a little mental shake—it went deep against her grain to trust magic (especially Sarkondish magic) when she could neither see its effects nor even had a clear idea of what it did. Still, Atheris had as much to lose as she did—or maybe more—if they were captured; to that extent, at least, she could trust him.

Her trust was stretched to its limit, however, as they approached the caravan. There were indeed guards, more than Peri had originally thought; they'd simply stayed much closer to the camp than was customary in Agrondish or Bregondish caravans. The guards were neither idle nor careless and wandered steadily among the wagons, and Peri found that reassuring; at least it confirmed what Atheris had said.

The first time Peri saw two of the guards turn in their direction she froze in fear, certain that discovery and attack was imminent; to her amazement, however, the men ignored her and Atheris completely. The guards continued past on their patrol, and Peri breathed out slowly again.

Atheris peered into one wagon, then another, and Peri assumed he was looking for a wagon whose cargo wasn't warded, with enough boxes and bundles to conceal them comfortably. This assumption proved correct, and when Atheris indicated a wagon and motioned her inside, she climbed in and rearranged the boxes as quietly as she could to make a hiding place. Meanwhile Atheris unwrapped his cut hand and opened the wound yet again, repeating the spell Peri had first seen him use and letting drops of blood fall along the slatted sides of the wagon bed. Peri held her breath again; if the caravan had a mage, as it must surely have, and that mage happened to be awake despite the lateness of the hour, Atheris's spell might be detected. But no alarm was raised, and Peri helped an utterly exhausted Atheris into the wagon, quietly moving the boxes again so they were completely concealed. Atheris slumped back against her makeshift pack, barely conscious.

"I know you're tired," Peri whispered. "But I need to

know how long your spell—or spells, or whatever—will keep us hidden.''

''Yes.'' Atheris's whisper was barely audible. ''The Bone Hunters will not be able to sense us as long as we remain in the wagon. That spell will remain active as long as I remain within its boundaries to feed it with my energies. The spell that allowed us to bypass the guards and magical traps and the like, for that I drew on the power and properties of the Veil— borrowed a bit of it for ourselves, if you will. As long as we remain near the Veil, it will hold firm. But it does not precisely hide us; it only renders us less . . . noticeable. So we must be quiet and cautious.''

Quiet and cautious wouldn't be difficult so long as nobody unloaded the wagon, and the wagon was, after all, traveling west, which was exactly where Peri wanted to go. *All right, then.* Tiredly Peri stood again, trying to figure the quietest way over the boxes.

''What are you doing?'' Atheris whispered. He was so exhausted that his eyelids were fluttering in their effort to stay open.

''We have a little water,'' Peri whispered back, ''but no food and nothing to treat your wounds. If you're too weak or sick to cast spells if we need them''—*you're useless to me*— ''we're both in trouble.''

Atheris made no answer; he had closed his eyes. Peri didn't know whether he thought it wasn't worth his trouble to argue or whether he'd merely passed out, but it made no difference. She'd followed his advice as far as she was going to. She hoped the Bone Hunters would be too busy chasing Tajin to notice her for the time she was outside the wagon.

Peri slipped quietly from the wagon and made her way stealthily to the next wagon, dodging a guard. She started to peer into the wagon but froze as the sound of a throaty snore emerged. Peri grimaced, shaking her head, and moved on to another wagon.

Nobody would trade over the border for something as basic as dried meat, but on a road like this, where hunting would be impossible, a caravan this large would have to have a supply wagon. And that wouldn't be warded, not when the wards would have to be reset every time somebody wanted a piece of cheese or a skin of wine. After considerable searching Peri found the wagon she was looking for; an old man, probably the cook, was sleeping under it, but she was still able to carefully withdraw enough food for a day or two, a skin of water, and a smaller skin of brandy. Retreating with her booty, Peri nearly collided with a guard, and she huddled against the wagon, heart pounding, for several minutes before she dared move again.

Guilty as a thief, she thought amusedly, then humor fled. *Oh, Mahdha, forgive me, I AM a thief. A common thief hiding in a caravan and stealing food.* For a moment she shook with self-disgust. Not only was she consorting with a Sarkond; now she'd fallen to thievery. How could she ever raise her head in Bregond again?

Peri's guilt, however, did not stop her from finding the caravan's handler and the kit he kept for tending the horses, and liberating some of what she found there.

Is it true theft to steal from outlaws? Would any man or woman in Bregond condemn me for taking what I needed from Sarkonds? Well, yes, they would, at least if they knew it was to feed and tend another Sarkond. But I need him to get home alive.

Atheris was still asleep or unconscious when Peri slipped back into the wagon with her loot, and she saw no reason to try to wake him. She couldn't tend his wound in the darkness, and she wouldn't have dared light a lamp even if she'd stolen one, which she hadn't. If he was hungry or thirsty, he could

eat and drink just as easily later. Peri herself swallowed a little
water, but exhaustion won out over hunger for her, too, and
she curled up as warmly as she could on the hard wagon
boards. Tomorrow they'd decide whether it might be safer to
abandon the caravan and cross the Barrier on foot or stay with
the wagon and wait for the merchants to cross—Peri had her
doubts about the wisdom of that; it was always possible that
it was the Bregondish merchants who came into Sarkond instead. Tomorrow she'd find out exactly who these Bone Hunters were and why they'd hunted Atheris even into Bregond.
Tomorrow she'd decide what she needed to do about Atheris
once they crossed the Barrier.

Tomorrow she'd . . .

2

PERI WOKE, PANICKING, TO A HAND CLASPED firmly over her mouth, a Sarkond leaning over her. Reflexively she reached for her dagger, preparing for combat—

"Hush," Atheris said, his face almost touching hers. "Stay quiet. We have a problem. Several problems, actually."

Atheris. Bone Hunters. The Barrier. Sarkond. The caravan. Memory returned in a rush and Peri held still, breathing heavily, until Atheris cautiously withdrew his hand. The wagon was jolting under her and Peri remembered the deep ruts in the road.

"What problems?" she whispered, despite the jolting and squeaking of the wagon.

"The blood spell on the wagon is intact," Atheris murmured, "but the spell hiding us from the guards is gone."

"WHAT?" Peri hissed as loud as she dared. "What do you mean, it's gone? How could that happen?"

"That," Atheris said softly, "is another problem. We have left the area of the Veil. The road, and the caravan, must have turned north hours ago to have gotten so far. I only woke a short time ago myself and felt that the spell was gone. I can no longer even feel the Veil."

Peri clenched her teeth, trembling.

"Why would they turn north?" she said, forcing herself to keep her voice low. "They should've followed the Barrier west until they met a Bregondish caravan. That's what *you* said."

"That is what I thought," Atheris whispered, shaking his head. "But there is another possibility. When you searched the other wagons, what did you find?"

Peri shook her head impatiently at the question.

"Typical trade stuff," she said. "These boxes and bags are candles. There's bolts of cloth, boxes of spices. Hams. Cheeses. Casks of wine—" Then she stopped, seeing Atheris's expression, and she felt a chill begin somewhere at the base of her spine.

"Sarkond," Atheris said, very, very softly, "has few such goods at all, and certainly none in such quality or abundance to trade them to Bregond."

"No," Peri whispered. "Oh no."

They weren't traveling west to meet another caravan to trade.

They were returning home after they'd already traded.

"We've got to get out of here," Peri whispered rapidly. "If we start back south now—"

"No!" Atheris's hand on her shoulder tightened. "There is nothing hiding us from the guards now, do you understand? If we try to leave, they will see us and kill us." He hesitated. "And there is something else . . ."

"What?" Peri looked into Atheris's eyes and the chill in the pit of her stomach deepened.

"The Bone Hunters?" she whispered.

"I—I believe so," Atheris whispered back very slowly. "They are too far behind for me to be certain. Nor can I know without doubt that they are following this caravan, or this road. But I . . . I believe at least some of them remain between us and the Veil, and I believe they are moving north. How many and how quickly, I do not know. Perhaps none of them were fooled by my spell."

Peri said nothing; she clenched her hands hard to stop their trembling. If what Atheris said was true, they were in very great danger indeed. If the Bone Hunters had seen through Atheris's trick that easily, what hope of escape was there, especially now that they no longer had the advantage of Tajin's speed?

Peri took a deep breath and sternly forced down her terror.

Panic, she reminded herself, *kills more warriors than the deadliest foe. The first priority is surviving the next minute. Second is surviving the next hour. Third is the next day. Fourth, the next week.*

All right. Use our advantages. Play strength against weakness.

"You're certain," Peri whispered, "the Bone Hunters can't sense us here?"

This time Atheris did not hesitate.

"I am certain," he whispered back. "I can feel the spell drawing on my energies. And if they knew where we were, they would either be here already, or they would have sent magic against us."

"Good," Peri murmured, nodding. "We're safe for the moment, at least from the Bone Hunters. There's that. Can you cast another spell to hide us from these people without using the Barrier?"

Atheris hesitated for a long moment, then reluctantly shook his head.

"I could cast such a spell, yes," he said softly. "But not—" He waved his hand illustratively. "Not like this. To perform a proper ritual I would need certain paraphernalia I do not have. I could improvise something, but for that I would require the power of a blood sacrifice."

Peri went very still.

"What," she said slowly, "you mean kill somebody?"

Atheris shook his head.

"No," he said. "For a sustained spell I need a living source to draw upon, as the spell on this wagon draws upon me, rather than the short but powerful burst of energies released by a death. But I am not strong enough to have two such spells drawing upon me, and were I to use your blood, then neither of us would be strong enough to defend or flee in a crisis."

Peri forced herself to ignore the surge of despair she felt at his words.

"All right," she said. "We'll think about that for a while. Right now that protection isn't critical. We're safe enough here. Nobody's going to go searching through a wagonload of cases of candles unless we give them a reason to. So for now we keep still, keep quiet, and we're all right unless the situation changes."

"Yes," Atheris whispered after a moment's thought.

"This caravan's big and illegal," Peri said, thinking out loud. "That means it's also expensive. Merchants minimize expenses. They'll operate out of the closest good-sized city to their trade point. That means that's the city we're headed for." She turned back to Atheris. "What city and how far?"

"I believe the closest city on this road is Darnalek," Atheris said hesitantly. "But as to distance, I cannot say. Unfortunately I am unfamiliar with this area."

Peri stifled an impatient sigh, trying to remember the quantities of food she'd seen in the supply wagon. It had seemed like a lot.

No. Wait a minute. There's no grazing or clean water out here. A lot of that had to be water and feed for the horses. They can't have planned for a very long trip, then. Not with only the one supply wagon. She breathed a sigh of relief.

Of course, a city's a whole new set of problems. As far as I know, we don't have any money at all, but that doesn't matter, because one look at my skin and features, not to mention my clothes, would mark me as a Bregond, and I'm sure my Sarkondish is as accented as Atheris's Bregondish. Well, if I get killed in the first Sarkondish city we come to, at least I won't have to worry about those Bone Hunters.

She closed her eyes, clenching her teeth.

I've been away one whole night now. Uncle Terralt will have all the guards searching for me—the guards at the garrison, too. And most of those guards are Bregondish, they'll be starting to wonder . . . Grimly Peri forced that thought away.

Right now her most pressing problem was Atheris's wounds, but there was nothing she could do about them with the wagon jolting so. Fortunately Sarkondish merchants liked their comfort as much as did their Bregondish and Agrondish counterparts, and the caravan stopped at noon for a hot dinner, and Peri took advantage of the daylight and stationary surface. By the time she'd picked splinters and fibers out of the wound in Atheris's side, cleaned it thoroughly with the brandy, and made a dressing with the herbs and bandages she'd stolen, she had gained a growing, if grudging, respect for the Sarkond. Although Peri knew she had to have caused him severe pain, he had held quite still and remained absolutely silent throughout her treatment, although he'd gone almost white and he'd clenched his hands so hard that he'd set the cut on his hand bleeding again. Peri cleaned the cut, decided it did not require stitching, and applied a clean dressing, then tended the cut on her own arm; then there was nothing to do but rest, eat and drink their stolen supplies, and wait.

They waited. Dinner ended and the jolting journey began again. Atheris drowsed, tired by sustaining his spell and by the pain he'd endured, but Peri fidgeted restlessly in her cramped position and thought thoughts that darkened her mood more than the hard floorboards of the wagon, the splintery sides of the box against which she leaned, the lingering ache of her bruised ribs, or the uncomfortable fullness of her bladder.

Mahdha grant that Tajin got past the Bone Hunters and that someone finds him quickly. Oh, Bright Ones, very, very quickly . . .

Uncle Terralt would have had guards out searching for Peri since soon after sunset the night before. They'd have ridden on to the garrison. Not all the guards were Bregonds, so perhaps the search would have been called off until morning; it was hard enough to locate someone on Bregond's plains, nearly impossible at night, and an unskilled searcher, or one who just didn't know the land, could easily become lost. But sooner or later the guards would have found the dead mare, the signs, the Sarkondish camp.

Not the Sarkonds themselves. Obviously the Bone Hunters had evaded detection despite their sleeping mounts, or Atheris would not be sensing them now. Perhaps they had mounts again, perhaps they were on foot; somehow, in any event, they'd managed to make enough progress to stay within Atheris's range, whatever that might be, despite the Mare's Sleep, despite the spell on Tajin, despite Atheris's magical concealment.

But meanwhile, back in Bregond, the guards would have found Tajin's trail and that of the Bone Hunters overlaying it, and that trail led directly into Sarkond itself. Unless they found

Tajin and read the message on his saddle, there would be only one conclusion they could draw.

That Peri had been captured by Sarkonds.

And that meant that in Bregond at least, Peri was dead—if not killed in battle by the Sarkonds, then, as custom required, honorably dead by her own hand. Her friends and kin would mourn her as dead. If she returned she could expect no welcome, no help, no acknowledgment whatsoever. She'd be an outcast even to Danber, and Mahdha, who whispered her secrets to the clans and carried the spirits of the honored dead on her wings, would forget her name. Even Peri's mother, despite the years she'd lived in Agrond, would never wholeheartedly welcome her daughter home.

No, Peri simply had to hope that Tajin would make it past the Bone Hunters. Someone would find him, read the message, get word either to Aunt Kairi or Danber. Then they'd only think Peri had run from her responsibilities—disgraceful but not disastrous. Unfortunately her exploits were not quite heroic enough to get her out of trouble, but at least she'd be able to return to Bregond. Life as Kairi's Heir, and later as High Lady, was no prospect she relished, but anything was better than total exile from the land she considered her home.

And she'd risked everything to rescue a *Sarkond*.

That thought piqued Peri's curiosity, but just as she was about to wake Atheris and ask him about it, the wagon slowed, stopped. Cautiously Peri peered out under the edge of the wagon cloth and immediately saw the reason. The sun was low in the sky, almost down. The merchants were camping for the evening.

"That's it," she murmured.

"What?" Atheris said softly, making Peri jump. The Sarkond was awake and watching her anxiously.

"I have got," she said between clenched teeth, "to piss.

Not tomorrow, not after midnight when everybody's gone to sleep. Right *now*."

Atheris gazed at her for a moment, his lips twitching suspiciously, then picked up a nearly empty waterskin. He quickly swallowed the last of the water and mutely handed her the empty skin.

Despite her foul mood, Peri had to stifle a laugh of her own at the waterskin and the look Atheris had given her; but a laugh would have brought the guards down on them, and more importantly, would have had very negative consequences on her overfull bladder. Instead she applied her wits and her knife to the problem, widening the opening so she could use the waterskin. Thankfully Atheris turned away without her having to ask—*Mahdha bless me, he's got good manners for a Sarkond!*—and when she finished, she just as silently handed him the skin and turned her back. When he was done she tied the skin off tightly and set it aside. Tomorrow, when she was certain nobody would see, she'd empty it out the back of the wagon.

"How's your side?" she whispered.

Atheris pulled up the edge of his tunic and touched the dressing, raised his eyebrow, and pressed a little harder.

"Very good indeed," he said softly. "I wondered why you did not simply use a spell, but then I realized that a mage in the caravan might have detected it, and perhaps you were wise to conserve your energies."

Peri grimaced.

"I didn't use a spell," she murmured, "because I don't have enough healing magic for spells, just a kind of knack for knowing what's wrong and what to do about it."

Atheris gazed at her for a long moment; then his eyes widened.

"You sacrificed your gift," he whispered, very slowly, "for *this*?" He touched her sword.

Peri irritably pulled out a strip of dried meat and chewed on it; she *hated* having nothing to do.

"I don't know what you're talking about," she muttered.

"Why would you forsake your magic for the sword?" Atheris persisted, looking disturbed, almost horrified.

"I didn't forsake anything," Peri said, annoyed. She gestured pointedly at Atheris's empty scabbard. "Why did you?"

Atheris's brows drew down.

"That is different," he said with great dignity. "The temple required my sword training. But you are a woman."

Peri rolled her eyes and shut her mouth hard before she could begin an argument that would probably lead to raised voices and subsequent discovery. She'd run into *that* attitude often enough in Agrond. She certainly didn't need more of it from a Sarkond.

Anyway, I'd value his opinion slightly lower than what I just put in that waterskin, Peri thought grimly.

"More importantly," she whispered, "we need to talk about your next spell. What've you got that can tell us how far we are away from this city, this Darnalek, and whether or not your Bone Hunters are following us, and if so, how close they are?"

Atheris scowled slightly, but he paused thoughtfully before he answered.

"The city would be only an elementary scrying," he said. "The Bone Hunters are another matter. Finding them is simple; preventing them from sensing my scrying in turn is another matter. That requires a more powerful spell."

"So?" Peri said.

"I am already sustaining the blood spell on this wagon," he said slowly and patiently, as if speaking to a child. "Casting the necessary scrying will weaken me greatly."

"Well, think about this, then," she said, just as patiently. "We have to get away from this caravan before we get into a city, or I'm dead. We've got to find some other place to hide, or you're captured. That means that we've got to know where the city is so we have time to get away from the caravan, and we've got to know where the Bone Hunters are so we have time to get away from *them*. Or do you have a better idea?''

Atheris was silent for a long moment. At last he spoke, sounding very tired.

"I will require a bowl," he said. "Or a cup."

And they had none. Peri thought about the problem for a moment, then nodded.

"Can you make fire?" she asked.

"Fire?" Atheris repeated. "By magic?"

"By magic, yes," Peri said irritably. "If I wanted somebody to hear me scraping away with flint and steel, I wouldn't have asked you in the first place. Can you make enough fire to light a candle? Yes or no?" This was a Sarkondish mage, true, not a Fire-Dedicated like her mother, but even Loris could've lit a simple candle.

"Yes," Atheris said very softly. "I can light a candle. But if I do, it will be seen."

"Not if you stop talking about it and do it before the light goes," Peri retorted. She had to remind herself sternly to be slow and quiet as she drew a candle out of one of the bags. "Hurry."

Atheris said nothing, although he clearly wanted to question, if not argue, but he only focused on the wick of the candle Peri held out; a moment later the candle flared alight. Peri handed the candle to Atheris.

"All right," she said, extending her cupped hands. "Drip the wax into my hands."

Atheris's eyebrows shot up, but he obeyed, tilting the candle sharply so that the wax melted rapidly. He glanced at Peri's face as the hot wax dripped down.

"I would think," he said slowly, "that that would be quite painful."

Peri grinned ruefully, carefully working the liquid wax with her thumbs against her palms into a bowl shape.

"Not much, actually," she said. "I've been studying the sword and herding horses most of my life. I've even woven baskets out of swordgrass. My hands are pretty callused and tough." She chuckled, thinking of her mother; the Fire-Dedicated High Lady, whom Peri had seen hold metal in the forge until it melted in her bare hands, would not have been impressed by a little melted beeswax.

And she and Father wouldn't be much impressed by anything else I've done so far, either, Peri thought sourly as she worked the wax. *And why should they be? So far all I've managed to do is rescue an enemy, get the both of us chased into Sarkond by magic-wielding assassins, and lose my warhorse. So much for convincing them I was meant to be a great warrior. A great idiot—now, THAT they might believe.*

"Enough," Atheris whispered, blowing out the candle. "The wax cup is deep enough, and the sun is low. Soon they would see the light from this wagon and investigate."

Peri carefully pulled her fingers free of the hollowed-out wax cup and handed it to Atheris. When he started to unwind the bandage around his hand again, however, Peri shook her head.

"Don't," she said. "If you keep opening that cut, it's going to need stitches, and the palm of your hand is the worst place to have a scar." She grimaced. *Why do I care if he cripples or scars his hand? Mahdha scour me raw, you'd think he was my clansman. Never mind—for now, at least, I need him unmaimed.*

"If you have to use blood," Peri said, forcing the words out, "can you use mine? You may need your strength for more spellcasting, and Mahdha knows *I'm* rested."

Atheris hesitated thoughtfully for a moment, then nodded. "Your blood will suffice," he said. "Your knife?"

"Right." Peri passed it over and pushed up her sleeve, indicating the fattiest part of her forearm beside the previous cut. "There."

That's another priority, she thought to distract herself while Atheris made the shallow cut, letting her blood drip into the wax cup. *If he has a scabbard, I assume he has at least some idea of what to do with a sword, mage or not. Whatever that horsecrap was about women and swords, two blades are better than one, even if one of them IS a Sarkond. I've got to find a way to steal him a dagger at least. I don't like eating with a knife that's been used in Sarkondish magic. And as long as I'm in Sarkond, at least, my grace-blade never leaves my boot sheath. If I were captured—* Peri resolutely did not finish that thought.

When Atheris released her arm, she bound the cut quietly, watching as he chanted in a whisper over the makeshift cup. At last his chant trailed off into silence; Peri saw nothing reflected in the blood in the cup, but Atheris's gaze became intent and the fleeting expressions passing across his face told her that the spell had at least revealed something of interest.

At last he closed his eyes, apparently breaking the spell, raised the wax cup, and to Peri's amazement, swallowed the small quantity of her blood in the cup. Atheris shivered as he swallowed, and Peri shivered, too, grimacing. She'd tasted the blood of her kills often enough, sharing the heart or liver on a successful hunt, but this was different. This was human blood, *her* blood.

"Why in the world," she whispered squeamishly, "did you do that?"

Atheris glanced at her curiously, as if the answer were self-evident.

"Your blood contains the emanation of your magic," he

whispered back, "and further was imbued with some of my own magic as well. What would you have had me do, waste its power and pour it on the ground for the Bone Hunters to track us by?"

Peri didn't grace that with an answer, but she privately resolved to empty her urine out the back of the wagon at the first possible opportunity, before she learned about any more bizarre Sarkondish customs!

To her surprise, however, she found herself weary, almost exhausted. She checked the cut on her arm, only slightly reassured to find it already closed, then sat back against the crates, closing her eyes, already drowsing. Certainly Atheris hadn't drawn enough blood to leave her this worn-out. This must be the magical draining effect he had mentioned. If that was so, no wonder he'd slept all day!

"So what did you see?" Peri murmured, forcing her eyes open. "Bad news first; I'm not sure I can stay awake for the lot."

"The Bone Hunters are definitely closer," Atheris said softly. "There are three who crossed into Sarkond, and they are far west of the point where they crossed. Whether they are tracking us somehow, whether they are merely paralleling the Veil by arrangement with their brethren on the other side, or whether they are following the trade road, deducing that we might take that path, I do not know. They are mounted—not the horses they rode before, so they have stolen or claimed others. They ride slowly but with purpose, not deviating from their path to search, so I must assume they have some idea of our course. And they move, of course, far more rapidly than this caravan."

"Oh, Bright Ones," Peri groaned, abruptly remembering their situation and quickly lowering her voice. "Is there any more bad news?"

"No," Atheris said softly. "The rest should reassure you.

The other Bone Hunters have not crossed the Veil, which indicates they are not positive we are still in Sarkond. That remains to our advantage.

"Judging the distance we have made from the Veil in one day," he continued, "we will reach Darnalek in two days, perhaps three. But we will wish to leave the caravan tomorrow."

"Oh, really?" Peri said, forcing herself to sit up straight. She shook her head as cobwebs threatened to smother her brain. "Why? And have you figured out how yet?"

"The 'why' will answer a part of the 'how,' " Atheris told her. "I have found for us a far better hiding place than this, and one which will quickly conceal us when we depart this wagon. There is a large pilgrimage of worshipers journeying to the great temple at Rocarran. The road the pilgrims are following joins with this one very soon, and the caravan will undoubtedly overtake the pilgrimage tomorrow in late afternoon. There are enough people on the road that the caravan will be forced to follow behind the pilgrimage until the worshipers take another fork in the road some miles beyond. Therefore it is almost certain that the caravan will camp near the pilgrims tomorrow night. We should be able to leave the wagons and easily hide ourselves among the worshipers, many of whom are sick or diseased. A robe and some bandages will conceal your outland features and clothing."

"That's fine," Peri said irritably, "except that it still leaves us with our two biggest problems—first, that we're going farther north when we want to be heading south instead; and second, that we won't have any nice wagon you can cast a spell on to hide us from those Bone Hunters."

"But that is the perfection of it," Atheris told her, smiling. "The worshipers are accompanied by priests of the temple, powerful mages themselves. Hiding within the crowd, the presence of the priests will conceal our emanations as certainly as the spell I used, and without taxing my magical energies in the slightest. And when the Bone Hunters find no trace of us, why should they search farther north when they know that is the one direction we would never choose to go? Surely they will assume that they have passed us and turn back eastward, and then we can make our way back to Bregond safely.''

Peri was far from convinced. Atheris's plan meant continuing north, so they'd have that much more of Sarkond to cross on foot to return to Bregond, with only whatever supplies and money they could manage to steal from the merchants before they left the caravan. Her every instinct told her to sneak out of the wagon this very night, steal a couple of horses, and head back for Bregond as fast as she could ride, with or without Atheris. And could she trust what he told her? Perhaps his whole goal was to get them deeper into Sarkond for purposes of his own.

But that made no sense. He'd clearly fled Sarkond into Bregond; she'd seen that for herself. And just as clearly the Bone Hunters had pursued him and captured him alive with the goal of taking him back. Atheris had no more to gain by venturing farther north than Peri herself. His motives might be questionable, but she was far too tired right now to press him for those answers. She could hardly form a coherent thought without nodding off.

"All right," she whispered at last. "We'll talk about it and make our plans tomorrow while the wagon's moving and we can make more noise. Right now I need . . ." Her eyelids were so heavy she could barely keep them up. "Need to—"

"Yes, sleep," Atheris urged, sliding their makeshift pack over for her to rest her head on. "Regain your strength. And tomorrow—"

But sleep swallowed whatever he might have said.

3

"**Y**ES," ATHERIS SAID, VERY SOFTLY. "THEY ARE definitely closer."

Peri sighed, rubbing her eyes. Her head was still fuzzy, her eyes scratchy, despite having slept all night and most of the morning.

"Bright Ones, I'm a mess," she whispered. "Was that scrying spell that strong?"

"The spell itself was not strong," Atheris replied. "It was intricate and subtle, and I had to substitute the energy of the blood sacrifice for properties normally gained over the course of the ritual. Unfortunately, as you say, the little magical force in your blood is quickly consumed and so your energies are exhausted more rapidly. I must avoid drawing on your strength unless it is unavoidable. You are better left to defend us physically." He sounded vaguely disapproving, and Peri bit back a retort that seemed likely to start the whole women-as-warriors argument over again. First chance she got, she'd happily demonstrate her ability as a warrior. She was less than pleased this morning anyway; to her embarrassment, when she woke she found that she'd cuddled cozily against Atheris in her sleep, and unfortunately, by the time she pulled away, Atheris had already wakened and noticed her position and her flaming cheeks. Thanks be to Mahdha, at least he'd kept his mouth shut about it; for that great mercy, Peri was willing to forgive him his idiotic view of women—for the moment, at least.

"Three priorities," she said shortly. "First: steal food, water, weapons, and money if possible. Second: get away from the caravan without anyone noticing. Third: hide ourselves in the pilgrimage, which means getting a robe and rags for me."

"This time let me manage the thefts," Atheris told her. "If you can only get away from the caravan and hide yourself temporarily, I will procure what we need."

"Really." Peri glanced at him narrowly. "And just how are you going to do that?" If anything, he looked more weary than she felt.

"I can cause sleep," Atheris told her, then added hastily, "in one or possibly two persons at a time. I could hardly so treat the whole caravan of guards and merchants. But with care I can find a guard by himself and so procure his weapons. I will gain money and supplies and your robe in a similar manner. Only leave the caravan and make your way around to the north side of the camp and wait for me. That way the pilgrims and priests will remain between you and the Bone Hunters."

"I can do that," Peri said unwillingly. It disturbed her profoundly, the idea of depending on Atheris and his magic so heavily. But she could suggest nothing better. And stealing ran contrary to everything she had been taught. However hypocritical it might be, she would far rather leave the stealing to someone else.

"I can do that," she said again, more strongly. Atheris had trusted her expertise before; here, now, deep in Sarkond, she had little choice but to trust his. And speaking of trust—

"Why do they want you so badly?" Peri whispered. "Those Bone Hunters, I mean."

She was surprised by the pain in Atheris's eyes before he glanced away, hiding his expression.

"It was—a temple matter," he whispered. "It would make no sense to an outlander. Pardon me—I need to rest, conserve my strength for tonight."

Peri ground her teeth in frustration, wanting to press Atheris for an explanation. Temple matter? Were these Bone Hunters not even associated with the Sarkondish military, but some kind of religious authority? Assassin priests, Atheris had said— and able to use magic as well. What kind of "temple matter" merited such pursuit? Peri wanted to shake Atheris, demand that he tell her—

But Atheris had already fallen into an exhausted slumber, and unwillingly Peri felt a pang of pity. He was weakened from spellcasting—part of it on her behalf—and recovering from a wound. Judging by what she'd learned of the Bone Hunters, he probably hadn't had a good meal or a sound night's sleep in days, and she couldn't quite bring herself to wake him now.

Oh, well, no matter, Peri thought with a sigh. *It looks like we're going to have plenty of time to talk. And if it's a "temple matter," it's got nothing to do with me anyway.*

Time passed, the wagon jolting along, Peri thinking and watching Atheris or peeping cautiously out the side of the wagon. The farther they traveled from the Barrier, the more normal the land began to look—it was poor, thin steppes, cold and bone-dry and rocky, a little blighted-looking grass and a few scraggly brambles the only vegetation, but at least it was not utterly blasted and barren like the land farther south. Slowly the sun lowered in the sky.

It was midafternoon when the caravan caught up to the pilgrimage. Peri dared not raise her head to look out the front of the wagon, but she knew it when the wagon slowed and she heard the merchants and the guards shouting back and forth. At last, peering cautiously out under the edge of the wagon cloth, she saw the stragglers wandering in little groups of one or two or three off to the sides of the road, and she bit her lip, shocked to a silence greater than caution.

Bregond had no pilgrimages. The temples were not places of worship; they were the homes of the Orders where Bregond's priests and priestesses were trained in the use of their magic, until they finished their training and left the temple to serve where they were most needed. In Agrond it was different; there were temples to many gods, and the priests and priestesses were only that, not necessarily mages, and there were pilgrimages to those temples. Once or twice Peri had seen such pilgrimages. She'd seen the weak and the sick, lepers and cripples being brought to the temples to pray to their gods for the miracles that healers could not provide.

This was different.

Peri's first thought was that she no longer wondered why Atheris had so blithely assumed that she could swaddle herself in robes and rags without anyone questioning. Half the pilgrims she saw—and admittedly those were the stragglers, the weakest—were so smothered in ragged cloth that they could have been Agrond, Bregond, Sarkond, elves, demons. But those hidden ones were not the worst.

The worst were the ones Peri could see.

In Agrond Peri had lived at court, largely sheltered from such sights as this; as a member of the royal family it was too risky for her to ride through the worst sections of town where such unfortunate souls took refuge. In Bregond, among the horse clans for the most part, there *were* no such sights. Bregond was a harsh land that did not coddle the weak. The maimed, the diseased either recovered on their own, or were healed, or they died—of their disease or by their own hand. It was as simple as that. She had seen injuries, sometimes horrible injuries, hunting accidents, herding accidents.

She had never seen the aftermath of a war of magic, or the offspring of a magic-blighted land.

They were twisted, withered or bloated, covered with lumpy growths or running sores, too tall or too short, too pale or too dark, skin peeling or scaly or scabby or slick and bald. One such creature hobbling near the wagon—Peri could not tell whether it was male or female—had a stunted, twisted third arm curling out of its left armpit. A woman carried a baby with neither hands nor feet; the infant wailed continuously, waving withered stumps in the air. A tall, almost impossibly thin man covered with knobby tumors hobbled along on legs which terminated not in feet, but in birdlike three-toed claws. A young girl with snakelike scales covering her skin dragged herself along on two crutches with the aid of feeble pushes from boneless legs. Peri could not turn away from the sight; horrified but fascinated, she stared out through her peephole until the waning light told her that the caravan would soon stop.

"Lend me your dagger," Atheris whispered, startling her.

Peri turned gratefully to face him, drawing the dagger but reluctant to surrender it.

"Why?" she asked softly.

"You do not need it to flee and hide," Atheris said practically. "And you have a sword if you must defend yourself. But I may need a sharp blade to cast my spells. And if I have to crawl into a wagon from the side, do you want me to cut the thongs binding it to the frame or chew through them with my teeth?"

Peri clenched her jaws tightly but handed over the dagger.

"Try to find yourself a blade," she hissed as Atheris tucked the dagger into his belt. "I cut food with that, you know."

Atheris chuckled very quietly.

"Believe me," he said, "that I am far more eager to hold steel of my own than you are to reclaim yours."

Then they sat quietly, cataloging the sounds of the caravan setting up camp for the night. Fires were kindled; tents were pitched for merchants who did not sleep in wagons and pallets laid for the guards. Watches were assigned. Supper was cooked and eaten, and guards who were not on watch lingered by the fires, drinking and talking.

Later there were other sounds. There were whores among the pilgrims, and the whores came to the merchants' fires in search of wealthier—and certainly healthier—bedmates. Sounds from the tents and pallets indicated that at least some were successful in their transactions. Peri wondered squeamishly whether the purchasers of the whores' services bothered to inquire what manner of healing the whores were seeking at the temple. Slowly those sounds too faded, replaced only by the occasional snore.

"We can go now," Atheris whispered very quietly. "Remember, make your way north of the camps as quickly as you can. I will get what we need and meet you there before sunrise so that we can join the pilgrim camp while the others are still asleep."

Peri nodded, inspected her makeshift bundle of weapons and supplies to make sure nothing would rattle to betray her, and fastened it securely on her back. She timed the guard patrols and waited until one had just passed before she climbed out as quietly as she could. She was both glad and dismayed to find the night as overcast as her first in Sarkond—glad because the poor light would help conceal her departure; dismayed because it concealed her footing and path just as thoroughly. She did not bother watching which way Atheris went; right now her concern was to hide herself, and if Atheris got himself caught in the middle of all these people, there was nothing whatsoever she could do about it. She had only moments to spare before the next guard on patrol walked by.

She scampered away as quickly as she could, hand on the hilt of her sword in case she needed to draw and fight— although how she'd fight in near pitch darkness and on uncertain footing she had no idea—and hurried out of camp in what she hoped was the right direction. Thankfully the Sarkondish guards were in the same fix as she; actually, Peri realized, she had a slight advantage in that she knew they were there, while hopefully they had no idea that she was.

Once she moved away from the wagon, however, Peri did not totally lack for light. Some of the pilgrims had managed to build fires, probably burning droppings from past caravans, and there was sufficient glow from their fires to give her at least an indication of where the boundaries of the pilgrim camp were. There were no stars visible to show Peri north, but to the best of her knowledge the road had been heading slightly northwest, so she could at least estimate where she was supposed to be.

She'd made it nearly halfway around the perimeter of the camp when a figure came lurching through the darkness. Peri froze, her hand tightening on the hilt of her sword, but the man only continued past her; a moment later she heard a telltale splatter of liquid and chuckled to herself. In her sudden fear she'd nearly done the same, but without benefit of a waterskin this time.

It was quite a job, avoiding the camp and the occasional nighttime wanderers, trying to mind her footing lest she make some noise falling, trying to locate some ridge or hollow large enough to hide her. At least she was no longer stumbling through ash and sand and sharp rock-glass.

Finally she found a hollow deep enough (she hoped) to hide her, Atheris, and a couple of packs. She settled herself as comfortably as she could and waited; if she was honest, she was waiting to hear an outcry, either from the caravan camp or the pilgrims, indicating that Atheris had been discovered and captured. But there was no outcry, and after an uneasily long time, Peri heard soft, careful footsteps.

"Peri?" Atheris whispered.

"Over here," she murmured back, almost dismayingly glad to hear his voice. "Sounds like you're heading right for me. Just follow my voice straight on."

Atheris nearly fell over her; his arms were loaded, and Peri hurriedly relieved him of some of his burdens.

"Stay down and quiet," she whispered. "I want to make sure nobody heard you."

They listened for several moments, straining their ears, but at last Peri sighed.

"All right," she said. "I think we got away clean. What did you manage to take?"

"I dared not steal a sword," Atheris apologized. "I wanted this to seem a simple theft by one of the pilgrims. But I have a good dagger, food and water and a blanket, a pouch of money that felt heavy—although it could be all coppers—and I have robes for us both and bandages for you."

Peri unwrapped the heavy bundle, wondering at its weight and Atheris's ability to carry it. She would have thought the magic he'd said he would use would have exhausted him, but on the contrary, he sounded strong and alert—if anything, stronger than before.

Peri touched the robes a little hesitantly.

"The people you took these from," she said. "They weren't—uh—diseased, were they?"

Atheris chuckled wryly.

"Perian, I did not stop to inquire into their state of health," he said. "Nor are the robes clean. I was in no position to be selective. Wear them over your clothes and be thankful if they fit."

"What now, then?" Peri asked, taking the robe before squeamishness could win over reason. "Move into the camp?"

Atheris nodded.

"Tonight we will lay our blanket at the edge of the camp," he said. "But as soon as possible tomorrow we should move deeper into the crowd for better concealment."

Peri thought of the people she'd seen today and shivered with a horrified pity that made the tiny hint of healer's magic in her ache with frustration.

"You know," Atheris said gently, "you should let me carry your sword."

Peri froze.

"Never," she said flatly. "Not until the day it falls from my cold, dead hand."

Atheris sighed with resignation.

"Then you must hide it well under your robe," he said. "Or—we could wrap you more thoroughly and pretend you are a burned and disfigured man. That would not be so difficult," he added thoughtfully. "You are tall and well muscled, and you must not speak anyway, or your accent would be noticeable."

"Fine," Peri said shortly. "I'm a man, then." She almost chuckled at the thought. There'd been times when she—and probably Danber, too—had wished she was a man in fact.

Fortunately Peri had always followed the Bregondish belief that a good blade needed no ornamentation; her own sword and dagger, while of excellent-quality steel and wonderfully balanced, had plain leather-wound hilts and plain scabbards well battered and scarred from riding through Bregond's tall grasses. No one would look at them twice.

Her clothing was more of a problem; she'd have to be sure to keep it covered with the robe at all times when someone might see her. Her tunic and trousers were functional rather than decorative, too, plain sensible outdoor gear, but they were obviously Bregondish in style. The leather jaffs which had protected her legs when riding through the sharp-edged Bregondish grasses she merely packed into their bundle of goods. They were useless in Sarkond and would certainly appear unusual to anyone who saw them. At least she could cut them up for leather if she had to. Her boots, thankfully, were well-worn and unremarkable. Many of the pilgrims were probably barefoot, but Peri had no desire to emulate them!

Only a few hours remained before dawn, and nobody took notice as Peri and Atheris worked their way closer to the pilgrims' camp, laying their blanket down close enough to appear to be part of the camp. There were no guards; why guard a crowd of sick and impoverished pilgrims? There were rocks aplenty to weight the corners of the blankets, but no sticks to hold up a tent, so Peri and Atheris simply spread their blanket and lay down on it. At least this area appeared dry enough that Peri doubted they'd be drenched with rain, despite the thick cloud cover. Atheris fell asleep quickly, but Peri had never felt less like sleep in her life, especially after her long sleep in the wagon not long ago.

Hours passed. Pilgrims turned, snored, gasped, wheezed, coughed, moaned weakly, wept. The sheer miasma of human misery around her made Peri sick. The sun rose almost reluctantly behind dense gray clouds. At "dawn" the camp's inhabitants began to stir, taking no notice of Peri and Atheris.

Atheris woke quickly, and Peri confirmed her puzzling observation of the night before—he not only sounded stronger, but looked it. Maybe simply freeing himself from the drain of the concealing spell helped; she couldn't imagine what he could have done to so replenish his strength otherwise. He moved quickly and efficiently, helping her to divide their belongings into two neat bundles, and, to Peri's combined annoyance and amusement, insisted on taking the heavier load himself. He'd obviously never carried a load without a pack before; Peri had to show him how to roll the bundle narrowly and sling it diagonally across his back, cloth ends over one shoulder and under the other arm and tying in the front.

In the morning light she realized the sheer size of the crowd of pilgrims with dismay. There were certainly more than a hundred of them, possibly almost two hundred, plus a handful of priests and a few acolytes, distinguishable by the fact that they rode horses or mules and that their clothes were marginally cleaner. Thankfully not all the pilgrims were as wretched as the ones Peri had seen the day before; probably half their number were merely ordinary peasants traveling to worship. Most of them had gathered their scant belongings by now, eaten if they had food enough, and were preparing for another day's walk.

Glancing to the south, she could see the caravan. Hardly anyone was stirring there; she remarked on it to Atheris. When the caravan had camped before, they'd been under way again at dawn.

"They have no reason to hurry," Atheris told her. "They cannot pass around the pilgrims and so are held to a much slower pace. They will break camp much later today to let the pilgrimage get far ahead of them and take the other fork in the road ahead; the merchants will lose no more speed that way and will not have to travel so close to the sick and cursed." He looked relieved himself, and Peri could guess why—the later the guards and merchants slept, the longer it would be (and the farther away Peri and Atheris would be) before they discovered his thefts of the night before and raised an outcry.

"Let's see that purse," Peri said in a low voice, turning her back to the pilgrim camp.

Atheris handed it over, and she untied the thong, glancing inside. She gasped, quickly knotting it closed again and hastily thrusting it into her tunic.

"You idiot!" she hissed. "It's chock-full of Bregondish gold pieces!"

Several expressions flitted across Atheris's face; he settled on anger and scowled at Peri.

"And what," he said coldly, "is wrong with gold? We need money."

"We need," Peri said exasperatedly, "to stay inconspicuous. Merchants won't send guards after a pilgrimage over the theft of blankets and a little food, but they certainly will over a pouch full of gold! And what happens if two characters as scruffy looking as us go into a town and try to spend gold coins, especially *Bregondish* gold coins? Where and how are we supposed to have gotten them?"

Atheris's mouth dropped open in realization and he grimaced, chagrined.

"Forgive me," he said softly. "I did not think." He flushed. "I am new at stealing. And there was no way for me to assess the pouch's contents when I took it."

He glanced unhappily at the other pilgrims, most of whom were packed now and readying themselves to leave.

"Must I attempt to return the pouch? Must we conceal it somewhere and leave it here?" he asked. "Any such action would surely be noticed."

"Well, we can't return it, and we're damned sure not leaving it," Peri said distractedly. The weight of the pouch in her tunic made her shiver. "Give me another of those rags."

As unobtrusively as she could, she transferred the coins from the pouch to the rag, knotted the rag tightly, and replaced it in her tunic. She scuffed a hole in the earth with her toe, surreptitiously dropped the pouch in the hole, and covered it with dirt. If someone had cast a tracking spell, it was most likely on the pouch, not the gold; that was generally the practice, because a thief might spend his loot at several different places, thus leading his trackers on a merry chase.

The priests approached their horses as if to mount, but one of the acolytes stopped them, gesturing at the camp. Peri looked around and saw nothing out of the ordinary until she noticed a small group of worshipers clustered together in the general direction the acolyte had indicated. One of the priests followed the acolyte back to the small group, and although they were too far away for Peri to hear any of their conversation, the priest appeared more annoyed than disturbed.

"What's going on?" she murmured to Atheris as quietly as she could. "Can you tell?"

Atheris glanced at the group of worshipers, then looked away, flushing.

"Someone died in the night," he said. "It is not uncommon in such pilgrimages, with so many weak and sick. Come, we will draw attention to ourselves by taking too much notice."

The priests mounted their horses and the procession was under way. No one stayed behind to burn or bury the bodies; Peri cringed at the thought of human beings, even Sarkonds, left out at the mercy of scavengers, but there was nothing she could do. She and Atheris fell in with the rest, on the outskirts at first, but as they walked they gradually worked their way into the midst of the group. Atheris seemed relieved as the distance grew between the pilgrims and the camp.

They had not gone far, however, when three of the caravan guards rode up and around the pilgrims, stopping the priests. Atheris tensed, and Peri found herself holding her breath; she thrust her hand into her tunic and shoved the wrapped gold into her sleeve, scuffing another hole in the ground with her toe. If the guards were going to search the crowd, she could drop the gold and bury it quickly, although she wasn't sure what good that would do. If she was searched, her disguise would quickly be penetrated, and she doubted that Bregondish spies discovered in Sarkond fared any better than thieves.

An animated conversation took place between the guards and the priests; one of the priests waved in annoyance at the crowd of waiting worshipers, and Peri went very still as the guards glanced searchingly over the crowd. She felt as if that gaze pierced right through the robes and rags hiding her. Two of the guards turned their horses and rode directly into the crowd, glancing to the left and right as they wove their horses slowly through the crowd, and Peri's heart leaped into her mouth as she realized they were probably looking for the stolen blankets or other recognizable goods taken from the caravan.

Peri forced herself to take a deep breath. There was nothing remarkable about her or Atheris or anything they carried openly—except for the fact that she was standing here staring and shaking like a child caught with his hand in the honey jar. Resolutely she relaxed, dropping her eyes, trying to mimic the vague curiosity she saw in the expressions of those around her.

One of the horses turned in her direction and Peri's heart nearly stopped. She shifted slightly, moving her arm so she could feel the comfortable solidity of her sword. At last, however, one of the guards shrugged, beckoning to the others; they turned their horses back south and rode away. Peri heard a sigh and glanced at Atheris; apparently he'd been holding his breath, too.

"Next time," she whispered, clenching her hands to stop their shaking, "*I'll* do the stealing."

"Yes," Atheris breathed, very softly indeed. He stared unwaveringly at the ground.

The procession started again and they walked on. Despite

the danger of her situation, despite the diseased and disfigured and sometimes horrifying pilgrims around her and the fact that she was walking ever deeper into Sarkond, Peri felt unaccountably cheered. The caravan guards hadn't found her, and at least she was out of that wagon walking in the open air. The leaden sky above her was still sky, the rocky and hostile land under her feet was still land, and the faint breeze carrying the smell of diseased and unwashed flesh was still a breeze.

They paused at midday; those who had food ate, and those who did not, rested. Atheris pulled bread and dried meat from his pack, and Peri squatted down, trying to find some way to get the food past the bandages wrapping her face; then a chill ran down her spine, a vague but growing certainty that someone was watching her. Fighting to keep her hand from her sword hilt, she turned slowly—

—and found herself gazing into the very wide eyes of a thin young woman, hardly more than a child herself, a weakly crying toddler in her arms. The baby's thin face was covered by an angry red rash, and the woman was staring not at Peri, but at the bread and meat in her hand. Peri held out the food, nodding encouragingly; the girl hesitated for a moment, then took it, mumbling her thanks. She started to turn away. Peri debated with herself one second longer, then touched the girl's shoulder, cursing her disguise, and gestured at the child. The girl's eyes widened and she clutched her baby tightly, protectively.

Atheris muttered a curse under his breath, which Peri heard, but he stepped forward, smiling reassuringly.

"My friend has helped treat the sick before," he said. "He wishes only to look at your child."

The girl hesitated again, glancing suspiciously at Peri.

"If he is a healer," she asked timidly, "why is he so covered?"

"He is not a healer, of course," Atheris said quickly. "He

only has a little healing lore. He was badly burned in a border skirmish, terribly scarred and rendered mute. When he could no longer act as a warrior, he served instead by assisting the healers in tending the wounded.''

The girl still hesitated, but at last she laid her baby down on the ground, unwrapping the cloth in which she'd been carrying it. Peri inspected the rash which dappled the baby's body; she'd seen the like before several times. Gesturing re-assuringly at the mother, she bent down to smell the baby's breath. Once more cursing the necessity of her silence, she pointed at the baby and made a retching sound, miming vomiting.

"Yes," the girl said timidly. "He is often sick."

Peri sighed. There was no possible way she could convey what she wanted to say by gestures. She stood and took Atheris's arm, pulling him aside.

"Watch my hands while we talk," she whispered, moving her hands and fingers through an intricate series of gestures. She knew she was safe enough using the hand talk, although of course Atheris probably didn't understand it; most countries used one form of it or another in hunts or in battle when silence was crucial. "When we go back, tell her that it's her milk that sickens the baby. He needs goat's milk—not cow, goat.''

"And where," Atheris whispered patiently, "is she to get goat's milk?"

Peri ground her teeth and hunkered down on her heels, huddling in on herself. She reached into her tunic and fumbled one of the gold coins loose. She scrabbled through the dirt until she found two rocks and as unobtrusively as she could slid the coin between them, then hammered the rocks together hard until the markings on the coin were completely obliterated. She continued hammering until she broke a piece off of the now shapeless coin; sliding the larger part into her pocket, she handed the fragment to Atheris.

"I've seen a couple goats in the crowd," she whispered. "That ought to buy one of them." She glanced around again. "Remind me to crush up the rest of those coins whenever we get a chance."

Atheris returned to the girl and her child. Peri did not hear their conversation, but she saw the girl take the bit of gold in trembling fingers, her eyes wide. Then the girl stood slowly, walked to Peri, and to Peri's profound discomfort, dropped to her knees in the dirt.

"Thank you, wise one," the girl whispered. "Bless you for saving my baby. May you find mercy and ease from your suffering in Eregis's touch which heals all ills." Then she was gone.

Peri shivered. Maybe it was her understanding of Sarkondish which was flawed, but the odd wording of the girl's blessing sent a chill down her spine.

"That was foolish," Atheris murmured, returning to Peri's side. "Others saw what you did. Now they will spread word that you have some of the healing art, and that is woman's magic, not man's. It will cause talk. We will be fortunate if that does not draw the priests' attention."

Peri ground her teeth again in frustration and said nothing. There was nothing to say. Besides, why should she bother to defend herself? She was mute, after all.

Fortunately, when Atheris might have pressed the argument, the priests mounted their horses and the procession was moving again. Peri fell in gratefully, not watching to see whether Atheris walked beside her.

They walked from midday to sunset without pause. For Peri it was no great hardship; she was well accustomed to walking, riding, or running long distances, and her load was not that heavy. She was surprised to see that Atheris also held up well under the pace. She'd had him pretty much figured as a temple-bound mage, brave enough perhaps, but soft. Still, there'd been the empty scabbard and his reference to sword training. And sheltered or not, he'd obviously done something sufficient to warrant all this pursuit.

And tonight she'd find out exactly what that was.

At sunset they camped at a crossroads; the merchants and their caravan took the fork in the road which presumably led to Darnalek, and a small group of pilgrims coming down the same road joined the camp. At Peri's surreptitious urging, Atheris traded another hammered bit of gold for a sturdy javelin carried by an ex-soldier with a withered arm. Carefully broken in half, the javelin made two serviceable tent poles and gave Peri a little badly needed privacy.

Peri checked Atheris's wound immediately, while there was still enough sunlight to see by. She was relieved—and Atheris amazed—to see that both the entry wound on his side and the exit wound on his back were well on the way to healing with no sign of infection. She made a new poultice and dressed the wounds again. The cuts on Atheris's hand and her arm were healing well also, and the exercise had largely eased the stiffness from her bruised ribs; all in all, she felt rather proud of her efforts.

When Atheris had secured the flaps of their tent for the night, however, and Peri would have unwound the rags hiding her face, he shook his head.

"No," he said, very softly. "There is too much danger of discovery. You must stay hidden so long as there are people around us."

Annoyed, Peri sighed, but she left the rags in place, settling herself back against her pack.

"Can we at least talk?" she whispered.

"How can we?" Atheris returned just as quietly. "You are supposed to be mute. And even were that not so, anything we could say to each other must not be overheard."

"Look," Peri whispered, nearly inaudibly. "I've done an awful lot, come an awfully long ways, on trust of somebody I've got no reason at all to trust, and a couple hundred years of reasons not to. I've gone about as far as I'm willing to go without some explanations. Now, either you're going to find *some* way to tell me about these Bone Hunters—who they are, why they're so interested in you, what's going to happen—or tomorrow this pilgrim's going to take her chances on this disguise in the city long enough to get hold of a horse and head back south. And you can take that to the market and trade it for ten sacks of grain and a cask of good wine."

"Ten sacks of—" Atheris said blankly.

"Never mind," Peri said irritably. "Agrondish saying. All it means is I'm deadly serious."

Atheris was silent for a long moment.

"Lie down," he said at last.

Peri took a deep breath to calm herself and settled herself on the ground as comfortably as she could. She almost bolted upright when Atheris curled up against her side, his arm around her waist. She could feel the wiry muscle in his arm, his chest against her side. She waited for a moment, breathing hard, her body tingling where he touched her, fearing some unthinkable advance on Atheris's part, but he made no further move and slowly she relaxed.

"We can talk now," Atheris murmured in her ear. "If anyone discovers us like this, two men apparently lovers, we will be driven out of the pilgrimage as deviates, but that would be less disastrous to us both than the course you suggest. You have no idea what the Bone Hunters would do with you if they captured you, and if you were to strike out on your own in this land, that they most certainly would do."

"All right," Peri whispered. Part of her ached to pull away

from him, but another part perversely took comfort in his solid human presence. "Tell me."

"I am under sentence of death by torture by the Bonemarch," Atheris said simply, "for forbidden magical practices."

Peri waited, but Atheris said nothing further, as if he had explained everything in that one sentence.

"What forbidden magical practice?" she whispered patiently.

"The practice of women's magic," he answered after a long pause. "Life magic."

"All right, skip that for the moment," Peri whispered. "Who's this Bonemarch?"

"They are the ruling council of the temples, nine priests and priestesses, one representing each of the greater temples," Atheris told her. "They dwell in the oldest temple, the one at Rocarran where this pilgrimage is bound, make and administer temple law. They judge crimes within and against the temples."

"What, such as practicing the wrong kind of magic?" Peri asked. She shivered, realizing it was growing colder out; unconsciously she scooted a little closer to Atheris.

"Exactly." Atheris was silent again for a moment. "My crime was considered almost unthinkable. I knew this when I committed it; I knew the punishment I would receive. But I hoped that I would accomplish something miraculous, something of such significance that my transgression would seem small in comparison with the benefits gained. Instead it went wrong and I accomplished nothing, only hurt one I cared for greatly. So I fled ahead of a sentence of death by torture, and the Bonemarch dispatched the Bone Hunters to bring me back at all costs. What I did was dangerous to the Bonemarch. That it might become known, even more dangerous. That I might successfully escape the judgment of the temples for my actions, more dangerous still—and that I might take all this knowledge to the lands of our enemies, most dangerous of all.''

Peri could have groaned. She'd set out to rescue heroically what she'd believed to be a Bregond captured by Sarkonds. Instead she'd abandoned her family and her duty to rescue (quite clumsily, in fact) not only an enemy, but not even an *important* enemy—a common heretic.

''I still don't understand,'' she said at last. ''I can see why they want you—if you can disobey temple law and get away with it, that not only makes your Bonemarch look powerless, but it encourages other people to do the same, maybe. But what's all that got to do with me? What good does it do these Bone Hunters if they capture me?''

Atheris chuckled dryly.

''That you brought upon yourself,'' he said. ''I fled into Bregond, and you, a Bregond, an enemy, chose to risk much to rescue me. Why? And why were you there in that remote part of the country at all? The Bone Hunters will not be satisfied until these questions are answered, and you hold the answers. At best, I might have imparted to you the secrets of the temple. At worst, you and I are part of a larger conspiracy by Bregond to plant spies within the temple, to spread heresy—who knows?''

Atheris raised himself up slightly, glancing at Peri.

''I would like to know myself,'' he admitted.

Peri shrugged.

''There's nothing to tell,'' she said. ''I was on my way back from Agrond. I saw scavenger birds circling where your mare was killed, and investigated. I saw Sarkondish soldiers with a captive, and it never occurred to me it was another Sarkond.'' She sighed.

Atheris chuckled again.

''I can believe such a coincidence,'' he said. ''But the Bone

Hunters will not. They will not rest until they have captured us both and returned us to the Bonemarch.''

Now Peri would have done more than sighed; she could have wept.

And I thought I was stupid before. Why should the Bone Hunters believe I'd rescue a Sarkond from them simply by accident? I can't believe it myself. I suppose there's some comfort in the knowledge that I could hardly muck this all up any worse than I already have. No, that's not true. Based on what I've done so far, I'd find a way.

''Tell me about these Bone Hunters,'' she whispered at last. ''You said they're assassin priests, and mages, too.''

''They serve the temples in many ways,'' Atheris said as if surprised by the question. ''They are the eyes and ears and hands of the temples across the land and among the people. They are the only priests trained in physical combat—when I was allowed to learn the sword, I began to wonder whether my elders were considering such a role for me.'' He grimaced. ''I suppose that thought was what finally spurred me to take such a risk as I did, the likelihood that I might be destined for such terrible service.''

Peri digested that.

''Everyone's afraid of them, then, these Bone Hunters?'' she asked at last.

''Of course,'' Atheris said, grimacing. ''There is good cause for fear. Bone Hunters know the most potent of magics, the most terrible methods of questioning, the most subtle techniques of assassination. They are castrated and their faces scarred and burned to prevent them from forming any human attachment to others, and as the final test of their training they are sent to kill each member of their own family. They are renowned for their viciousness and lack of mercy. They live solely to use their terrible skills in the service of the Bonemarch, and therefore their appearance invariably bodes ill for someone. Likely the only happiness in seeing them results from learning that someone else is the cause for their visit.''

''Mmmm. And they sent *five* of these fellows after you?'' Peri asked skeptically, shivering a little at Atheris's description. Atheris's arm tightened slightly around her, and to her surprise, she didn't mind. ''Seems a little like going after a fly with a battle-ax, doesn't it? Either that or you've really been holding back on your magic. Mahdha knows *I* haven't seen anything that impressive yet.''

Atheris said nothing, and the silence grew awkward. Peri turned over to look at him.

''So what's this terrible magical thing you were trying to do?'' she said. ''Make Agrond and Bregond drop off the edge of the earth? Raise up an army of demons from the Hidden Realms? Destroy the Barrier?''

Atheris raised his eyebrows.

''We were trying,'' he said slowly, ''to make rain.''

Startled, Peri rolled over to face him fully.

''Make rain?'' she repeated blankly. ''Is that all? My aunt K—'' Peri stopped abruptly, remembering her resolution that she keep her identity a secret. ''My aunt can pull rain into Bregond even in high summer. And specialized weather mages in Agrond can turn the finest spring mist into a raging storm in only a few hours.''

''I did not speak of bringing rain from elsewhere,'' Atheris said patiently, ''nor of molding what is already there. We were trying to *make* rain.''

''To *make* rain?'' Peri asked stupidly. ''You mean out of nothing?'' She'd never heard the like before. Everyone knew a mage couldn't *invent* weather, only manipulate it; otherwise dry Bregond would have surely been rendered as rich and lush as Agrond by now. And that was as it should be; let Agrond keep its farmers and Bregond its nomad herding clans, each to their place.

"Not out of nothing," Atheris corrected. "Out of magic."

Peri shook her head. That was an ambitious idea, all right—
as presumptuous as her own hope that she'd invent a qiva of
her own. At least if Peri failed she harmed no one, disappointed no one but herself. But manipulating magic on such
a grand scale, using it to spit in the eye of the natural order
of weather—the very daring of it filled her with a grudging
admiration.

"Bright Ones," Peri breathed. "How did you plan to do
that? I mean, everything I've ever heard about magic says it
can't be done."

"Man's magic cannot do it," Atheris said softly, shaking
his head. "Nor can woman's. But I—we—thought the two
together might succeed where each alone had failed."

"We?" Peri whispered, chuckling slightly. "Sounds like
there's a woman in this story."

"Of course," Atheris said after a brief hesitation. "My
cousin Amis. I convinced her—" Then he stopped. "It was a
foolish idea." Abruptly he rolled over, turning his back to
Peri.

Peri scowled but said nothing; she was, in fact, just as glad
to have Atheris farther from her. She'd been taking entirely
too much comfort, almost pleasure, from the contact. Well, he
was a comely man—for a Sarkond, that is—and she was a
woman, and just as well they keep their distance. And whatever he'd started to say, it hardly mattered; she knew what she
needed to know:

First, that Atheris was useful to her only as long as she was
stranded in Sarkond. Once she made her way back across the
Barrier, he became a liability. A common heretic wasn't worth
taking to Aunt Kairi for questioning, as tradition demanded.
Even so, practical though it might be, she quite couldn't bring
herself to turn him over to his Bone Hunters now, or toss him
to one of the nomad clans to be slaughtered. Still, any debt

Peri owed him surely extended no further than some money, a horse, and directions to the shortest route out of Bregond.

Second, that these Bone Hunters wanted Atheris—and by extension, her—quite badly, and so far, at least, nothing Atheris or Peri had come up with had managed to throw them far off the trail. That meant that Atheris's concern was probably warranted, and little as Peri might like depending on a Sarkond, she was safer with Atheris and his magic than without him, and she'd be wise to follow his advice—at least here and now.

Peri rolled over on her side, her back to Atheris. There were things, she knew, that he wasn't telling her. Fair enough; there were things she wasn't telling him, either, and had no intention of doing so. Much better if nobody knew there was a member of the Agrondish ruling family—and soon-to-be Heir to the throne of Bregond as well—stranded on foot and all but helpless in Sarkond. As long as Peri could keep that a secret, as long as she could remain free, she hadn't burned all her bridges in Bregond. Mahdha would remember her name, she could return home—

That is, as long as someone received the message on Tajin's saddle and sent it on to Peri's kinfolk, and as long as they believed that message. Because failing those two things, she was dead—or as good as—anyway.

4

PERI ROUSED BEFORE DAWN TO A PERSISTENT
scratching at the tent pole. Checking the rags concealing her face, she at last pushed aside the tent flap and
peered out. A young man crouched there, ducking his head
apologetically.

"Forgive me, healer," he murmured, not meeting Peri's
eyes. "My name is Minyat. I saw how you tended the girl's
baby yesterday. There is a wise woman traveling with us who
says my wife is a fool to go with the others who have no
hope, to seek Eregis's touch in the temple. She tells us to go
to Darnalek instead. Please, will you look at my wife and tell
us your thoughts before we abandon the road to Darnalek and
commit ourselves to Rocarran?"

Peri hesitated, then turned. Atheris was already gazing at
her in weary resignation. He simply pulled on his boots,
handed her hers, and followed her without a word.

Minyat and his wife appeared more prosperous than the average pilgrim; they had a tent, at least, and some supplies; a mule was tethered to a small wagon or a large cart, depending on one's definition, beside the tent. The young woman on the pallet in the tent appeared healthy enough except for the huge lump swelling on the side of her neck. The frail, elderly woman kneeling at her side, however, sent a warning twinge through that intangible healer's sense. Sharp gray eyes gazed at Peri out of the seamed face, and she shivered at the canny glance which seemed somehow to pierce her disguise.

"My wife, Irra, healer," Minyat said apologetically, gesturing at the young woman on the pallet.

Tearing her eyes away from the older woman with some difficulty, Peri knelt beside Irra. Unlike the girl with the baby, Minyat's wife seemed unafraid, not flinching as Peri carefully probed the round swelling. Peri bit her lip, marveling. She'd always thought Sarkonds barely human, horrible death-dealing raiders always poised just beyond the Barrier, waiting for an opportunity to sweep down and raid Bregondish clans or caravans. But apart from the Bone Hunters, she'd seen little so far to support her imaginings. These were people, and only that—plain human folks, a little strange in their coloring and the cast of their features, but ordinary hard-worn human beings nonetheless, subject to the same hurts and illnesses as her own kinfolk. Peri found the revelation strangely unnerving.

A small noise drew her attention; she found the old woman gazing sharply at her again.

"I know you are . . . unspeaking," the old woman said dryly. "But I understand the gesture language of the unspeaking. Your thoughts?"

Now Peri hesitated uneasily, sensing a trap, but she could not back out now. Any profession of ignorance now would seem more suspicious than a true answer. She could only pray that the gesture language was the same in Sarkond as it was in Bregond.

No healer is needed, she signed. *She needs fish and salt from the sea and will heal on her own in time.*

"Interesting," the old woman said. She coughed into a rag; once again Peri felt that sharp warning pang through her senses.

"I myself, when I had a shop and stock at my disposal, prepared a potion for this ailment," the old woman continued after she had stuffed the rag back in her sleeve and relayed Peri's signals. "One of the ingredients was sea salt."

She turned to the young man.

"Sea salt can be purchased in Darnalek from alchemists," she said. "Not cheaply, but I trust you'll manage." Abruptly she turned back to Peri. "Walk with me, warrior."

I know what you are, her hands signed.

Peri went very still.

"Walk with me," the old woman repeated.

Peri rose slowly, and when Atheris would have followed, not understanding, she held up her hand to stop him. The old woman ducked out of the tent and Peri followed.

Can I kill her? Peri thought sickly. *I've never killed anyone in my life. I've never had to. Could I kill a sick old woman, even a Sarkond, to protect my secret?*

A few pilgrims were rousing as the sky slowly lightened. The old woman did not stray far from the tent; she stopped and coughed again, and this time Peri saw the rag before the old woman tucked it away. It was spotted with blood, old stains and new.

The woman followed Peri's gaze to the rag, then chuckled.

"Yes," she said dryly. "It is my death. Feel here." She took Peri's hand and pressed it against her side. Peri felt the hard nodules under her skin, the heat of the disease consuming the frail old body.

You think you will find healing at the temple? Peri signed, cringing inside as she felt the presence of human death clearly and unmistakably for the first time in her life. There were powerful healers, she knew, capable of halting such diseases, but she doubted even they could offer much hope at such an advanced stage.

The old woman chuckled again, hoarsely.

"No," she said. "I journeyed to the temple for Eregis's touch, as is my duty, but I foresaw that I would never reach it alive. A bottle of Black Sleep waits to end my pain. Now that I have met you, I need wait no longer."

Once again Peri froze with shock. Reflexively she almost spoke her denial, almost betrayed herself. A dry old hand on her arm silenced her.

"I sought the vision path," the old woman whispered. "I knew my own death; there was little enough to lose. I saw with my spirit the face you seek to hide from my eyes."

You are the enemy who comes as a friend, she signed. *You are the one blessed with the warrior's skill of death, and cursed with the healer's gift of life. You seek to flee us and we force you deeper into our heart. You bring death and destruction to our only hope, and in destroying it, you will save us despite yourself. The blessing of Black Sleep will spare me from witnessing these things come to pass.*

She paused to cough into the rag again.

"The price of vision is obscurement," she said. "I know only that obstacles in your path only guide you more surely to your goal. Therefore I will hinder you in the only manner in which I can—by giving you aid and nurturing the gift that curses you."

She thrust a leather bundle into Peri's hand.

"Take it and be damned," she whispered. "I thank Eregis that death will spare me from the gifts you bring. Do not look upon me again." She muttered another word that Peri assumed to be a curse, turned away, and picked her way slowly, stiffly through the camps, leaving a stunned Peri standing where she was.

Atheris appeared at her side as if by magic. Peri felt a surge of relief for the simple fact that his presence kept her from going after the old woman. Any Bregond would respect her right to death. Any Agrond would at least try to talk the old woman out of it. Peri was Bregond enough to let her go, Agrond enough to feel guilty about it.

"What was that all about?" he asked, scowling.

Peri shook her head.

"Near as I can tell," she said, glancing around to make sure nobody was close enough to hear her, "she hates me, so she decided to help me. She started muttering about prophecies, shoved this bag in my hand, and walked off."

"Prophecy?" Atheris said slowly. "What prophecy?"

Peri shrugged.

"She was just a sick, crazy old woman talking nonsense," she said.

"But what was it she said as she walked away?" Atheris pressed.

"I don't know," Peri said impatiently. "I didn't understand it. Sounded like *ni'chuatai* or *niachuatai* or something like that."

Atheris shivered.

"Well, which was it, *ni'chuatai* or *niachuatai*?" he insisted.

"I don't know," Peri said, forcing herself to patience. "I never heard either word before. I wasn't even really listening. What do they mean?"

"*Ni'chuatai* means 'misborn,' like some of these unfortunates," Atheris murmured, gesturing unobtrusively. "*Niachuatai* means 'harbinger.'"

"Well, given the conversation, it could've been either one," Peri said irritably. "Look, it's over, she's gone, people are waking up. We'd better go strike our camp before somebody hears *our* conversation, hadn't we?''

Atheris took a deep breath; to Peri's surprise, he was shaking with tension, and for a moment she thought he'd insist on continuing their discussion despite the danger.

"Very well," he said at last, with apparent reluctance. He followed Peri back to their camp; Peri was relieved (and a little surprised) to see that their belongings appeared untouched—Sarkonds were all thieves, weren't they, and how could they resist such easy loot?—but Atheris took it in stride. He silently helped Peri bundle their supplies into two packs; when she would have absently shoved the leather bundle into her pack, however, he laid a hand on her arm.

"What did she give you?" he asked.

"I don't know." Peri examined the leather. It was a rolled bundle tied with thongs, the beaded leather cracked with age but surprisingly well preserved otherwise. She untied the thongs and carefully unrolled the bundle; from the old woman's remarks, she half expected some venomous beast to leap out at her. What she found, however, surprised her even more—an obviously old but carefully maintained healer's kit, needles and lancets not of the usual carved bone, but of painstakingly polished silver, small horn vials and little pouches holding what investigation showed to be a fair assortment of herbs and powders, some of which Peri recognized, some she did not.

"It's a healer's bag," she said, rolling the bundle back up and tying it securely. "A good one, too. My clan's healer had one that was newer but no better."

"You had none?" Atheris asked, raising his eyebrows slightly.

"I think I told you before," Peri said from between her teeth, "I don't have enough of a gift to be of any real use as a healer. I never had any gift at all until a few sevendays ago.

For the last time, I have no training, I have no magic worth the name, I have no skill—"

"I disagree," Atheris murmured, shouldering his pack. "I have seen you without the use of spells, without training as you say, diagnose two illnesses with a facility any healer might envy. You used no magic in their treatment, but their condition did not require it." He touched his side. "You tended my own injury with amazing skill; I still can hardly believe it did not fester under the circumstances. There is no denying you have a true gift."

—*cursed with the healer's gift of life.* Peri grimaced. It was a curse, all right. Enough of the healer's gift to twist the path of her life all awry; enough to leave her constantly frustrated among all these sick and malformed people, but not enough to help most of them. She sighed. Ironically, she actually might have done some good in Danber's clan. They had a competent healer already, but a halfway decent herbalist and healer's assistant was always more than welcome in the nomadic clans to ease the healer's burden, tend minor cases, and do field treatments in the hunting parties and patrols. Her ability to sense water would be equally valuable.

But only to Danber's clan, Peri thought bitterly. *By Mother's logic my gifts will serve all of Bregond as Aunt Kairi's Heir. Even if I never actually used the gifts themselves—and I wouldn't, either. Bregond's High Hall has about as much use for a pitiful healer and water mage—or a swordswoman, even a damned good one—as a grasshawk has for horseshoes.*

She shouldered her pack and turned around, surprised to see Atheris watching her intently, a troubled expression on his face. Peri tightened her lips; as far as she was concerned, the subject was closed, and anyway, the other pilgrims were awake and bundling up their own goods, preparing for their day's journey.

"Heal—good sir!" Peri jumped and whirled, her hand on her sword hilt, and Atheris turned just as quickly, only to find the man Minyat behind them.

"Forgive me," Minyat said, his eyes wide. "I only wished to thank you, good sir, for your aid, and ask if there was any compensation I might make you for sparing my wife and me the journey to Rocarran." He hesitated. "I spent most of our coin buying the wagon and supplies so that Irra might make the pilgrimage, so I can offer you no money, but if there is anything we own that you desire—"

Peri shrugged negligently, but Atheris's eyes widened.

"You will journey to Darnalek, then?" he asked.

"Most immediately," Minyat said, nodding. "We will pro-cure a good supply of the sea salt before returning home. There is surely little enough of it to be found in Sarkond at all, and none in our small village."

"We, too, would profit from a visit to Darnalek," Atheris said quickly. "Could you make room in your wagon for us?"

Minyat raised his eyebrows.

"Of course," he said. "But it is only a short road to Dar-nalek, probably only a day's steady ride in our wagon. That is scant compensation for such service as your friend has so kindly rendered my wife and me." He gave Peri a look of such gratitude that she scowled under her disguise. She'd only spared them an inconvenient trip to a temple for healing; it wasn't as if she'd saved Irra's life, after all.

"For us it is compensation enough," Atheris said gravely. "Come, if this arrangement is satisfactory to you, my friend can assist your wife, and I will help you load your wagon." He gave Peri a significant look.

Peri frowned, confused, and found herself following Minyat and Atheris uneasily. What was Atheris up to now? Not long before, he'd agreed it was vital to avoid the city; now he was abandoning the safety of the pilgrimage, which he'd maintained so staunchly, to go to Darnalek. She could hardly refuse or argue now, either. A day or two ago she'd have rejoiced at an alternative to moving deeper into Sarkond; now the abrupt change in Atheris's plans only made her uneasy and suspicious.

Peri had no chance to question him, however, for as soon as they returned to Minyat's tent, Atheris busied himself with Minyat loading the wagon, and she had little choice but to help Irra pack up the couple's belongings. The woman was friendly but, thank the Bright Ones, not talkative, perhaps awkward in Peri's presence. Peri began to understand Atheris's strategy, however, when she glanced over and saw him surreptitiously dripping blood from a cut thumb onto the wagon frame.

When the wagon was loaded, Peri and Atheris tucked their packs in and climbed on the back. Minyat did not attempt to guide the wagon through the crowd of pilgrims, but waited for them to gather up their belongings and move ahead, clearing the way, before he turned the mule north toward Darnalek.

There was no way for Peri to talk to Atheris, not with Minyat and Irra sitting right in front of them, so she could only settle herself as carefully as she could on her lumpy and rather precarious seat and fume in silence as the wagon jolted up the road.

Although from what Minyat had said, they had to be near the city, they passed no one on the road except small groups on foot that Peri suspected were bound for Rocarran, and the countryside remained every bit as bleak and dry and empty as she'd seen so far. From time to time she saw what appeared to be houses, but these were empty and obviously abandoned, many fallen to ruin. There were no farms, no inns, no small settlements, no shrines—not even the bands of raiders that she had always thought must populate the whole of Sarkond. Peri wanted to ask Atheris about it and ground her teeth in frustration that she could not.

Minyat and Irra seemed more cheerful now, probably relieved at the prospect of returning home, and they chatted amiably with Atheris, occasionally addressing a remark to Peri rather abashedly, as if they had forgotten she was there (and, she thought sourly, despite their gratitude, they probably had). From their conversation she gathered that the couple lived rather northeast of Darnalek in a small town. Minyat traded in copper pots and utensils, information which, to Peri's mystification, seemed to impress Atheris greatly; Irra, childless herself, practiced as a midwife, which explained to Peri the woman's ease with healers.

"At least Irra's trade thrives," Minyat said, shaking his head. "Not so with mine. Everyone flocks to Rocarran now to hear the Whore. I'm glad enough to stay away. These are strange times, friend, dangerous times—too strange for a simple copper trader. Not that I question the prophecies," he added hastily, glancing back at Atheris and Peri as if to make sure he hadn't overstepped himself. "We pray every day for the awakening, make our offerings regularly. When the healers said there was no cure for Irra, I vowed to seek Eregis's touch at her side. But Eregis be praised, wise one, you—"

He broke off again, then said, with obvious relief, "Look! The walls of Darnalek."

Peri looked, then grimaced. She hadn't expected a city the size of Tarkesh, the capital of Agrond, or even Olhavar, Bregond's capital city, but Atheris had implied that Darnalek was of a fairly respectable size. From what Peri could see, it was no bigger than a good-sized town, and certainly no richer. The "wall" was a stockade of thick upright posts in rather poor repair, lashed together with vines, and the thick wooden gate hung apathetically ajar. One lethargic guard drowsed at his station atop the wall beside the gate, and the cart passed without acknowledgment.

The city itself impressed Peri no more than the wall. The wooden buildings were neglected, some of them badly deteriorated, and clustered so thickly that the narrow lanes seemed to close in around the little cart. Although the street was so hard-packed and dry that she knew there must have been a recent extended drought, and although the streets were amazingly clear of dung, a rotten smell rose up from the gutters in a fetid miasma. Peri grimaced, for once glad of the rags over her nose and mouth.

The people of Darnalek looked as worn and neglected as their city. A few thin, sickly children played apathetically in doorways or in the filthy gutters. The adults leaning in the doorways or windows and staring lethargically at nothing in particular, or shuffling wearily along at the side of the narrow lane, looked as drab and thin and unhealthy as the youngsters.

A gasp made Peri turn and glance at Atheris. The shock in his expression was plain as his eyes flitted over the dismal scene.

"I have never been so far south before," Atheris said, very softly. "I had no idea things had gotten so bad here."

Irra glanced back at him.

"Some of the towns are better," she said. "Our well taps a very deep spring and there is less demand made on it. But little grows on the farms. There is no life left in the soil even that far to the north."

Atheris made a small sound of dismay, and Peri was surprised by his distinctly guilty expression. What in the world was *he* bothered about? He'd said himself that he'd never been this far south before. Whatever had blighted this land had obviously happened long ago, probably during the war, and Atheris looked young enough that he'd probably not even been born then.

"If you are familiar with Darnalek," he said, very quietly, "and could direct us to an inn, I would be most grateful."

Minyat and Irra exchanged glances.

"There are a number of respectable inns," Minyat said slowly. "But—" He glanced at Peri and fell silent.

"Ah," Atheris said softly. "I see."

"I have a cousin who lives here with his wife," Irra said at last. "He does not run an inn, only a stable, but he has a large loft he sometimes rents to boarders of good character. If I speak to him, I am certain he would sympathize with the plight of a warrior disfigured in the defense of the country, and especially one who has rendered us such kindly service."

"You are too kind," Atheris murmured, but he said it absently, still gazing out, brooding, over that terrible half-dead city. He looked so deeply shaken that without thinking, Peri reached out and took his hand, squeezing his fingers. Atheris glanced at her, startled, then mustered a faint smile. Peri felt her cheeks heat under the rags, but it was too late to withdraw the gesture.

Thankfully the southern fringe of the city nearest the least-used gate was apparently the worst of it; the buildings nearer the center of the city showed somewhat better care, at least enough that Peri stopped worrying that the roof might tumble down on their heads or the floor fall out from under them in the night. A few of the shops even had a touch of color to them, paint on the signs or a swath of colorful cloth curtaining the window, and once or twice a more appetizing aroma reached her nose even over the stench of the gutters.

Minyat stopped the wagon outside a house that appeared not terribly shabby. Glancing apologetically at Peri and Atheris, Irra climbed out of the wagon by herself. A homely, tired-looking woman answered her knock on the door, smiling at Irra in welcome, and they talked quietly for a few moments. At one point during the conversation, the woman glanced uncuriously at the wagon and its passengers, then returned to her quiet interchange with Irra. At last she nodded, waiting in the doorway while Irra stepped back to the wagon.

"My cousin Orren is gone to the market for the morning, trading for feed," Irra said apologetically. "Lina says you are welcome to the loft, and for board and breakfast and supper she will charge you four sestis a day for the both of you, or two for board without meals. An inn would cost you at least five."

"The lady's offer is more than generous," Atheris said quickly. He pulled out his pack and Peri's. "And we thank you both for the transport and your kind efforts on our behalf. May Eregis favor you both with prosperity, and may your cure be swift and easy, lady."

Peri simply climbed out of the wagon after Atheris, patting Irra's hand and nodding to Minyat. They followed Lina silently into the house; to Peri's surprise, the woman barred the door behind them although it was only late afternoon.

"Madmen, murderers, and thieves," Lina said briefly. "No one is safe. Come, I will show you to the loft."

When Lina opened the door at the top of a flight of stairs, Peri sighed, blessing the good luck that had led her to Minyat and Irra. The loft was huge, covering the house and stable alike, plain but clean; fortunately the nights were warm enough that the single small coal brazier would heat it sufficiently. There was no bed, but straw mattresses on the wooden floor would make pallets certainly more comfortable than the ground. The latching door was thick and solid, as were the floor and walls, and stout shutters fastened over the windows; here, at least, Peri could speak and even practice her swordplay with little fear of being overheard. Even the nasty smell from the gutters and the more familiar aroma of horses and manure from the stables wasn't too bad up here with the shutters closed.

"This will more than suffice," Atheris told Lina, although Peri somehow had the suspicion he'd have said the same if the woman had shown them to a closet full of lice. "We are most grateful for your hospitality, lady." He pulled out a few of the pounded bits of gold. "I regret we have no sestis. If this gold will not suffice to pay a week's board and food in advance, I could quickly change it for coin for you."

Lina silently picked up one of the bits, eyeing it critically, unfazed; then she nodded, scooping up the other bits.

"Gold will do," she said briefly. "Chamber pot's in the corner. I'll bring you up a bucket of water. No guests in the room. You get drunk and break things, you go. Breakfast at dawn, supper at sundown. We don't open that door sunset to sunrise, so be in by dark or not at all."

She glanced at Peri and her expression softened slightly.

"You've had a bad journey, I can see," she said. "I'll bring up some bread and cheese with your water. It's still a few hours to supper."

"Thank you most kindly, lady," Atheris said, still absently; he waited almost impatiently until Lina returned with the bucket and a covered basket, and as soon as she was gone, he latched the door and turned to Peri.

"Now that we are out of the wagon, the Bone Hunters can find us if they try," he said. "I must protect this room. But it must be your blood to set the spell."

Peri remembered how much that spell had weakened her the first time and rolled up her sleeve rather reluctantly.

"Why mine?" she said.

"Because one of us must remain within the wards to sustain the spell," he said, "and one of us must go out tomorrow and find a mage and purchase better protections and supplies. And you cannot speak in the city, and you have no knowledge of the magic we will need, so it must be you who stays." He grimaced slightly. "I doubt that my errands in this city will be so enjoyable as to leave you envious of my freedom.''

Peri thought of those stinking, narrow lanes and the gray denizens of Darnalek and shivered.

''All right,'' she said. ''I can't argue with that.''

When Atheris had drawn a little of her blood and sprinkled the edges of the loft, Peri kindled a small fire in the brazier and set the bread and cheese to toast while she relievedly discarded her robe and bandages.

''I don't suppose there's any chance of a bath?'' she asked wistfully.

Atheris shook his head.

''Our host and hostess most likely have a steamhouse,'' he said. ''Coal is cheap enough but water is precious. If the steamhouse is inside the building, you will still be inside the wards. Or use what is in the bucket, if you prefer.''

Peri glanced into the bucket and grimaced. The water was not too murky, but it had an odor, a flat, dead smell that she didn't like; she hesitated even to wash herself with the stuff, especially with the healing cuts on her arm.

''A sweathouse is fine,'' she said, shrugging. Danber's clan used sweat tents when water was scarce—hardly an infrequent occurrence on Bregond's dry plains—and a good long steaming sounded appealing in this rather cold and dismal city. She set the bucket aside. Atheris would simply have to buy more wine, or good water, if he could find it, while he was roaming the streets of decaying Darnalek tomorrow. And while he was at it, he could price horses. The Bright Ones knew they had gold enough to purchase a couple of nags sound enough to get them back to Bregond.

Atheris went downstairs to consult with Lina and returned with the news that a steamhouse was indeed available at a slight additional cost, which he had paid with a tiny shaving of gold, and he had brought back clean cloths and a bowl of soft soap.

"I mean you no disrespect," he said, glancing at Peri sideways, "but it would rouse suspicion if we wasted the water to use the steamhouse separately."

Peri disliked that idea intensely, and Atheris's spell had left her tired and lethargic, but the prospect of relative cleanliness, even though she had no fresh clothes to wear, was too tempting.

"All right," she said shortly, but when she took the bundle of their gold with them, she took her dagger, too. She wouldn't spoil her sword in the heat and moisture of a sweathouse, but as her mother said, there was a word for people who took even a few steps outside their front door unarmed. And if anybody thought Peri an easy mark, she'd teach them that word.

The loft was so bare that Peri had to search for some time before she found a crack in the eaves in which she could hide her sword. She didn't bother to hide the healer's bag, although it was probably the most valuable thing they owned, apart from the gold. Fate had dropped it unwanted into her hands; if somebody stole it, she wouldn't complain.

The sweathouse was a tiny room, hardly larger than a big closet; Peri could see that its size had been reduced, most likely to conserve the precious water. Lina had lit the brazier, and the coals (and the room) were already quite hot; Peri scooped out a dipper of water and sprinkled it over the metal grate, producing the first hissing cloud of steam. She turned away from Atheris and undressed briskly, settling herself on one of the benches and drawing her knees up in front of her. She should've thought, she realized, to wear the loincloth she kept in her emergency pack to hold the rags on her moon days. She'd never felt self-conscious in the sweat tents of her clan, shared by men and women alike to conserve water, but Atheris was no clansman. This was a *Sarkond*.

Atheris undressed slowly, apparently as reluctant as Peri,

keeping his back turned, but for the life of her Peri couldn't resist peeping at him out of the corner of her eyes. When she'd tended the wound in his side she'd noted his wiry muscle, and now she couldn't help a certain reluctant admiration. He didn't have Danber's robust bulk, but there was nothing of the soft city mage about him; his dusky skin was stretched tightly over muscles that silently boasted of long hours of sword practice. Sweat and condensation ran down his back and his skin gleamed; Peri took a deep breath, helplessly watching the droplets' descent—then, as Atheris sat down, she glimpsed something that shocked her healer's sense into a clamor.

"Bright Ones, what *happened* to you?" Peri said, rolling back to her feet, modesty completely forgotten. She pushed Atheris's hands aside, gaping at the straight, narrow scar running down his chest from just below his collarbone to a point just above his groin. "You look like somebody gutted you!"

Atheris hurriedly turned sideways on the bench, pulling his knees up and wrapping his arms around them, hiding the scar.

"It happened many years ago," he said stiffly. "It is none of your affair."

Peri sat back down on her bench, shivering. The scar was too thin and even to be a battle wound or even hasty field surgery, and Peri could think of no illness or injury that would require such extensive cutting anyway. That horrible wound had been deliberately made. She thought of the blood spells Atheris had cast, and the burn scars on her mother's hands, and her stomach heaved.

"That's something to do with your magic, isn't it?" she said sickly. "By Mahdha, Atheris, you said women's magic was life magic. Just what kind of magic is it men use? Death magic? Necromancy?"

Atheris turned eyes full of pure outrage on her, then looked away again. When he spoke, his voice was tight and controlled.

"Necromancy is an obscenity," he said acidly. "You could perhaps call men's magic death magic, since female mages are barred from those arts of death which would taint their power—battle magics and combat. It is true that my magic retains a link with death, for I had to allow death to touch me"—he touched the long scar pensively—"to fully understand and master the energies of life." He ran his fingers slowly down that narrow line, his eyes closing. "It is a test that leaves its mark upon the spirit even more than the body."

Peri grimaced. She wanted to ask him whether he'd let someone else cut him open, or whether he'd done it himself— and then she realized she didn't want to know. To cover her confusion she turned away and dumped another dipperful of water on the grate, producing a new cloud of steam. Sweat and condensed water slickened her skin and she dug soap from the bowl, scrubbing roughly while she gathered her thoughts.

"You think me a monster," Atheris said after a long silence. "Some evil demon who lives to cause death. But you are wrong. I have never used my magic to deliberately cause harm to another, although I do not deny I have the ability to do so. Only the Bone Hunters and battle mages use their power to such a purpose. And I had no desire to become either."

Atheris dug soap out of the bowl and began lathering his skin slowly, as if choosing his words carefully.

"The difference in our magics," he said slowly, "lies mainly in their source. Women draw their magic—the power of healing and growth—from within themselves. It is a power that gives life where there was none before. Men draw upon the energies of life that exist within all living things, themselves or others, such as the spells you have seen me cast. It is a magic that *takes* life, molds it, uses it. Do you see?"

Peri shivered. Now she regretted allowing Atheris to use her blood for the protective spell he'd cast upstairs; it seemed somehow unclean.

"I don't want to talk about this anymore," she said bluntly. She threw a little more water on the grate and picked up the scraper, sluicing the lather off her skin. Her braids felt gritty, but her hair would have to wait; she had no intention of unbraiding, wetting, lathering, rinsing, wringing, combing, and rebraiding her hair here in a sweathouse with this Sarkond. She pulled her pilgrim's robe on over her damp skin, wrapped the towel securely around her hair and lower face, and hastily gathered up the rest of her belongings, leaving Atheris to finish his steambath alone.

Back in the loft, Peri barred the door—Atheris could knock or, as far as she was concerned, sleep on the stairs—and hurriedly stripped off the dirty robe. She pulled on her linen breastband and hose, wishing she hadn't sacrificed her undertunic for bandage material; it left her with only her grimy linens and an even dirtier tunic and trousers. Sniffing the tunic, she grimaced and unhappily sloshed it and the trousers through the water in the bucket, which smelled marginally better than the fabric. If she stayed in the loft another night, tomorrow she'd wash her breastband and hose.

Chores done, Peri wanted nothing more than to crawl into her bed and sleep, she was so utterly weary. But she knew the moment she lay down, Atheris would rouse her again, knocking at the door. Besides, this was her first moment of privacy in what seemed like ages; best enjoy it while she could.

Forcing herself back to her feet, Peri slowly worked her way through the limbering stretches and lunges, each with its breathing pattern, that Danber had always insisted she perform before sword practice. As always the familiar exercises, the smooth and powerful sensation of her muscles moving under her skin, calmed her, bringing her chaotic thoughts back into focus.

I am Perian. I am warrior. I am earth, deep-rooted and strong, mother of steel. I am wind, swift and light. I am fire, steel's father, dancing, all-consuming. I am water, unbounded, ever-changing. I am warrior. I am Perian.

"That is beautiful," a voice said softly behind her.

Peri whirled, her hand instinctively reaching to her hip before she realized that her sword was still in its hiding place, her dagger on the bed. To her dismay, Atheris stood there, the door closed and barred behind him.

"You didn't tell me," Peri said between clenched teeth, "that your magic includes the ability to walk through walls."

"It does not," Atheris said, smiling slightly. "But it requires no magic to open a door when you have neglected to pull in the latchstring." He shrugged apologetically, then gestured. "Besides, when does a dancer mind an audience?"

"I'm not a dancer," Peri muttered. She picked up the discarded robe and pulled it on hurriedly over her linens. "It's part of my sword practice."

"Truly!" Atheris raised his eyebrows. "I have heard it said that in Bregond, swordplay is a ritualistic art, but I never believed it. Apparently the rumors are true."

"I suppose the Ithuara does look kind of . . . ritualistic," Peri said, tying the robe securely.

"I know the Ithuara," Atheris said absently, looking at her rather strangely. "That was something different." Abruptly he stepped closer, touching Peri's shoulder, and his eyebrows shot up. Involuntarily Peri remembered the sight of those droplets of water trickling down his skin—she hurriedly shrugged his hand off, stepping back a pace.

"It has more than the appearance of ritual," he said slowly. "You feel stronger now, yes?"

"Of course," Peri said irritably. "That's the whole point, to build focus and concentration."

"It has built more than that," Atheris told her. "When I used your blood for the protection spell in the merchant's wagon, you were greatly weakened. Do you feel weak now?"

Peri paused, taking a deep breath to bring her temper back under control. Sure, she'd felt tired almost immediately when Atheris had cast his spell. She'd almost stumbled with weariness walking down to the sweathouse.

But she certainly didn't feel weak and tired now. She felt calm, focused, alive.

"All right, I'm not tired," she said cautiously. "What does that mean?"

"What that means," Atheris said gently, "is that either your exercises were purposefully designed with the goal of generating life energy, or else you have unconsciously taught yourself to use them to that end. In either case the end result is the same." His eyes sparkled. "Will you show me again?"

Peri clutched her robe more tightly, cynically certain that Atheris was more interested in seeing her in her breastband and hose than he was in her practice techniques.

"Why?" she asked. "You said you know the Ithuara yourself."

"I know the Ithuara," he said patiently. "But I have never seen the movements you were making. Obviously Bregonds have augmented the qivas with this preparatory ritual, of a purpose which interests me greatly. If you have a means of increasing the magical energy at our disposal, can you not see the importance of that?"

Peri took another deep breath.

"All right," she said. "But I don't know anything about generating energy. To me they're just exercises."

"Fine," Atheris said, nodding. "Just show me."

Peri reluctantly untied the robe and laid it aside. She began the opening breathing patterns, moving slowly through the initial stretches.

"Nothing is happening," Atheris said, breaking her concentration. "Are you certain you are doing it properly?"

Peri ground her teeth.

"I can't do much of anything if you keep interrupting me," she said. "You wanted me to do this, I'm doing it. Now let me do it."

Atheris started to speak again, then closed his mouth with a sigh. He sat down on the floor.

Annoyed, Peri started over—breathing, stretches, moving into the first patterns, her blood flowing fast and strong now, breathing controlled. She breathed out anger, breathed in calmness, clarity, strength.

I am Perian. I am warrior. I am earth, deep-rooted and strong, mother of—

"There!" Atheris said suddenly, interrupting her again. This time Peri was more startled than angry, a little frightened by the intensity of the Sarkond's expression.

"Fascinating," he said softly, his gray eyes sparkling. "From a ritual designed for warriors—death givers—you generate *within yourself* true life energies. But how can that be?"

"*I* don't know," Peri said self-consciously. "Look, I don't know how many ways to tell you this. I don't know anything about magic, life energies or death energies, or whatever. I know swordplay, I know horses, I know how to mix you up a wonderful poultice for a heat rash. What do you want from me?"

"I want to understand," Atheris said rather wistfully, "how it is that without even knowing how you do it, you have learned to do what I have dreamed all my life of achieving, what I made myself a heretic and criminal attempting."

"If I knew what I was doing," Peri said with embarrassment, "I'd tell you." The room seemed darker, she realized, and glancing at the windows, she noticed that almost no light came in through the cracks in the shutters anymore. "Look, it's sunset and supper will be ready. Would you mind fetching it up?" She shrugged self-consciously. "My tunic and breeches are wet."

"Yes, yes," Atheris said, shaking his head. He left still shaking his head, returning a few minutes later with a basket and a deep covered bowl.

"Bread and vegetable stew," he said. "After days of dried journey food, it smells wonderful."

Peri was less impressed. The bread was hard and stale and the vegetables seemed old and limp, and apparently nobody in Sarkond had heard of putting herbs and spices in their food, much less salt, but at least it was hot and thick and plentiful and, as Atheris said, it wasn't dried journey food. She ate prodigiously and silently, and thankfully Atheris kept quiet, too, as if lost in thought.

"There are only two blankets," Atheris said softly when they had finished. "Will you be warm enough if we light the brazier?"

"I'll be fine," Peri said shortly. She lit the brazier and made up her pallet. She'd sleep colder than Atheris in only her linens, but with the robe laid over the blanket she'd manage. She crawled into her pallet, turned away from Atheris, and closed her eyes, trying not to remember the night before and the warmth of his back against hers. Once more her years with Danber's clan served her well; strange bed notwithstanding, she was asleep in moments.

Sometime during the night she half roused, shivering; before she woke entirely, however, she grew warm again—*Atheris must've built the brazier up*—and drifted back into sleep.

Peri woke grudgingly, still tired and sore, to some sound in the room. She sat up, rubbing her eyes, and saw Atheris closing the door behind him. He was carrying another bowl.

"Hot porridge," he said by way of explanation. "Come, you must eat."

Blearily Peri pushed the blankets off—*blankets?*—yes, sometime during the night Atheris must have laid his own blanket over her. She flushed.

"Thanks," she said, plucking at the blanket. "You didn't have to do that."

"You sustain the spell that protects us," Atheris said simply. "You need rest and food to maintain your strength. I suggest you perform your exercising ritual again after you break your fast, while I try my luck in the city."

Peri ate, not arguing when Atheris left her most of the porridge. He had plenty of money; he could easily buy something to eat in the market—probably something better than porridge, too.

"If you leave this house," she said slowly, "won't the Bone Hunters know where you are?"

"Hopefully they either followed the caravan, discovered we were not there, and turned back, or followed the pilgrimage and are too far away by now to sense me," Atheris said, sighing. "But even if not, I have little choice. We must have supplies, horses, too, if I can find them; but if possible, what I would most like to purchase is a talisman to replace the blood spell that conceals us. Mages' shops will be warded, and at least while I do business there I am concealed, if nothing else. I will certainly try to minimize my visibility as much as I can."

Peri sighed, too, but she could not argue with his logic. With any luck, the Bone Hunters would have either doubled back south, or, better yet, ridden on west after the pilgrimage. A couple of fresh horses and a hard ride straight south was surely her best option now. She and Atheris had traveled far enough west that once they crossed the Barrier, it wouldn't take them long to reach one of the border garrisons, and from there, Olhavar and safety. But it would have to be a fast journey. She didn't have any illusions that she could outride a magical attack.

"Don't buy horses," she said. "Just look at what's available. Better yet, ask Orren if he knows of any good horses for sale. When I can go out with you, we'll look over the best of what you found, and I'll see if there's anything that'll get us to the border reasonably fast.''

"Gladly,'' Atheris said rather wryly. "I know nothing about horses.''

"Well, I hope you know something about water,'' Peri said. "See if you can buy us something fit to drink. No wonder most of the people I've seen look sick. This stuff's got to be tainted somehow to smell that bad. Buy wine or beer or ale or something if you have to.''

Atheris looked at her oddly.

"I smelled nothing in the water,'' he said.

Peri grimaced.

Right, she thought wearily. *Water magic. Well, at least it's doing me some good for once.*

"I've got a touch of water sensitivity, so maybe it isn't really a smell. Or maybe all the water in Sarkond is this bad,'' she said. "If you're used to it, you probably don't notice it. To me it smells flat and dead, like water that's been stagnant for a long time, and in Bregond, we don't drink water like that. So see if you can find us something else to drink. The Bright Ones know we've got money enough. And by the way, don't take it all with you, in case someone tries to rob you.'' She'd have been embarrassed giving most people such obvious advice, but Atheris had a kind of—well, perhaps not näiveté, but a slightly distracted air about him that made Peri wonder whether he, like her mother, had had a rather cloistered youth.

"As you say, then,'' Atheris said, giving her another odd look. "I will be back as quickly as possible. Attend to your strength and remember to keep your bandages close at hand in case our host or hostess should knock on the door.''

When he was gone, Peri latched the door, remembering to pull in the latchstring this time. She washed her breastband and hose in the bucket and considered her tunic and trousers, but they were still damp; she hoped they'd be dry before Atheris came back. Peri sighed and rooted in her emergency pack for her loincloth. At least it provided some covering, and if anyone knocked at the door she'd just pull on the horrible robe.

Peri was so tired that it was an effort to force herself to begin her exercises, but as always, the movements soon had her warm and limber and strong again. This time nothing interrupted her and she moved on to practice the qivashim, first defensive, then offensive, as best she could without a partner or even a practice dummy or post. The limbering drew the last remaining soreness from her bruised ribs, and Peri noted with satisfaction that the last few days of missed practice had not dulled her edge; her timing and form was as good as ever and she flowed evenly from one qiva to the next.

Waterdance, however, continued to elude her. Her uncle Terralt was right. Her blade work was fine; it was her feet that were getting her into trouble. Even barefoot and on the solid wooden floor, nothing at all to trip her up, she couldn't keep her footing. She had thought—and still did—that balance was the key to Waterdance, but there wasn't much to be gained in throwing off her enemy's balance if she lost her own as well.

But that's the problem, isn't it? she thought, frustrated. *Two people step onto the deck of a rolling boat and they're BOTH off balance. The only question's who falls first.*

That thought nagged at her, as if she was missing something vital, but the more she chewed at the problem, the more insurmountable it seemed. At last she disgustedly returned to the defensive qivashim. She'd worked through most of them when Atheris finally knocked on the door; to Peri's surprise, judging from the light in the cracks in the shutters, it was midafternoon. She'd practiced most of the day away. She hurriedly pulled on her still-damp tunic and trousers and let Atheris in.

He dropped several heavy bags in the corner; to Peri's relief, there was a sword in his scabbard now, too.

"Here is your ale, the best I could find, and I fear it will not impress you," he said rather grimly. "Conditions in the city are worse than I suspected. I am told there has been no rain for months, and many of the wells are dry. There is no water to be bought of better quality than what our hosts give us, and you are right, healers have linked bad water with several fevers rampant in the south."

"In Bregond, the clans boil water they aren't certain is safe," Peri said slowly. "Supposedly boiling the water makes it so uncomfortable that any demons living in it are forced to flee. My father says that's just superstition, but it's true that the nomads never seem to get pond fevers or black squats from their water. If we can't find anything else to drink, it's worth trying. Are there any horses for sale?"

"Few," Atheris said shortly. "And what there are, are of poor quality, even to my inexperienced eye. There is little grazing here, you see, with the drought, and feed is terribly expensive. But our host, Orren, recommended a merchant who was not in the market today. He should be there at midweek, tomorrow."

Peri grimaced.

"Any good news?" she said.

"Yes," Atheris said with a sigh. He pulled out a braided leather cord with what appeared to be metal and bone beads, incised with strange designs, knotted into it at regular intervals. "I was able to purchase spells that will protect us from any manner of magical detection. I put mine on immediately." He pushed up his left sleeve, showing Peri the cord tied around his wrist. "Fortunately, being on the road to Rocarran, Darnalek at least attracts mages. The spells were not cheap, and I had to spin a lie of considerable complexity to explain their purchase. The curiosity of that mage troubles me, in fact, although it may have stemmed from my payment in gold rather than what I purchased. I changed some gold for coin later, though I got a miserable rate, so that we can prevent such notice in the future. But at least I can dissolve the blood spell on this building, and we have some money we can spend safely, and you can venture outside in your disguise if you are careful to remain silent.''

"Yes, and we can plan to ride south as soon as we find horses," Peri said with relief. "I was afraid we'd have to buy a wagon or a cart, something you could cast a spell on, and that'd slow us down too much—not to mention that I'm not sure we could even *get* a wagon across some of that terrain near the Barrier, much less across the plains in Bregond. Look, if we can find a couple of horses that are in even halfway decent health and a couple skins of something drinkable, I can get us back. You worry about those Bone Hunters, I'll worry about the rest.''

Atheris smiled gravely and pulled a bundle out of one sack.

"These are for you," he said rather awkwardly, handing her the bundle. Peri unrolled it and found, to her surprise and delight, a plain but sturdy tunic and trousers, a linen undertunic, and a set of men's smallclothes and hose. The cut of the garments was strange and the fabrics coarser than she usually wore, but Peri couldn't have been more pleased if every piece had been of the finest, softest ikada wool.

"I looked at your tunic and trousers for size this morning, while you still slept," Atheris said a little uncomfortably. "I dared not buy female garments, nor anything too fine, lest someone remark on it, but in those at least you can pass without attracting too much notice.''

"They're fine, they're fine," Peri said happily, overwhelmed by the gesture. "Oh, Mahdha blow you the scent of your prey! I swear, if I *never* have to wear that filthy, stinking robe again—''

Without thinking she pulled off her tunic and trousers; it was not until Atheris gasped that she realized she was wearing nothing under it but a loincloth. Peri flushed, but the damage was done; there was nothing she could do but hurriedly pull on the linens and then the new tunic and trousers. When she finally forced herself to look up, she was startled and a little uneasy to see Atheris still staring at her, apparently not at all embarrassed. At last he made an apologetic gesture.

"Forgive me," he said abashedly. "I have never seen a woman like you."

"What, a Bregond, you mean?" Peri asked, concentrating on buckling her belt to cover her embarrassment. Bright Ones, breasts were breasts, and hers were nothing remarkable. Besides, he'd seen her the day before in the sweathouse, although with all the steam he'd probably not gotten much of a look.

"No, a warrior," Atheris said, flushing slightly. "There are a few Sarkondish women who are warriors, I know, but I have only met women who serve in the temples, and they never learn the arts of death. I have never seen a woman muscled like a swordsman."

Peri grimaced. Somehow it had sounded rather more complimentary when Danber had told her she looked healthy and strong. Then she frowned again, not liking it that this Sarkond's opinion even mattered to her. She quickly turned the conversation by asking a question that had nagged at her since the day before.

"You said you know the Ithuara," she said. "I didn't know it was practiced in Sarkond." That was as polite a way to ask *When did Sarkond steal it from us?* as she could think of.

Atheris glanced at her rather narrowly.

"The Ithuara was *first* practiced in Sarkond," he said. "Or at least by the clans that later became the Sarkondish people. They were a race of nomads, with no good lands of their own, so they lived by conquest of other peoples. They developed a style of swordsmanship that encompassed and countered each style of swordfighting they encountered, offensive or defensive, in a qiva of its own, and thus the Ithuara grew.''

Peri felt her back stiffen with anger.

''I was taught,'' she said coolly, ''that the Ithuara was born in Bregond in the same way—not because the clans were vicious murderers out to steal other people's lands, but because nearly every race of people have tried, at some time or other, to take ours.''

Atheris's lips thinned slightly, and Peri was almost gratified to see some hint of a warrior's pride in him at last. Any Bregondish clansman worth his salt would have challenged her for that remark.

''If the Ithuara grew in Bregond,'' he said between his teeth, ''explain how it came to be known here, since no Bregond would ever teach it to us?''

Peri gave a bark of laughter.

''I could ask you the same question,'' she said. ''And I could ask you another one, too. If the Ithuara's Sarkondish, tell me how it is that Sarkonds don't even know the preparatory stretches and breathing patterns that even the youngest Bregondish warriors learn?''

''Your ritual preparations,'' Atheris said slowly and patiently, as if to a child, ''are obviously a Bregondish invention and no part of the Ithuara. You surely could not expect to work your way through all those exercises in combat.''

''And you can't expect to be a proper swordsman if you don't understand the importance of flexibility and focus,'' Peri retorted scornfully.

''That sounds like a challenge,'' Atheris said, scowling.

''Then take it as one.'' Peri drew her sword. ''Have a guard?''

Atheris flushed.

''I did not buy this sword to play with,'' he said defensively. "And we cannot risk the injuries of even a guarded blade. Scabbards only."

Peri sighed and shrugged, laying her sword carefully aside. She unbuckled her scabbard and raised it, sketching a half-hearted salute and assuming a neutral stance. Let Atheris choose offensive or defensive; she'd trounce him quickly enough either way.

You've done well, Peri, Danber had said. *You have the steel in your blood—the strength, the reflexes, but more importantly, the gut.*

Peri was surprised when Atheris fell easily into a tight offensive, not taking the obvious Charging Boar qiva but choosing the much more difficult Diving Hawk, forcing Peri into Shifting Gusts, an equally tricky defensive qiva. He was pushing himself hard and testing her just as adroitly, and she was impressed; she'd never known a mage, Agrondish or Bregondish, to have either time or opportunity to master swordplay to any degree of skill.

Damn all, Peri, learn to THINK! Danber scolded. *You can't expect to hammer every opponent into the ground with sheer boldness.*

Differences of opinion and race forgotten, Peri looked at Atheris now as warrior to warrior and paid him the compliment of tacitly acknowledging his skill, pushing back just as hard, falling into patterns she'd never risk against a lesser opponent for fear of hurting them. She turned his attack and took the offensive, gave him Stalking Cat, and he responded with Leaping Flame, a daring and risky counteroffensive she'd never seen before, so unexpected that it nearly forced her back on the defensive.

I won't be able to practice with you much longer, Danber told her, half in admonishment, half with pride. *You want it too badly. You take it to a level I won't, not in practice, Peri.*

If you don't learn to discipline yourself, you're going to burn up in that fire.

Heart pounding, full of a savage exhilaration, she barely recovered, transmuting Stalking Cat to Mahdha's Fury, one of her best offensive qivashim, and at last Atheris's defense began to show signs of weakness. It soon became apparent to Peri that while Atheris had a thorough acquaintance with the qivashim, he simply did not have the sword-in-hand practice hours to build stamina and train his reactions to the edge she had achieved.

The realization apparently occurred to Atheris at the same time; the thought flickered in his eyes and he raised one eyebrow; Peri dipped her chin briefly in acknowledgment and abruptly the contest became the daring and cooperative dance of practice.

You take too many chances, Peri, Danber said. *Too many risks. You overextend yourself—*

She dropped her offensive and Atheris took it, Peri almost giddy with the ability to trust her opponent and test her defensive limitations, hone the rough edges of her skill against a partner who knew when to draw her out and when to back off, and let her work out a problem on her own. She reciprocated when she took the offensive again, pacing their dance so that Atheris could keep up with her, playing to his range rather than to raw strength and endurance. He acknowledged the gift with a half smile, and in a sudden burst of confidence, heart pounding, blood pumping hotly, Peri dropped her attack, leaving Atheris an opening, and flowed as easily as breathing into Waterdance—

Enough, Peri. Danber meeting her eyes coolly.

Defiantly: *Maybe you don't want it badly enough, Danber. Maybe, Peri, you want it too much.*

And for one single, breathless instant, it almost worked.

Atheris's eyes widened with surprise, his pattern faltered, breaking—

Then Peri stumbled and, to her complete disgust, fell heavily, her teeth clicking shut on her tongue in sudden exquisite pain, so hard that she faintly tasted blood.

An extended hand appeared in her field of vision and she glanced up, flushing with utter humiliation. To her surprise (and relief), Atheris's expression held none of the ridicule that she had expected; his gray eyes were sparkling excitedly, and as he helped her up, his smile was encouraging, not mocking.

"That was marvelous," he said. "I can barely remember the last time I had the opportunity to spar with a true master of the art. But what was that last qiva? Some Bregondish invention? I would swear I never saw it before."

Peri grimaced.

"I've been working on a new offensive qiva," she said with a sigh. "For a moment there I thought I finally had it. It's a water qiva, meant to throw an opponent off balance, like when you step onto the deck of a boat on rolling water."

"You—are *creating* a new qiva?" Atheris murmured, his eyes widening again.

Peri shrugged self-consciously.

"I know," she said. "Pretty presumptuous of me, isn't it?"

He chuckled.

"Given my level of achievement, I am scarcely qualified to judge," he said. "It is an ambitious idea, true. But someone, after all, must invent the qivashim, and perhaps only those who are truly gifted are inspired to do so."

Peri took a deep breath.

"Thanks," she said quietly.

Atheris raised his eyebrows questioningly, saying nothing.

"For not telling me I was jumping blind off a cliff for the sake of ambition," she said a little abashedly.

Atheris grinned ruefully.

"I am scarcely one to make such an accusation," he said. "But I believe sometimes that a leap is the only sane path to take." He touched her shoulder. "And you *are* strengthened, are you not?"

"Strengthened?" Peri chuckled. "I feel—"

Then she met Atheris's eyes and there was that flicker of recognition again, acknowledgment, and without thought Peri found his lips crushing hers, her fingers digging hard into his shoulders, not to push him away but to pull him closer. The hot coppery taste of blood from her bitten tongue was in both their mouths, and Atheris smelled of sweat and the slightly grimy leather of his tunic; then the tunic was gone and there was the heat of his skin against hers and the hardness of the wood floor against her back, then his, then hers, then his as they rolled heedlessly in combat no gentler than the dance of steel.

Peri's blood boiled in her veins, pounded in her ears; this was no play now, no tentative experimentation. This was an Ithuara in flesh and blood, two warriors meeting on the battleground, the fierce ring of steel kissing steel, testing each other's limits and then drawing back only to begin anew, asking no quarter and giving none. Atheris's long, sweaty hair was in her eyes and mouth, his chest crushing her breasts and making her bruised ribs twinge; then Peri's braids hung down around her face and the scar running down Atheris's chest was smooth and strange under her tongue and his nails bit into the skin of her shoulders.

And at the end came a qiva against which there was no defense, and with that a surrender that was still victory, or perhaps just the opposite; and afterward, lying half on and half off one of their pallets in a sweaty tangle of hair and limbs and half-shed clothes, Peri admitted to herself with a sigh of something less than regret that the battle had, without a doubt, ended in a draw.

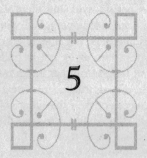

5

"I KNOW," ATHERIS SAID QUIETLY. "I WAS shocked, too. I still somehow expected it would not be so bad."

Peri glanced up hastily, guiltily; then she realized he was talking about the marketplace and bit her lip to stifle a sigh of relief.

Atheris had cause for shock. Back in Agrond, the great market in Tarkesh was a marvelous place, so huge and full and noisy that it seemed like one great yearlong festival. Bregond had nothing to rival it, of course, but even tiny towns too poor to manage more than a few carts at the center of town once a week were lively places where friends gossiped and laughed or argued with each other and haggled with the merchants.

Darnalek's market was gray and all but silent; the loudest sounds were the creak of cart wheels and the clop of hooves or boot soles against hard-packed dirt. A few listless men and women made a cursory attempt at bargaining with equally apathetic vendors, then paid or walked away just as indifferently. No wind ruffled the drab garments hanging out windows to dry. No urchins or thieves or dogs ran the streets. No beggars called out to passersby. Peri couldn't even hear the rustling of rats from the alleyways.

The market stank of decaying garbage and emptied chamber pots, and under that a less definable but no less discernible smell, the same odor that Peri had detected in the water—a flat, stagnant, dead smell. Every piece of wood seemed riddled with worm tunnels or crumbly with dry rot. The very stones of the foundations seemed to be rotting away. The few vegetables and fruits for sale were not only wilted but strangely colorless and withered. Even the air seemed somehow gray.

And it matched Peri's mood.

Battle heat, she thought resolutely. *Danber warned me about it, the firing of the blood after a good fight. All my sword instructors warned me.*

Maybe last night, relaxed and sated and unthinking, she'd had no regrets. This morning she'd had plenty of time to think. Plenty of time to regret.

If she'd thought her parents—not knowing of her "arrangement" with Danber, of course—less than approving of her sneaky tumble with Loris, she didn't even want to imagine what they'd think of this. She hardly knew Atheris; he was practically a stranger—worse, a *Sarkondish* stranger. Even Danber's understanding didn't stretch that far, and battle heat seemed no excuse at all, even to her. Nobody she knew could possibly understand, much less condone, such disgraceful conduct.

Peri stifled a groan, glad the rags hid her burning face. What in the world could she have been thinking? Well, she *hadn't* been thinking, unless it was with her loins; that was plain enough! She hadn't felt like a trollop after her night in Loris's bed—just vaguely disappointed. *All this fuss for THAT?* But today she felt so—so—

And the horrible thing about it was that last night it had felt so *right.* Loris, probably trying to be considerate of her inexperience, had been gentle, careful, slow, almost polite.

Kind of like the way most Bregonds think of Agronds, Peri thought with a sigh. *Where's the LIFE in these people?*

With Atheris it had been different, hunger meeting hunger, strength meeting strength.

Ithuara, "steel's kiss." That was us, steel meeting steel. She shivered at the memory. *Would it be that way with another warrior? With Danber, if he'd wanted me? Or was it just battle heat after all?*

She shook her head disgustedly. Atheris had seemed troubled over breakfast this morning, too, quiet and pensive as if he, too, didn't quite understand what had happened.

Atheris wants something from me. What, I don't know. It all seems so complicated. Last night for a little while it seemed simple for once—we both wanted something, and we took it. I felt more MYSELF than I'd felt in a long time, strong and sure and free, like I used to feel riding with the clan or working out tricky qivashim with Danber. But it wasn't simple at all. Just stupid.

She bit her lip.

Oh, Mahdha, Breath of Bregond, blow me home. I've lost the trail and I'm riding blind.

"There," Atheris said quietly, interrupting her thoughts, and Peri glanced up again, startled.

"What?" she whispered as quietly as she could. She must've missed some comment, some explanation.

"The horses," Atheris said, gesturing a little impatiently. "Orren said they were the best for sale in town. You wanted to look at them before the owner knew we were buying. There they are."

Peri grimaced, remembering the conversation now.

Bright Ones, Perian, pay attention! You'll look a pretty fool if you trip over your own feet and fall face-first in that stinking gutter, won't you?

She looked at the horses in the pen across the square and grimaced again. Not a one of them would have made it past Danber's first and most superficial cull. Even in Agrond most merchants wouldn't have thought these lifeless beasts worth the trouble of taking to market.

"What about the bay near the gate?" Atheris suggested after Peri's extended silence pronounced its own judgment.

"It's half-blind," Peri whispered.

"The brown-and-white closest to us?"

"Going lame in the near hind," Peri said, shaking her head. "Couldn't outrun a sick turtle. All right. The gray gelding at the water trough and the buff mare at the east end."

"That foul-tempered thing?" Atheris protested as the buff turned and nipped savagely at her neighbor.

"I can handle 'that foul-tempered thing,'" Peri muttered. "The gelding's for you. Now listen. When you go in, don't ask the merchant about either of them; go look at that black-and-white gelding in the middle. That's his showpiece. Show some interest, then try to talk him down to half of whatever he asks. He won't go that low. When that doesn't work, shake your head and ask about the dark brown gelding, the one with the white patch over his eye. When the merchant quotes you a price, act like you're interested. Then look in the brown's mouth, give the merchant the nastiest look you can manage, and start walking away. Don't say a thing. He'll stop you and offer you a decent price on the gray and the buff. Offer him three-fourths of what he asks. He'll take it."

"How do you know he'll do all that?" Atheris asked, raising his eyebrows.

"Because you'll have proven to him you know what you're

doing, and he knows those two are the only horses he'll have even a chance of selling you. The kind of buyers he's getting are too green to take that nasty buff mare, and the gray's just too flat-out *ugly* for an easy sell. Trust me. He'll go for it. Make him have both of them reshod. The gray's about to throw his right front shoe. And tell him to deliver them to Orren's stable so nobody notices us with those horses before we leave.''

Atheris shook his head, but walked away, giving Peri a skeptical glance over his shoulder. She ignored it and turned away, wandering among the stalls. There was no excuse for someone looking like her to be hanging around the horse pens, not unless she wanted to be mistaken for a horse thief.

The aroma of relatively fresh food cooking was sweeter than perfume in this decaying city, and Peri followed her nose. A vendor was frying meat-and-turnip pies in a kettle of hot oil, and after days of no meat except the leathery trail food, Peri wasn't inclined to inquire too closely what animal had given its life to fill those pies. The vendor appeared less than pleased by the appearance of his swathed and silent customer, but coin was coin and at length Peri walked away poorer by two copper coins and richer by four hot pies.

Walking back toward the horse pens, she nearly collided with a smugly smiling Atheris.

"Did you get them?" Peri whispered, handing him two pies.

"Just as you said," Atheris admitted, chuckling. "He said he would have the horses reshod and at Orren's stable tomorrow before sunset. And I thought *I* was the mage."

"There's no magic to it," Peri said, after glancing around to make sure nobody was close enough to hear. "Horses lose their value fast penned up like that—they founder or get hoof rot and their muscles soften up. Pretty horses sell easy to stupid marks. Ugly sound ones—I wish I could say *good* horses, but not these two—only sell to horsemen. That was you. So he jumped on the sale.''

Atheris grunted, biting into a pie.

"I still say it was magic," he muttered, his mouth full. He raised his eyebrows. "Hmmm. I see you found the horses that failed to sell."

"Oh, good," Peri said, glancing at Atheris out of the corner of her eye. "I was afraid it might be dog or rat or something."

To her disgust Atheris only gazed at her gravely, although the corner of his mouth twitched.

"No," he said seriously. "Rat is much gamier."

They made their way back to the other end of the market to look at saddles and bridles; there Peri dared not send Atheris in alone. Fortunately she had proper Sarkondish clothing now, and while a swathed and presumably disfigured warrior helping to purchase tack for two horses was certain to attract attention, a filthy and presumably disfigured pilgrim buying the tack would have seemed a great deal more suspicious.

Peri was surprised to see what appeared to be a large number of pilgrims in the city, judging from the bundles of belongings they carried; there certainly were no large temples in Darnalek from what she'd seen. When asked, Atheris explained that the pilgrims were likely here to join the next pilgrimage to Rocarran, and that surprised her even more. Why, the last pilgrimage had hardly passed by here. If the pilgrims felt safe in waiting here in the city for the next group, instead of hurrying northwest to catch up with the others, such pilgrimages must occur with amazing frequency. Even in Agrond Peri hadn't seen such activity except during large religious festivals or other significant occasions. She tried to press Atheris for a further explanation, but from his brusque and often vague answers she quickly realized that it was an uncomfortable subject for him. Of course, he'd served in a temple himself. Obviously it was painful to be reminded constantly that he'd been cast out of the little world that had been his whole life, declared a heretic. Peri let the subject go and Atheris seemed vastly relieved.

As they walked back, Atheris stopped abruptly, so suddenly that Peri barely avoided colliding with his back. He was staring at something across the street. Peri herself saw nothing remarkable, only a few shabby shops—a baker, a fortune-teller, a potter.

"What?" she asked as loudly as she dared. "What is it?"

Atheris was silent a moment longer, then abruptly started walking again.

"Nothing," he mumbled. "I thought I . . . felt something. But I was wrong."

The sun slowly lowered in the west, and reluctantly Peri followed Atheris back to Orren and Lina's house carrying their goods in coarse sacks. She hated this gray and lifeless city, hated the unhealthy stench and the silence of it, but at least while she walked the foul streets with Atheris she could avoid talking to him and facing him. In the privacy of their loft there would be no more excuses.

To her surprise Atheris seemed reluctant, too, dawdling in the stable after they'd told Orren of the impending arrival of their horses, then lingering scraping his boots at the door, until Lina appeared on the threshold, gazing pointedly at the setting sun. In the loft, Peri busied herself settling their tack in a corner, lighting the brazier. Atheris took an unusually long time fetching their supper, but when it came, the stew was fresh and hot and floating with dumplings, and there were even chunks of meat in it, and Peri gratefully took the food as another excuse to postpone the inevitable confrontation.

"So tell me," she said, picking out another tough chunk and chewing vigorously, "what's this, dog or rat?"

"Goat, actually," Atheris said, chuckling.

"Oh, yeah?" Peri bit into some vegetable she neither recognized nor liked, grimaced, swigged bad ale to wash away the taste, and grimaced again. "How do you know? Not gamy enough for dog?"

"Hardly," Atheris said wryly. "Yesterday when I asked Orren about the horses, he mentioned that he had taken two rather elderly goats in exchange for stabling a merchant's horses for a month. Knowing that the goats were not worth the money to feed them, I merely applied the same sort of magical deduction you made." He shook his head. "Meat twice in one day. The south must be finally recovering, despite appearances."

Peri seized eagerly on the subject.

"Yes, what happened here?" she said. "There couldn't possibly have been any magical attacks this far north during the war or the earth would be blasted like it is near the border, and I can't imagine magical taint from the Barrier could reach this far—it certainly didn't in Bregond. But I've never seen anything so unhealthy as this land. Everything here seems dead."

"Not dead," Atheris said softly. "Lifeless."

Peri raised her eyebrows.

"There's a difference?" she said.

"Oh, yes." Atheris glanced down at his bowl almost guiltily. "Do you remember what I told you about men's magic?"

"Right, death magic," Peri said, trying to remember what he had actually said. "Or—no, magic that *takes* life, uses it, right?" Then realization struck her silent for a long moment as she digested the implications.

"You mean," she said very slowly, "somebody just . . . sucked all the life out of every living thing here?"

"More than living things," Atheris said softly. "During the war our battle mages wielded such potent magics that they drew all the life out of the very soil, deep down into the bones of the land. Few crops can grow because the soil, even the water, is utterly barren of life.''

He made a vague gesture at the loft.

''Do you know how Orren and Lina live so prosperously?'' he asked. ''Not because of the income from what few boarders they take in. Not from the stabling fees few here can afford to pay. No, Orren makes his money selling the manure and old bedding from the horses to farmers to spread upon their fields.''

Peri remembered the noticeable lack of dung in the streets and grimaced. On a good market day in Tarkesh she wore her highest boots just to walk down the streets. Fostering in Bregond, she'd never taken for granted the lush fertility of Agrond's soil, but—

''Why would they do it?'' she asked softly. ''Why would Sarkond's mages suck their own land dry of life?''

''Because of a prophecy,'' Atheris said, sighing and closing his eyes as if it pained him to utter the words. ''A prophecy of our god, Eregis, He Who Sleeps. We were promised that when He woke, His power would deliver us from poverty and hunger, that we would dwell thereafter in lands of plenty. Our priests said that meant that we would conquer the rich lands to the south, and they believed that time had come. The Sign had come to pass, you see—or so we were told by our sources south of the border.''

''The Sign?'' Peri asked uncomfortably. Sources south of the border? Traitors. Bregondish or Agrondish traitors. There were whispers in Bregond of a great scandal among the temples shortly after the war. She had asked her mother about it, but High Lady Kayli couldn't—or wouldn't—explain.

''The Harbinger,'' Atheris said very softly. ''Born to nobility, destined to walk between two worlds, embodying both life and death—well, no matter.'' He shook his head. ''Our priests believed it was the Lady Kayli of Bregond, she who wed to unite Agrond and Bregond and wielded the most potent and lethal fire magic, who fulfilled this prophecy. But she was not the one, and it was not the time, a mistake our warriors and priests did not realize until far too late. Eregis did not wake, and Sarkond was defeated—more, nearly destroyed. By Agrond's and Bregond's magic, yes, but even more so by what our mages had done to our country in the hope of that victory.''

Atheris was silent for a long time. When he spoke, his voice was flat and tired.

''Were we betrayed by our god or by our own misunderstanding?'' he said. ''No one knows. The people could only wait and hold on to the hope of the prophecy, that the Sign had not yet come, that the promise was yet to be fulfilled. And the temples have kept the faith alive. They—we—have . . .''

Atheris's voice trailed off and this time the pain was visible in his eyes.

''And you thought the prophecy was wrong,'' Peri said as gently as she could. ''You went looking for some other hope for your people, some other answer. And they called you a heretic for it.''

Atheris closed his eyes again and nodded silently. At last he opened his eyes but stared at the floor, not facing Peri.

''Before He slept, Eregis was once called the Father of Waters,'' he said. ''I thought the answer lay in a symbolic, not a literal interpretation of the prophecy. That by combining the polarities, the magic of man and that of woman, a great power could be wakened to bring life back to our land, just as the joining of man and woman brings new life. My cousin Amis shared this belief, and she was powerful in her healing magic. We hoped to make rain in a desperately dry land—only a first step, but a tangible one, one that must be recognized.''

He grinned rather bitterly.

''I understand your ambition to create a qiva,'' he said,

shrugging. "What Amis and I attempted was no less presumptuous, and utterly forbidden as well. Not only is the magic of life forbidden to priests, so is the act of life itself."

"What, sex?" Peri said, taken aback. What a notion! Why, her brother Estann's Awakening had been celebrated with a festival throughout most of Agrond.

Atheris only nodded, still gazing resolutely at the floor.

"I thought such restrictions mere dogma," he said. "I was wrong. We raised a power indeed, Amis and I, but not as we meant to do. She summoned up the energies from within her, but I—I did not know how to share, only how to take. I nearly killed her."

Peri grimaced. Bright Ones, no surprise that only disaster came of a system of magic and religion that so twisted and distorted the natural order of the world. Men's magic and women's magic indeed!

Atheris met Peri's eyes at last.

"Our joining last night was a mistake," he said quietly.

"It certainly was," Peri said flatly.

"I have no excuse," Atheris said, shaking his head. "Eregis forgive me, I should have known better. But Amis was so quiet and tender, vulnerable—and you were so different, strong and full of life, and it felt—"

"—right." Peri sighed, her skin shivering into gooseflesh and her heart pounding hard at the memory. "Like our fight. Blade meeting blade, not needing to hold back, able to take a chance without having to worry about a misstroke—"

"—or to fear giving harm or receiving it," Atheris said, his eyes sparkling. "Only the dance—"

"—the kiss of steel—" Peri breathed, her hands trembling. Slowly, almost unwillingly, Atheris leaned closer.

"—in flesh and—"

And Peri groaned, lost and damned, and pulled him to her. Late in the night, Peri roused to a faint sound. She lay still, her hand creeping to the hilt of the dagger under the edge of her pallet. There was only a little light from the cooling coals in the brazier, and it took her a moment to realize that the figure moving stealthily through the loft was Atheris. Peri held perfectly still, kept her breathing even. What in the world could he be doing?

He pulled the pouch of gold out from under his pillow, and Peri heard the clink of coins as he withdrew a handful, shoving them into his pocket. He moved to one of the windows, opened the shutters. He climbed quietly out onto the stable roof, closing the shutters behind him but not latching them.

Peri sat up, alarmed, but a quick glance in the corner showed that their packs and sacks were still in place. They had no horses yet; he hadn't taken anything but his weapons and the gold.

Peri hurried to the window, opened the shutters just a crack. Atheris had climbed down the side of the stable and was working his way up the street toward the market, trying to be stealthy about it, darting from doorway to alley to doorway, but he obviously didn't know much about cover and evading—rather than fleeing—pursuit. To anybody who had ever done any night hunting he might as well have rung bells as he moved.

Peri quickly retrieved her sword and dagger, pulled on her boots, and slipped out the window. Orren and Lina barred their door, but apparently they'd never considered the possibility of somebody climbing the roof, because it was a simple matter to drop down from the stable roof and wouldn't be too much more difficult to climb back up.

She set off down the street after Atheris. The streets were empty, eerily so—she'd expected guards, beggars, whores, drunks returning from taverns, or at the very least pilgrims too poor to pay for a room and opting to sleep in doorways instead. But there seemed to be nobody about.

Or was there? Once or twice Peri heard scuffling noises from the darker alleys, sounds that she hoped were made by rats or stray dogs but seemed somehow too large—and besides, she'd already noticed the lack of such animals in the city. She peered down one of the alleys and thought she saw someone duck furtively around a corner, but the light was too poor for certainty. Peri took a deep breath and continued on. She couldn't afford to delay if she wanted to keep up with Atheris.

Speaking of her quarry, he'd nearly reached the market at the center of town. He slowed now, glancing around him nervously, and Peri had to mind her cover as the wider streets and open market area provided more light.

To her surprise, Atheris stopped near the point where she'd almost collided with him, quickly crossing the street; amazingly he approached the foretune-teller's shop, where the windows were still lit. Peri stopped where she was, blinking in astonishment. He'd done all this, sneaked out here in the middle of the night just to get his fortune told? But sure enough, Atheris knocked on the door, and shortly thereafter it opened, a middle-aged man conversing briefly with him, then stepping aside to let him enter.

Peri waited until the door closed behind Atheris, then crossed the street as quickly as she could. Because of the light in the windows, she was far too visible in the front, and the shops on either side were both closed. She glanced around and saw an alley that looked promising, and ducked into it.

There was almost no light in the narrow space between buildings, but Peri heard none of that eerie rustling here and concluded that she probably wouldn't encounter anything more deadly than rats and mice. She ran her hand along the wooden wall beside her until a gap indicated a perpendicular alley leading in the right direction; to her relief, dim lights in two windows implied that the fortune-teller's shop had, as she had hoped, a back door. She crept up as quietly as she could, peering in one window, then the other. There were curtains drawn inside both windows, giving her only a thin line of visibility, and worse, the shop was apparently divided into a front and back room. Fortunately the connecting door was open, probably to heat the front room from the coal stove Peri could see in the back room. She could see a table in the front, and part of the fortune-teller's shoulder and back, but only the side of Atheris's head, and the murmur of their voices was muffled.

"Many paths converge in your future," the stranger said in a louder voice. "You are approaching a point of decision. You see the signs but fear to act. You are the fulcrum, but another is the lever. You are chosen for a great and terrible deed, a betrayal that will bring death and salvation. More than that I cannot see, except that danger approaches rapidly and—"

A crashing sound. Peri saw the fortune-teller bolt to his feet, knocking over the table, but now his back blocked her view. Cries now, thumps. Alarmed, Peri tried the door; it was locked securely, probably barred.

From inside, she heard Atheris's voice raised in a cry that was suddenly cut off. Hurriedly Peri backed away from the door. She'd have to try to break it down and—

Hands grasped her, pulled her backward and off balance. Peri's head slammed into a wall, half stunning her; before she could regain her balance or her senses, she was jerked backward again, borne down to the garbage-littered soil of the alley under the weight of her assailant. Dazed, she tried to struggle, but strong hands pinned her wrists to the ground. The weight of her attacker's body settled on her abdomen, and Peri groaned as her bruised ribs protested.

"Careful," a voice hissed in Sarkondish. "He may be with the other one."

"What of it?" her assailant answered. "The priest is the

one *they* want. We get no bounty for this one.''

"Who is he?'' the first voice asked. Then there was light, suddenly, dazzling Peri's eyes as a lantern was unhooded, and she heard two gasps, one after the other.

"By Eregis, a Bregond!'' the watcher muttered.

The weight on top of her shifted.

"And no man, either,'' her assailant said, shock melting into amusement. "Only a girl in man's clothes.'' One hand released Peri's left wrist and roughly squeezed her breast. "Nay, no girl—a woman, rather. His doxy, no doubt.''

"No doubt,'' Peri snarled. One wrist free was all she needed, even though she couldn't reach her daggers or her sword. Her eyes were still too dazzled to see, but the sound of her attacker's voice, the location of it, had told her more than enough.

She bent her hand back, smashing the heel up into his nose with all her strength. She felt cartilage and bone shatter and collapse inward, but her assailant only screamed and rocked backward, releasing her other hand—she hadn't driven the bone up into his brain, only smashed his nose completely. Still, half a victory was better than none; she could see now, and now her other hand was free.

She struck again, this time for his eyes, and this time her aim was true. Her attacker screamed and tumbled backward, rolling over her legs and then away entirely, blood and other fluid running out from under the hands he'd clasped over his eyes. Peri didn't wait to hear what the other man was doing; she rolled to her feet, knives in hand before she'd even consciously decided that quarters were too close for her sword.

Another sound, behind her, and Peri reacted without thinking; Leaping Wolf, striking out with a lightning kick, the impact and a cry telling her she'd connected, not stopping to see where, flinging one knife at the lantern bearer and readying the second knife. The lantern fell and its bearer stumbled backward, Peri's blade in his shoulder, but she didn't pause either to retrieve her knife or finish the job.

No time to bother with the door or windows now; Peri snatched up the fallen lantern—fortunately it hadn't broken—and darted back through the alleys to the street. The door to the fortune-teller's shop gaped open, but only a brief glance inside told her that nobody was there but the unconscious or dead proprietor lying limp on the floor. But nobody—not even several people—could travel too fast carrying a body or an unwilling captive, and Peri had time to glimpse several figures disappearing around a corner at the other side of the market plaza. She didn't worry about stealth now; she lit out after them as fast as her boots would carry her.

She paused at the corner, hooding the lantern and peering around the corner more cautiously. There were four of them, less than she'd feared, and Atheris, carried between them, was beginning to stir. Gods, if she could only get around in front of them, surprise them from an alley—but she knew nothing of this city, and she'd do Atheris no good at all if she lost herself in dark alleys. She couldn't even follow too closely—the men kept glancing behind them, probably waiting for the other ones who had attacked her in the alley.

Look at what I'm doing, Peri thought wryly. *I'm risking my life to save a Sarkond—the SAME Sarkond—again. And why? I've got supplies, money, protection from those Bone Hunters' detection. The horses will arrive tomorrow. I should go back to the loft, get a good night's sleep, and tomorrow get out of Sarkond as fast as I can ride. Anyone I know—Agrond or Bregond—would say so. I've got every reason to go and no reason at all to stay. But no, not me, not the mighty warrior. Tumble a man a couple of times and look what it does to me. I just can't leave him to die, that's all. I can't.*

Scuffling noise in the alley. Peri started, then darted into another doorway to hide, then another, following as close to the Sarkonds as she dared. She'd do Atheris no good—nor herself, either—if somebody else managed to sneak up on her tonight.

Atheris's captors approached another shop with lit windows, a mage's shop.

Mage? Oh, yes—Atheris said that mage was a little too curious, didn't he? Bright Ones, if a mage gets hold of him, slaps a geas on him, and sticks him down in some cellar— NOW what do I—

Fortunately the same thought must have occurred to the recovering Atheris; he suddenly struggled violently, kicking and flailing.

Well, so much for stealth and caution. No point in drawing her sword or throwing knives—in the dark with five struggling people, she'd as likely hit Atheris as his captors. Never mind, her unarmed qivashim were well honed, and after her scuffle in the alley she was certainly primed for combat. A short sprint across the plaza and she dropped the first man with Springing Lopa, knocking a second off balance in the process and forcing them to drop their squirming burden. She didn't wait to see whether Atheris was up and moving yet; she reached for her sword, and now it was Mahdha's Fury that greeted them—

And before she could get her sword free of its scabbard, a solid weight struck the backs of her knees and she realized her mistake—that because she'd hit the second man, she'd assumed he was down. She held on to her sword hilt desperately as she fell—*A warrior must never lose her sword, Perian, not until it falls from your dead fingers. It's the greatest humiliation a warrior can suffer. Besides, you might land on it*—but at least the one who had struck her was still down, half-pinned under her.

Which left only two now fully armed Sarkonds ready to descend upon her, thankfully wielding daggers instead of swords, maybe that would give her time to—

Then Atheris rolled over as one of the men stepped over him, and his hand wrapped around a leather-booted ankle—and the man's eyes rolled up in his head and he collapsed limply to the ground, as simply as that. The last standing man saw and barely hesitated, but that moment was all Peri needed; she lashed out full force with both feet, catching the unprepared Sarkond solidly between the legs, hard enough to send him flying backward with a sound more whimper than shout. He fell hard, the dagger flying from his hand, and lay where he landed, groaning hollowly.

Peri didn't take time to gloat or congratulate; she rolled to one side, jumping to her feet and preparing to settle the Sarkond who'd tripped her, who was even now struggling free of her weight and trying to rise. Even as she raised her sword, however, Atheris reached out and touched the Sarkond's arm, and he slumped back to the ground, as limp and unmoving as his companion.

Atheris scrambled to his feet, touching the back of his head and wincing.

"We had best hurry away," he said. "I am unprepared to deal with that mage, should he decide his henchmen cannot be trusted to subdue me alone."

"Right," Peri said grimly. She checked one last time to make sure none of Atheris's attackers appeared likely to pose a threat—not immediately, at least—and paused just long enough to scoop up his weapons, which one of the men had dropped, and hand them to him; then she followed Atheris back across the plaza as fast as they could run.

As soon as they'd put a little distance between themselves and the mage's shop, however, Atheris ducked into an alleyway and slumped against the wall, his hand clutching his side, breathing hard.

"Wait," he panted. "I have to stop."

"Are you mad?" Peri demanded. "If that clamor hasn't

brought guards down on us, then it's certainly brought thugs. We've got to get back inside before someone comes.'' Even now it was too late, she feared; there were voices approaching, and they seemed to be coming along the road Peri had taken— which put them between Atheris and her and their loft.

"I know," Atheris gasped. "I know. You should—go on."

"You *are* mad," Peri decided. She strained her ears; the voices were definitely closer. Several. At least five or six. Guards, thugs, didn't much matter; she wasn't wearing her bandage disguise. "Look, if we hurry around the corner, double back on a cross street—"

"Perian, I—" Atheris grimaced, taking his hand away from his side. "I have a small problem." He held out his hand.

It was wet with blood.

Peri groaned.

"Hoof rot and tainted springs." Peri yanked up her tunic and heedlessly ripped away a swath of her undertunic. She pulled up Atheris's tunic more gently to look. As she'd feared, he'd torn the entrance wound in his side open again. It didn't seem life-threatening to her, but there *was* a fair amount of blood on his tunic; better be safe and treat it as if it *was* serious until she could see better. Peri wadded up the piece of tunic and packed it firmly against the wound, using another strip from her undertunic and Atheris's belt to secure the dressing as tightly as she could.

"All right," she said, guiding his hand back to the wound. "Hold that *tight*. Put your other arm around my shoulder and tell me if you start feeling faint or dizzy. We'll go slow, but we've got to get out of here before someone sees us."

She started to peek out of the alley, hoping they had time to flee in the opposite direction, but even as she glanced out she saw dark-clad figures hurrying across the plaza, and she hurriedly stepped back into the shadows.

"All right, alleys it is," Peri said grimly, remembering the sounds she'd heard. She held Atheris's arm securely over her shoulders and steadied him with her free hand, careful to avoid the wound, and guided him back into the alley.

"By my calculations," Peri panted as they walked, "we're heading south right now. That's not too bad, but we need to turn east in a few minutes to get back to Orren's. I want to get out of these alleys and back on the main streets as soon as we can. Lina was barring the door for *some* reason, and in this hellhole, I'd just as soon not find out what it is."

They stumbled through the alley, Peri holding them to a snail's pace, straining her ears and cursing herself for leaving the lantern. Once or twice Atheris bumped into the side of a building and gave a little groan. Peri realized to her dismay that she could smell the blood on his tunic, even above the seemingly omnipresent stench of the rotting city.

Only a moment after this realization, Peri froze, pulling Atheris to a halt and pressing him back against a wall despite his gasp of pain.

"Something touched me," she whispered, drawing the scavenged dagger. She'd felt it quite clearly—a cold, almost slimy, rubbery sensation brushing along her arm, sending a chill through her. She turned her head, her ears straining, sniffing. Whatever had touched her, it couldn't have been anything human.

Then it came again, that horrible questing touch on her skin. Her stomach seemed to flip over, and a sort of shivery nausea ran through her. Ignoring it, she slashed out with her dagger— for a moment it seemed as though she contacted something, like cutting through jelly. Behind her Atheris stiffened.

"Feeders!" he hissed.

Peri didn't know what he meant by "feeders," but she knew she'd felt something, and she knew that any creature her knife cut could bleed and die. She slashed out with her dagger again, but this time contacted nothing. For a moment she thought whatever it was had retreated; then that awful cold touch came again, the sick, weak sensation worse this time.

Atheris stepped to her side, raising his bloody hand palm outward, chanting in a clear voice. The cold touch seemed to cringe away from her, but returned again, stronger this time. Peri struck out more desperately, but although her blade slid through *something,* her attacker appeared undisturbed.

Suddenly a flash of bright light seemed to pulse outward from Atheris's hand. For a bare instant Peri saw *something* through dazzled eyes, something tall and supple and semisolid like a shadow half made flesh, long boneless fingers outstretched, gaping dark sockets where eyes should have been, slick and hairless skin gray as stone, toothless mouth opened in a silent shriek. Then the light seemed to slice through it as her blade had not, and before Peri's tearing eyes the thing seemed to shiver into smoke.

"Hurry," Atheris gasped, seizing her shoulder. "Where there is one there will be more. The scent of blood will draw them. We must get inside, and very quickly indeed."

"Right," Peri said, trying to still her own shaking. She took a deep breath, telling herself ferociously that she would *not* vomit, would *not* piss in her pants, would *not* faint like a puling invalid. Atheris leaned on her much more heavily now, and Peri didn't dare ask him whether his weakness was due to blood loss or exhaustion from his magic; at the moment there was nothing she could do about either.

She pulled him through the alleys more rapidly, caution forgotten. If their noises drew guards or thugs or even Bone Hunters, so be it. She'd rather fight any number of real human beings than meet another of those horrible creatures.

It was impossible to keep a straight course; the alleys twisted and turned and even curved until Peri, despite years of training in tracking, began to worry that she was lost. When she finally spotted a section of more open road, she couldn't have cared less what part of the city she found herself in, but was delighted to see that they'd emerged on the right street, albeit some distance past their destination. Peri was so relieved that she could only manage a further dim gratitude that the streets were still empty; Atheris was stumbling weakly now and there would be no nimble darting from doorway to alley to hide their progress. She simply dragged him up the road, leaning him against the stable wall when they reached it.

Now she had a new problem. Even if she thought Orren or Lina would answer a knock at the door—and given the state of the city, Peri very much doubted that—she didn't want them to know that she and Atheris had been out, in case questions were asked around the city about the disturbance in the market. That meant she had to get Atheris back up on the roof and through the window into the loft.

"I can climb," Atheris panted, as if reading her mind. "You will have to help me, but I can make it. I must."

Peri nodded, inwardly cursing her lack of foresight in not buying rope. She could've made a harness and pulled Atheris up much more easily, not risked tearing his wound open again—She shook her head. *As the westerners say, there's no calling back an arrow you've shot.*

Wearily Peri boosted Atheris up as he climbed, supporting him as far as she could; then she climbed around him to the roof and pulled him the rest of the way up. By the time they crept into the loft and closed the shutters behind them, he was completely exhausted and Peri felt utterly drained, but she forced herself to keep moving. She lit two candles, enough to see by, and lit the brazier as well, laying the blade of her dagger in the coals—if the bleeding was too bad, she might need to cauterize the wound. When the blade was glowing she carefully unwound the dressing.

Peri had been right in her first estimate—the wound wasn't as bad as it had looked. It didn't need cautery, but it certainly needed stitching now. Atheris was relieved by the report.

"I find myself wishing, however, that you could simply cast a spell," he said wryly. "Never mind, I have endured worse."

"Well, don't say that just yet." Peri chuckled. "I've never stitched a human being in my life, only horses and a few ikada." She stirred a few herbs in some of their ale and gave it to Atheris. "Drink that. It isn't very strong—I don't dare, not in the state you're in—but it'll at least help with the pain. And try to stay quiet. This is a good solid loft with a thick door, but I bet our host and hostess would still hear if you screamed."

Once again Atheris kept quiet, and once again Peri could not help but be impressed by his stoicism. Then again, there was the long scar running down the front of his torso. Compared with that, a few stitches probably didn't amount to much.

"So," Peri said as she worked, "want to tell me what those things were, those feeders?"

Atheris grimaced.

"Accidents," he said. "I told you how our priests drew life from the land to fuel their magics, sometimes from great distances—you know for yourself how far Darnalek is from the Veil. To do this they had to create—well, proxies, if you will, taps upon points of power through which the energy could reach them. Sometimes the connection between a mage and this tap was prematurely severed—by the mage's death, by broken concentration, by magical intervention, who knows? Most often those stray bits of magic die. Sometimes they do not, and as they were created to do, they seek energy, life. One alone is not so dangerous, not to a healthy adult able to flee. But to the young, the weak, those taken by surprise . . ." His voice trailed off.

Peri tied off her stitches painstakingly.

"So they're what's sucking the life out of everything

here?'' she said, grimacing. Then she had another thought, one that made her shudder. ''Are those feeder creatures all over the south end of Sarkond? Mahdha's wings cover me, why didn't you say something? We've been camping out there, no watches, no protection—''

Atheris raised a hand, shaking his head.

''A feeder does not live, does not feed to sustain itself, but its purpose is to absorb energy to feed its creator,'' he said. ''On the barren plains where there is nothing to sustain it, a feeder would simply dissipate.''

''But in a city,'' Peri said softly, ''there's always food of one sort or another. So people stay off the streets, bar the doors. But you said there's mages here. Why don't they simply wipe them out?''

Atheris grimaced again.

''They may be more useful to the city's mages alive. If a mage can tap a feeder, he can harvest the energy that feeder absorbs. That is its purpose, after all. And there are few enough other sources of power for mages here.''

Peri fell silent, wondering why Atheris hadn't volunteered this information earlier. The dead city, the barred doors— surely he must have had some suspicion. Why hadn't he warned her?

Well, he'd never expected her to be out in the city after dark. And speaking of that—

''Are you ever going to tell me what you were doing to-night?'' Peri asked conversationally.

Atheris sighed.

''I am so tired, Perian—''

Peri said nothing, but after a moment Atheris sighed again.

''I saw the fortune-teller's shop this afternoon,'' he said. ''I felt the emanations of magic and concluded that the proprietor was a true foreseer, or at least a farseer. I wanted to ask him . . .''

"What?" Peri said when Atheris paused.

"About Amis," Atheris said at last, very softly. "Whether she lives or not." But he didn't meet her eyes, and from what Peri had heard of the fortune-teller's speech, she thought Atheris was lying.

"Well, did you find out?" she said at last.

Atheris glanced at her, his eyebrows lowering.

"What?"

"Whether she's alive or not," Peri said patiently.

"Ah. No, he could not tell me," Atheris said, his voice flat. "But I am almost certain she is dead—if not from the harm our magic caused her, then executed as a heretic." He was silent for a long moment. "I would like to rest now, Perian."

Peri sighed.

"Right," she said.

A poultice, a few bandages, and some brandy later, Atheris was soundly asleep. Exhausted as she was, however, Peri found no such release from her troubled thoughts.

Atheris was lying about the fortune-teller; she was certain of it. That meant there were other facts he was concealing. She didn't like what she *had* heard, especially the bit about betrayal. The plain fact remained that although she'd slept with this man, matched sword to sword as an equal, and risked her life for him several times over, she still couldn't trust him. But, oh, she couldn't lie in her pallet next to his and not smell the earthy scent of his hair, not taste his sweat, not see in her mind those eyes that seemed to know her so well—

Traitor, Peri thought grimly, helplessly, burying her head in her arms. *The betrayer in this loft isn't Atheris. It's me.*

In the morning, by tacit agreement they simply ate their breakfast and stayed in the loft waiting for the delivery of the horses. Atheris dozed, probably recovering his strength; Peri practiced with her sword, by herself this time. When Atheris woke, it was almost suppertime. Peri checked his wound, pleased to see it was healing cleanly.

"I've been thinking," she said when she'd fetched up their bread and stew. "I wonder if we shouldn't wait and leave in the morning. Nobody in this city seems to go out at night, and now we know why—if there *is* a guard at the gate, it's going to look pretty noteworthy if we ride out after dark. I'd hate to run into any more of those feeder things, either. Tomorrow we could slip out pretty easily with all the pilgrim traffic going in and out—we saw how slipshod the gate watch is during the day. Besides, you can probably use another good night's rest in a comfortable bed before we start a hard ride south. Once we're out in open country, where we might be riding right into your Bone Hunters, there's no stopping."

Atheris considered her words for a moment, then nodded.

"There is wisdom in waiting," he said reluctantly. "I would prefer to leave quickly, but—" He sighed. "You are correct that we would draw less attention leaving openly by daylight. And I would enjoy a last visit to the sweathouse before we go. Very well, then. It will be as you say."

Just as well that Atheris had agreed, for their horses arrived just at sunset, the merchant's man delivering them hastily and departing just as quickly. Orren grumbled at having to accept the animals so close to dark, but Peri was pleased by the care with which he stabled, groomed, and fed them. Then there was nothing to do but check the packs and tack one last time, sit in awkward silence sipping ale, and sleep.

In the middle of the night Peri sat up in the darkness, listening to Atheris's slow, deep breathing. She could see his profile in the dim light from the brazier, and a sudden stab of desire, an answering sharp pain in her heart, took her by surprise. She bit her lip hard, shaking her head, and slid out of her pallet, quietly pulling her clothes on, then her boots. Atheris slept on, as she knew he would. The herbs she'd slipped into the cup of ale she'd brought him before they'd settled down for the night assured that he'd sleep deeply and long. Long enough, at least.

She took nothing but her blanket and weapons, the healer's bag, her saddle and a skin of water, leaving Atheris the rest of the supplies, and, after a moment's silent debate, all the money except the few slivers of gold in her pouch. It wouldn't take her more than a day to reach the Barrier, and once past it she could find food and water. Atheris would need the supplies—and the money—far more than she would.

Peri crept quietly downstairs and through the side door into the stable. The horses roused at her arrival and she soothed them before they could make enough noise to alert Orren. The buff mare, as Peri had expected, was not as bad-tempered as she'd looked; an evening in a comfortable stall with bedding and good food had mellowed her enough that she stood quietly while Peri saddled and bridled her and led her out of the stall.

The outside door to the stable was locked, of course, but as Peri had seen when the horses were delivered, there was a key hanging *inside* the stable. Orren was wary of horse thieves, but not nearly wary enough of his houseguests. Peri unlocked the door and led the buff out; she locked the door again and, by dint of considerable maneuvering with her dagger blade, managed to push the key back into the stable through the crack under the door, then to the side where hopefully nobody would hook it back out. All right; she'd done her duty by her hosts. Now it was time to go home.

Guilt was a bitter taste in Peri's mouth, and she hesitated outside the stable doors. Atheris would wake in the morning to find her gone, leaving him alone to make his way back out of the country where he was a wanted criminal and then through Bregond where he was a hated enemy—

Peri shook her head grimly.

I can't help it, she thought. *I can't stay with him anymore.*

I can't trust him, and he does—something—to me that I can't—I mustn't—allow. He's got the supplies and the money and as good a horse as I could get him. With any luck those Bone Hunters are long gone, and they can't sense us now anyway—and even if that protection fails, they'll follow me, which is fine, since I'm the better rider. He should make it out of Sarkond all right without me.

But once he gets to Bregond, anyone who sees him will kill him! a small inner voice said almost desperately.

He knows that, Peri told herself firmly. *He knew that when he rode into Bregond the first time. He has magic to protect himself, to hide. The only good my presence would do him is maybe—MAYBE—I could get him just thrown into prison and tortured instead of killed on sight.*

How will he find his way? that annoying voice insisted. *He's wounded, worn-out, and doesn't even know his way around his own country, much less Bregond. And even if he doesn't get hopelessly lost on the plains, he doesn't have enough supplies to make it all the way across Bregond. He doesn't know how to find food and water there.*

If he's smart, and he is, he'll ride east to the border of Agrond, Peri told that inner voice. *Food and water's plentiful enough there, and cover for him to hide in, and he can follow the edge of the wetlands all the way south. Once he's out of the Three Kingdoms he's safe.*

But there's garrisons all along the border. There are patrols and—

I can't be responsible for him! Peri thought desperately. *I can't stay with him and make myself more of a traitor than I've already done! He's a Sarkond. He can't be trusted. He—*

He saved my life. And he needs me. And I—I—

Peri groaned, leaning her head against the saddle skirt. *Traitor! Traitor!*

Peri groaned again and slowly turned the mare around, back toward the stable—

Then she froze, her hand on her sword hilt. Her horse's hooves hadn't made that scraping sound, nor her boots—

Pure instinct saved her; she'd whirled and jumped away from the horse, sword drawn and raised to block, before she had time to think. Steel rang on steel and Peri guided the stroke aside. There was plenty of moonlight, but the buildings were clustered so closely that she could barely see a faint outline of her opponent, just enough to assure her that she wasn't fighting a feeder this time. The darkness didn't matter, he couldn't see her either; what mattered was the swift and silently lethal skill that one single stroke had showed. Peri barely blocked a second stroke, tried to dance aside, only to find her opponent had anticipated her.

Got to take the offensive somehow. My defenses aren't good enough, he'll have me in a minute—

If Atheris hadn't used Leaping Flame against Stalking Cat, she would never have thought of it, but the risky maneuver took her opponent as much by surprise as it had Peri. She immediately moved into the wind qivashim, her strongest offensives, but even so, her barely seen opponent countered easily, almost effortlessly, and Peri was immediately forced back on the defensive, dread settling around her heart—

Whoever this is, he's a master. I haven't got a chance.

Despite her best efforts, her guard faltered and too late she knew she'd left an opening for a killing blow—

I'm dead!

And then, to her utter amazement, she was still alive, a fine line of fiery pain down her thigh but nothing too serious, sheer reflexes keeping her moving as she realized—

He wants me alive. He wants me alive, or I'd be dead already.

Well, Peri had no such compunctions, and that one small

advantage was all she had. Grimly she ducked under a stroke and leaped into the offensive, recklessly now, Diving Hawk becoming Summer Lightning, Leaping Wolf, Mahdha's Fury; to her amazement her attacker fell back a pace, then another, then another—

And then he faltered, his guard dropping for the instant that was all Peri needed, and her blade slid through the flesh of his throat, all but severing his head. For a moment longer her opponent stood still, wavering on his feet; then he toppled stiffly, like a tree falling—

And behind him, a familiar figure numbly released the handle of the pitchfork whose tines were still firmly embedded in her attacker's lower back.

"Congratulations," Atheris said, his voice shaking. "You just killed a Bone Hunter."

Peri, stunned and shaking with reaction, dared not hesitate, dared not give shock time to set in. She wiped her sword and sheathed it.

"Hurry," she said. "Help me get him up on the horse."

Atheris did not question; he silently helped her wrestle the heavy corpse into the saddle. The mare shied at the scent of blood, but stood at last.

"Is your horse saddled?" Peri asked, panting from her exertion.

"Yes," Atheris said softly. "The only reason I was so far behind you is that I had to carry all the bags down by myself. I had just finished loading him when I heard the fight outside. But it took me a little while to find the key on the floor." Then, after a slight pause: "Mages quickly learn to recognize the taste of local herbs in potions, you know."

Peri sighed, wishing she could manage to regret the failure of her plan, wishing that she could silence that small part of her heart that shamefully rejoiced in Atheris's continued presence.

"We've got to get this body away from here and hide it," she said. "If we leave it anywhere nearby, Orren and Lina will certainly be questioned about us, and they're the only ones who can give a good description of both of us—well, as much of me as they could see, anyway—and our horses. Fetch your horse and let's get out of here."

Atheris hesitated.

"You are hurt," he said softly. "I can sense your blood."

Peri reached down and touched the cut on her leg. It didn't feel deep enough to need stitches and the bleeding wasn't severe. It would simply have to wait.

"Nothing serious," she said shortly. "Now let's get going."

Again Atheris obeyed silently, and Peri slid up behind him on the gelding, pulling the buff after them. Fortunately the other citizens of Darnalek appeared every bit as wary of the city after dark as Lina had been; they met no one, no guards or Bone Hunters or thugs or feeders, and between the two of them they remembered their way through the gray, silent streets and out of the decaying city. Once they were safely out of sight of the walls, Atheris pulled his horse to a stop.

"What now?" he said softly.

"That depends," Peri said. "Can you feel any of the other Bone Hunters, where they are?"

Atheris was silent for a moment; then he shivered.

"Yes," he said, very quietly. "I can feel the other four. Three are south of us, scattered east to west, but I think they were all following the road. They are approaching quickly, with purpose. They must have sensed the other's death. The last one is in the city somewhere—where, I cannot say. There are too many mages and priests and feeders in Darnalek. It confuses me."

"Oh, Bright Ones," Peri breathed. "We're caught between them. The ones to the south—if they can't sense us, are they separated widely enough that we can slip through, or maybe go around them?''

After a long moment Atheris shook his head.

"I think not," he said. "Off the road we could not ride with any speed—remember the ground there? And on the road we would certainly be seen."

Peri took a deep breath.

"All right, then," she said. "Here's what we do. We dump the body here and ride as fast as we can to that crossroads where we camped. Once we get there, we take off these protective charms—"

"*What?*" Atheris hissed.

"—and take the northwest fork," Peri said firmly. "Let them think we're heading for Rocarran to hide ourselves in a pilgrimage again. We ride hard till we catch up with the first pilgrimage we meet. Then we put the charms back on, leave the road, and turn back south."

"Ah, I see," Atheris said slowly. "Another false trail, but this time baited with ourselves."

"Exactly," Peri said grimly. "They've seen through every other trick we've played, or at least it looks that way." She slid off the gelding's rump. "Now help me with this body."

Atheris helped her pull the Bone Hunter's body off the dun, and for the first time Peri had sufficient light to get a good look at her attacker. He was tall and lithe, rather than heavily muscled—the build of a hunting cat, made for swift attack rather than sustained strength. His entire head was covered by a black leather mask with holes cut out for ears, eyes, nose, and mouth—remembering what Atheris had said about mutilation, Peri really didn't want to see what was under that mask—and the rest of his clothing was bone-beaded black leather, sturdy but nothing spectacular. The only other item of interest was a long string of short bones hanging around his neck.

"Fingerbones," Atheris said shortly, following the direction of Peri's gaze. "Tokens of successful hunts."

To Peri's surprise and disgust, he rapidly searched the body, stuffing the Bone Hunter's purse into his pocket.

Hoof rot and stagnant water, she thought, sickened. *Robbing the dead. The man I slept with, the man who looks at me with those knowing eyes, is looting a dead man. Mahdha flay me with grit, don't these folk have any* honor?

She said nothing, however, only mounted her horse and set as swift a pace down the road as she dared in the dim moonlight. The ride between the crossroads and Darnalek had seemed almost interminable in the cart, but it seemed amazingly brief on a sound—if not exactly swift—horse; in fact, knowing she was riding *toward* her pursuers, it seemed altogether *too* fast. But there was the crossroads. Not slowing the buff mare, she turned to take the northwest road; glancing behind her, she held up her wrist and pulled off the talisman, seeing Atheris mirror her gesture, and tucked it in the saddlebag. Hopefully taking it off her person was enough to negate the talisman's effects, because she couldn't throw it away; she'd need it later when they turned back south.

Compared with Tajin, the mare was a hopeless plodder, and Peri chafed at the slow pace, but in the end she realized miserably that it hardly mattered; slow as the mare might be, Peri had to rein her in several times to let the gray gelding catch up. Atheris might have found time to learn swordplay as well as magic, but he hadn't managed the miracle of expert horsemanship as well. Every such delay made her more impatient; judging from what she'd seen already, these Bone Hunters were certainly more than adequate on horseback, and there was very little doubt in her mind that they'd somehow managed to acquire far better mounts than these pitiful excuses for horses.

And these horses aren't going to get any faster, Peri thought grimly. *Not as long as we're driving them at their best pace over land where there's little grazing and no water. If we don't get back across the Barrier and into Bregond soon, we're going to be on foot again.*

Her knee touched a sticky spot on the saddle skirt. It was blood, the Bone Hunter's blood, blood of a man who'd nearly killed her, and that knowledge made her rather nauseous.

Shock, she told herself. *I've never killed a human being before, not even those thugs last night as far as I know. Danber told me to expect it.*

"Have you ever killed?" Peri asked softly.

Danber nodded gravely.

"Twice," he said. "Once bandits tried to raid the herds and I killed one of them. The other was my uncle Berestan. He fell from his horse in a stampede and was badly trampled, his spine crushed beyond healing. He asked me for grace and I gave it to him."

Danber shook his head.

"Both times I did as I had to," he said. "But I will never forget their faces, that moment when the light of life faded from their eyes. When you kill, Perian, you drink in a little of your victims' death. You must accept the responsibility for what you have done and grieve for it or that death you have swallowed will poison you. Every true warrior learns that."

"Grieve?" Peri asked confusedly. "Why should you grieve when you know you had to do it?"

"There is always an honest cause for grief," Danber told her gravely. "If not for the life you have ended or the act you committed, then at least for the necessity of committing that act. Or for what you've done to yourself by committing it."

Never mind that I was only defending myself, Peri thought. *Never mind that he was a vicious assassin, that I had no*

*choice at all. A human being is dead by my hand. All the years
he would have lived, all the things he might've done for good
or ill—none of that will happen now because I swung my
sword and spilled his blood. I've become a warrior who has
killed. I've become just a little more like him. I'll never again
be the same person I was yesterday.* She felt a pang on her
heart and a coldness on her face; she raised her hand, surprised
to feel the moisture on her cheeks.

Danber's right, she thought, surprised. *There was something
to grieve for.*

She wiped her eyes impatiently but the tears didn't stop; to
her disgust she felt even sicker, weak, as though all her
strength was flowing out with her tears. She clung to the saddle, feeling the wind-chilled tears dropping from her face.

Mahdha preserve me, Peri thought dizzily. *How much of his
death could I have swallowed? He kept enough of it to die
himself, didn't he?*

To her amazement, Atheris was riding beside her now—
how was he keeping up? He shouted something at her, but the
storm was growing worse and she couldn't hear him over the
wind, the thunder, the beat of the dragon's wings overhead,
Mahdha's voice whispering all around her. And Atheris
reached for her, but she pulled impatiently away—

"Let me alone," she muttered. "Let me grieve it all out."

And suddenly the ground was there, right in front of her,
flying toward her—*earthquake?*—and she clung to it tightly
as it spun and shook beneath her.

And then the feeders and the Bone Hunters and the rotting
dead were upon her, dozens of them, cold rubbery hands tearing at her, horrible disfigured faces riddled with disease leering
down at her, and maggots dropped out of their rotting mouths
and empty eye sockets and fell on her face and she drew her
dagger, slashing desperately, blindly all around her—

And then a terrible bright pain in her head, and the light became darkness.

Peri woke slowly, painfully. Every inch of her body ached and throbbed and she felt horribly weak and hot. She tried to raise her hands to her pounding head and couldn't move them; for a moment panic seized her. Then realization; her hands and feet were securely bound. Momentary relief, then new panic—

Light in her eyes, too bright, blinding. She winced away and the light dimmed. Faces, voices, one familiar, the other not.

"Demons in his blood," a strange voice said. "You must open a vein, bleed them out of him."

"He is too weak," the familiar voice protested. "He will die if—"

"Huh?" Peri muttered hoarsely. "Wha—"

A hand promptly fastened itself securely over her mouth, separated from her skin by cloth—oh, yes, rags over her face—

"Thank you for your help," the familiar voice said hurriedly. "I will attend to him."

One less presence near her. The hand over her mouth was withdrawn, then a face appeared in her field of vision. Sarkond—enemy—familiar—

"A-Atheris?" Peri mumbled.

"Here. Drink." A cup at her lips. Peri swallowed hot metallic-tasting water. More. More. At last the cup was withdrawn.

"Peri, listen to me," Atheris said urgently, his face close to hers. "The wound in your leg—the blade must have been poisoned. You are badly fevered. There is no healer in the camp, and I do not know any healing magic. Tell me what to do for you."

"Let—let me see," Peri said. "Help me see." Her tongue

felt thick and clumsy, like the time when she and Danber had slipped out of camp and drunk two whole skins of lingberry wine, gotten silly and confiding—

"Perian, you are my dearest friend, and I have a secret I want to share with you, only you—"

Atheris pulled her up to a half-sitting position, bracing her against his shoulder. Peri looked down at her leg. Atheris had cut her trousers away from her thigh. The long cut wasn't deep, but the skin around the wound had a greenish-gray hue that looked decidedly unhealthy and her thigh had swelled alarmingly.

Not a true poison, said that indefinable healer's sense with a surprising detachment. *More like an infection. Not a natural infection but—*

"Healer's bag," Peri muttered. "Have to—"

Then the bag was untied and lay in her lap and her hands were untied as well; Peri dimly noted that the beaded cord was back around her wrist. She fumbled through the vials and pouches, wishing she'd taken the time to acquaint herself more thoroughly with their contents. She found what she wanted by scent.

"Four drops of this in a cup of water for me to drink," she rasped, handing Atheris the vial, then a small pouch. "Open the cut and wash out the pus, then sprinkle it with this powder and burn it. Then pack the wound with clean mud. Clean mud. Then wrap it, but not tight."

Then she was lying flat, her hands tied again, and Atheris's face loomed over her.

"Forgive me," he said gently, just before he stuffed a wad of rags into her mouth and tied it securely in place despite Peri's struggles. Then she was glad of the rags to bite on as throbbing agony shot out from her thigh. Brief wonderful respite from pain—then something glowed orange in Atheris's hand, and she heard a sizzling sound and smelled the sickening odor of burning flesh.

Then the pain came again to carry her back into darkness.

Peri opened her eyes. There was canvas above her—a tent roof, perhaps—lit by the flickering glow of a lantern. She shifted experimentally; her hands and feet were free. Her leg throbbed miserably and every muscle in her body ached worse than the time Tajin had stumbled and fallen and rolled over her. She tried to sit up, only to find herself too weak and dizzy for more than a token attempt.

She did, however, succeed in attracting attention; almost immediately Atheris appeared by her side, cup in hand. The relief was so plain on his face that Peri wondered uneasily just how serious her illness had been. And at the same time—

He didn't leave me. Bone Hunters on our heels, me a Bregond, and he didn't leave me. He could've let them find me, gotten away cleanly with horses, supplies, gold. But he stayed. Even after I tried to abandon him, he stayed.

"I am overjoyed to see you awake," Atheris said with a relieved sigh. "Here, let me help you."

He raised Peri a little higher and pushed a pack under her shoulders to brace her, then held the cup to her lips. The water was almost too hot to drink, and it tasted harsh, metallic, but to Peri it might as well have been the finest wine. She drank every drop, and when Atheris refilled the cup, she drank that, too.

"Do you need more medicine?" Atheris asked, reaching for the healer's bag.

"Not—" Peri's voice came out hoarse; she paused to clear her throat and sip a little more. "Not till I have a look at the wound first. Help me up, would you?"

With Atheris supporting her shoulders, Peri was able to sit up, although he had to cut the bandages on her leg and peel off the dressing for her. She winced as the hardened mud pulled away burned skin, but the flesh under it was pink and healing cleanly.

"You did not say whether to repeat the drink and the powder," Atheris said apologetically, "so I did, once a day. As you suggested, I boiled all the water."

Almost exhausted, Peri let Atheris ease her back to the pallet.

"Once a day?" she muttered. "How long—"

"Two days," Atheris said grimly. "And for the first I was certain you were going to die—on the second, only *half*-certain. You are made of hard steel, Perian. The poisons of the Bone Hunters have never spared another, to my knowledge."

"If they were treated for poison, probably not," Peri said wryly. "It wasn't a poison; it was some kind of magic-bred infection, probably easily cured if you know the right counterspell. I guess you were half-right. They may want us alive, at least enough not to kill us outright, but they'll gladly settle for dead rather than let us escape."

She looked up at the tent roof again, then abruptly realized that a tent had not numbered among the purchases she and Atheris had made.

"Two days," she said again. "Where are we?"

Atheris grimaced.

"In a small pilgrim caravan bound for—"

"Don't say it," Peri begged.

"—Rocarran," Atheris said with a sigh. "Peri, there was nothing else I could do."

Two days! Peri shook her head weakly, trying to remember. The fight with the Bone Hunter. The ride out of the city. The body, the crossroads—then things got fuzzy and strange, unreal.

"What happened?" she asked confusedly.

"I knew the Bone Hunters would quickly arrive, even as we planned," Atheris told her. "But it was clear you could not ride. I hardly dared move you at all." He sighed again. "I carried you on my saddle for a short time, but you were delirious and struggling, and I had to stop. I found some rocks to hide us for the day. Two Bone Hunters rode past not long after. I thought they would surely find us."

Atheris shook his head.

"By nightfall I realized you were growing worse, too weak even to be carried," he said. "So I stayed where I was and waited. You were lost in dreams, talking strangely." He glanced at Peri oddly. "You spoke of grieving for your dead. At last I had to gag you for fear you might be heard.

"The two Bone Hunters rode back past near sundown; only a little later this caravan arrived and stopped for the night. I hoped they might have a healer. They did not, but they offered food and water and a place by their fire."

Peri started to protest, but Atheris cut her off.

"You needed shelter and care," he said flatly. "You were in no condition for a hard ride across country, not even with me carrying you." He looked at her strangely. "It is nothing less than a miracle that you survived at all."

"But the tent," Peri murmured.

"I traded the horses for it, and for a place in one of the wagons," Atheris said without preamble. He held up a hand, once more cutting off her protest. "They had no use for gold on the road, and we had no feed or water for the horses. By the time you recovered they would be useless. You could try to buy them back, I suppose."

Peri groaned softly to herself. Horseless, weakened, disguised, and being drawn ever deeper into Sarkond—why did this situation seem so depressingly familiar? Was there no escaping Rocarran?

I know only that obstacles in your path guide you only more surely to your goal. That was what the old woman had said, wasn't it, something about the inevitability of—

Peri grimaced. That was one danger of prophecies; they were usually couched in terms so vague and general that it seemed impossible to distinguish a lunatic's or common charlatan's ravings from the far rarer true foresight.

The other hazard, of course, was that those who allowed such prophecies to rule their lives were fools. Dangerous fools.

"So we've been traveling toward Rocarran ever since?" Peri asked softly at last.

Atheris nodded.

"The others have been very kind," he said. "They gave me blankets and furs to keep you warm, broth to feed you, a lantern, even a small brazier for our tent."

"Comparing the cost of a sound horse to a tent, they can afford to be kind," Peri said wryly. "How much farther is it to Rocarran, do you know?"

"Three more days, or so I am told," Atheris said softly. "The road is very poor for wagons and our progress has been slow. Peri, even if we had horses, I do not see how you would be able to make such a ride as we had planned, not within that time."

"Half-dead or sound asleep, I can ride if I have to," Peri said grimly. "We'll steal the horses back if we must." *Mahdha forgive me, look what I'm becoming—a thief robbing half-starved pilgrims who helped save my life.*

Atheris must have had some similar thought, for he gave her an odd look.

"First you must regain your strength," he said slowly. "If I bring you food, can you eat?"

Peri chuckled dryly.

"To tell you the truth, if our horses had gone into the stewpot, I'd hold out my bowl and ask for seconds," she said. "Bring it on."

To Peri's surprise there *was* meat in the thick soup Atheris brought her and carefully fed her, but she knew old, stringy chicken when she tasted it and didn't bother to inquire after the horses' health. The soup, the tent, the wagons, though—those added up to give her pause. Obviously these pilgrims were of a much wealthier class than those she'd seen previously.

"Yes, these are not ordinary pilgrims," Atheris said rather shortly when Peri asked. "These are lesser priests and acolytes from Tarabin."

"It seems like everyone and their fifth cousin is on the road to Rocarran," Peri said, scowling. "What's happening there?"

This time Atheris hesitated a long time before answering; he gave Peri another odd look.

"It is an important time in the temple," he said. "They come to make sacrifice and hear the words of the Whore."

"The *what*?" Peri murmured disbelievingly.

"A priestess and prophet," Atheris said slowly. "In the temple we show her respect and call her the Golden One, but she is better known among the people as Eregis's Whore. Eregis speaks through her, and she attends over the sacrifices."

"Sacrifices?" Peri said, remembering what he had said once. "Blood sacrifice?" Then she saw the expression in Atheris's averted eyes and something inside her went cold.

"Human?" she whispered.

Atheris's lips thinned.

"I cannot discuss the mysteries of the temple with a non-believer," he said rather stiffly. "Perhaps I have said too much already." Then his expression softened slightly. "Besides, you should rest. You must regain your strength if—if we are to attempt to leave for Bregond before reaching Rocarran."

His words made sense, and Peri did not object as Atheris covered her warmly, extinguishing the lantern, but she was troubled nonetheless. Something in his attitude had changed since Darnalek in a way she did not entirely like. Obviously the encounter at the fortune-teller's and later with the Bone Hunter had affected him strongly. Well, no surprise in that; it had affected her strongly, too, and she'd trained and prepared for such attacks all her life. Atheris had led a far more sheltered life than she; the Bone Hunter was probably his first kill, too. And it had been an agent of his own temple—and not even to save his own life, but in defense of Peri, a Bregond, an enemy. She had certainly felt guilt chewing at her stomach often enough since she'd rescued Atheris; not too surprising if he was starting to feel the sharpness of those teeth himself.

Despite her weakness Peri slept poorly, feeling unaccountably more threatened and vulnerable than she had in days; when she half roused during the night she saw Atheris sitting at the tent flap gazing out, and she wondered dimly whether he felt uneasy, too.

In the morning Atheris helped Peri don her bandage disguise and, despite her protests, picked her up and lifted her carefully into the wagon, where a comfortable pallet had already been prepared for her. Apparently the priests and acolytes were in a hurry, for the caravan set out as soon as there was light enough to see the road. An acolyte riding on a mule passed from wagon to wagon, distributing bowls; to Peri's surprise there was a share for her and Atheris as well. The bowls contained reasonably fresh bread, sharp cheese, and an unappetizing-looking but fragrant mishmash which Atheris explained absently was dried fruit fermented in honey and wine. Peri had never heard of eating such a thing for breakfast, but the stuff was a perfect vehicle for the restorative mix of herbs she needed to take with food, and it turned out to be the tastiest meal she'd had since she left Tarkesh. She reflected with some amusement that in this respect at least Sarkond was closer to Agrond than to Bregond—rather than practicing any form of self-denial, priests here appeared to live more comfortably than the worshipers who supported them.

Peri was surprised when the caravan stopped at midday—not for dinner, as she might have expected, but for prayer. There was some elaborate little ritual that took place outside of her view, although she saw that one of the acolytes left with a live piglet and returned with a dead one. Peri certainly wasn't bothered by the sacrifice of a pig that was probably destined for the stewpot anyway—the Bright Ones knew there were messier and more wasteful sacrifices in some of the temples in Tarkesh—but this time, in light of what Atheris had said (or avoided saying), she found it rather disturbing. He had said that male mages raised power by the release of life energies, and what greater release could there be than at the moment of death?

And if such animal sacrifices served to raise power for the priests, what manner of magical operation could the release of energy from a *human* sacrifice empower?

Atheris stayed with Peri rather than joining the priests at their worship, and Peri wondered briefly at his motives. Perhaps he found the practice somewhat distasteful himself; perhaps those feelings had formed part of the reason he'd attempted the dangerous experiment with his cousin. She fervently hoped so. The Bright Ones knew Atheris had had plenty of opportunities to raise a little power of his own in a far more bloody manner if he'd chosen to do so, either in Darnalek or when they were with the—

With the—

Peri froze, her mouth suddenly dry.

Someone died in the night. It is not uncommon in such pilgrimages, with so many sick.

Peri suddenly felt her gorge rising.

Mahdha spare me, she thought sickly. *Bright Ones look with mercy upon me. Oh, gods, all the gods—any gods—grant that I haven't been a party to cold-blooded murder.*

"Peri?" Atheris said quietly. "Are you unwell? You suddenly went pale."

Peri swallowed hard. She couldn't confront Atheris now, not when she had to keep her voice low and controlled for fear of the priest in the wagon seat hearing her.

Mahdha forgive me, I can hardly bring myself to think about it, Peri thought.

"I'm all right," she whispered, just loud enough for him to hear her. "Just . . . tired."

Atheris's expression softened.

"Sleep, then," he said gently. "There is nothing else for you to do while we travel."

Peri closed her eyes, but sleep eluded her.

I've shared my bed with this man. He's saved my life, protected me when he had no reason to stay and every reason to go, faced me honestly on the practice floor. He's tended my wounds, fed me—and kept me clean, too, or I'd stink of my own waste. If he could be such a monster as I hardly dare imagine—what does that make me?

The afternoon passed with excruciating slowness; exhausted, Peri finally drowsed uneasily, but she jolted awake when the wagon stopped. The sun was almost completely down. The priests must indeed be hurrying, to push on so late that they had to make camp in the dark.

Atheris set up their tent—to Peri's relief, well apart from the others—and returned to help her out of the wagon. Peri had almost worked up her nerve to ask about the dead pilgrims, however much she dreaded Atheris's answer, but as soon as he settled her comfortably in the tent, he hurried back out to fetch fuel for their brazier, water, and blankets for Peri. He returned only long enough to make up her pallet, light the brazier, and set a pot of water to boil; then he left again to fetch back their supper—as Peri had expected, tender young pork, cut into small pieces and threaded on skewers to roast quickly.

The food and herbs had helped; this time Peri, to her considerable relief, felt strong enough to sit up on her own and feed herself, and she thought she might even be able to walk a little once her supper had settled. She finished the food, bracing herself to ask—

"Peri," Atheris said suddenly, not meeting her eyes, "while you were fevered, you said many things, but what did you mean when you spoke of grieving for your dead?"

She shrugged uncomfortably.

"That Bone Hunter was the first human being I've ever killed," she said. "A dear friend of mine once told me that when you kill, you drink in a little of the death, and if you don't grieve it out, it poisons you."

Atheris grimaced.

"You grieved," he said disbelievingly, "for a Bone Hunter, an assassin who nearly killed you?"

"I don't expect you to understand," Peri said shortly. "I didn't grieve for him. I grieved because I had to kill him."

"I . . . see," Atheris said remotely. "And this cleanses you?"

Peri sighed.

"That's the idea," she said.

He was silent for a long time, staring into the brazier.

"There are not enough tears in the world," he said at last, very softly, "to cleanse me of what I have done."

Peri swallowed hard, taking a deep breath.

"And what's that?" she asked, barely loud enough to be heard over the crackle of fire in the brazier.

Atheris gazed at her a long moment, his eyes unreadable.

"I am a traitor," he whispered, "to everything I believe."

And when Peri would have asked him what he meant, his lips on hers silenced her; and when his skin was hot against hers, she told herself she was too weak to fend him off, and too cold and frightened and alone to try.

But later, in the silence before sleep, sharing his warmth under the blankets, she felt the sting of tears in her eyes and felt the presence of a poison that she, too, had not tears enough to wash away.

He's a traitor, she thought numbly. *And so am I.*

6

THANKS TO HER RESTORATIVE HERBS, PERI WAS able to sit up in the wagon the next day. For once she had no difficulty maintaining the silence her disguise demanded; she felt no desire whatsoever for conversation. She simply sat on her pallet and stared moodily out the back as the wagon jolted onward.

The landscape here differed little from the lands just south of Darnalek—not absolutely barren and blasted, but rocky and poor, the scant vegetation pallid and sickly looking. Peri sighed, hating to admit that Atheris had been right about the horses. Maybe Tajin, bred to manage on little water and poor fodder, could have survived a few days in this barren country—and then again, maybe not. The already underfed nags she and Atheris had bought in Darnalek would certainly have starved, if they didn't die of thirst first.

Peri stared at the sickly land, thought about the implications of it, and shivered. Was all this land sucked utterly dry of life, too, during the war, or had it been this bad before? Was drought alone responsible? Surely not; compared with this barren territory, even Bregond's dry, harsh plains fairly teemed with life. Surely no land could be this dead short of curse or blight or something of the sort. The thought didn't rest easily in her mind.

What if it WAS this bad before the war? Compared with this, even Bregond is a paradise. What if the raids, the invasions, even the war, were never about greed and conquest, only about desperation and survival?

Would anyone in Agrond or Bregond have even cared about the distinction?

Peri rubbed her eyes wearily.

It doesn't matter. Unless the northern lands are just amazingly fertile and productive, there's no way they can grow enough crops or breed enough livestock to feed the people. If they weren't desperate before, they certainly are now—at least those who aren't too hopeless even for desperation. And desperate people are dangerous. They'll do anything, take any risk, because they've got nothing left to lose.

She glanced at Atheris; he was also gazing out the back of the wagon, brooding at the barren land.

A desperate religion might cling to outrageous prophecies to keep its people's hope alive. A desperate temple might make human sacrifice in the hope of waking a god who has abandoned his worshipers. A desperate priest and priestess might risk their lives experimenting with forbidden magic. Oh, Bright Ones, what have I blundered into here? What pot's about to boil over at this temple in Rocarran? And if they knew the daughter of the High Lord and Lady of Agrond and the Heir to Bregond was being dragged all but helpless through their country, would that add another coal to the fire under that pot?

Oh, Bright Ones, Peri thought helplessly. *I've GOT to get out of here.*

Whatever thoughts troubled Atheris, he kept them to himself. In silence they rode from sunrise to midday; in silence they sat in the wagon while the priests performed their worship; in silence they rode again from midday to sunset. Then there was the tent to set up in the twilight, and Peri even managed to help a bit, although Atheris had to bring their packs from the wagon, fetch fuel for the brazier and dinner for them, and make up their pallets as before.

"Tonight," Peri said, finally breaking the awkward silence after they'd eaten. "We've got to get the horses back and get out of here tonight." To her unease, another small group of pilgrims had joined the caravan at a crossroads not long after midday; she assumed that the closer they got to Rocarran, the more frequent such meetings might be.

Atheris sighed patiently, staring resolutely at the glowing coals in the brazier.

"Peri, we cannot," he said. "You are still too weak."

"I can ride," she said stubbornly.

"Likely you can." Atheris shrugged. "But, Peri, if I cast the spell to make us unseen so that we can take the horses and leave, I will exhaust myself to the point where I will require *your* assistance. One of us at least must have the strength to get us both across very difficult terrain in the darkness, and you are far too weak to sustain the spell for me. We will have to wait until tomorrow night."

"What if there's twice as many pilgrims all around us tomorrow night?" Peri demanded.

"That matters nothing to a spell of concealment," Atheris said quietly. "You can walk unnoticed past one man or twenty, as long as you do not stumble over him in your weakness."

Peri bit her lip. Every instinct told her it was a chance worth taking to get away a day sooner, but she couldn't argue with Atheris's logic. As little as she liked to admit it, she stood very little chance of getting away without his help; nor could she contest his greater knowledge of magic or of their pursuers. And Sarkond or not, dead pilgrims notwithstanding, how could she mistrust him after he'd risked everything to save her?

And Atheris was right; she *was* weak despite the restorative herbs, weaker than she would have expected even after so severe an illness. Judging from his explanation of Sarkondish magic, she wondered whether the Bone Hunter's "poison"— or perhaps even his sword—had some sort of life-draining property she hadn't suspected. But she *was* recovering, albeit slower than she should be, and surely tomorrow she'd have the strength to make her escape. She'd simply have to. It would be her last chance to avoid Rocarran.

The tent was too small to permit a comfortable distance between the two pallets, but to Peri's relief Atheris seemed as determined as she to avoid any intimacy; after they ate, they dived into their respective bedrolls with as little conversation as possible.

Peri, however, found sleep elusive; she was too full of unanswered questions and uncomfortable thoughts. Despite her physical lassitude she felt unaccountably restless and uneasy. After sitting up and fretting for some moments in the darkness, she realized she was almost holding her breath listening to Atheris sleep, the rhythm of his breathing, the faintest rustle of movement every time he shifted. A warm and disturbing hunger had settled into her body at some point. Stifling a groan, she leaned her head into her hands.

How can I want him? How? For all I know he's a murderer. And why should I expect any different, anyway? He's a Sarkond! An enemy! I can't trust him, I can't want him, I can't— can't—

This time Peri did groan softly to herself, clenching her fingers in her braids.

There are traitors and criminals in Bregond and Agrond, she thought desperately. *I never would have believed it before, but I've seen for myself that there are ordinary, kindly folk in Sarkond, like Orren and Lina, or Minyat and Irra. Why can't I just tell myself that Atheris is a good, decent fellow fleeing from situations and practices that don't sit lightly on his soul, and leave it at that? And if I can't do that, why can't I tell myself he's a Sarkond, an enemy, and put him out of my mind—my heart? What's the matter with me?*

"Peri?" Atheris's voice in the darkness was very soft. "Is something wrong?"

"No. Nothing's wrong." *Oh, Bright Ones, don't let him speak to me that way, his voice like that. Don't let him—*

Then Atheris's fingers, shaking slightly, touched her hand ever so gently, and Peri bit back a sob, knowing herself lost once more. His mouth tasted like wine and despair, and the air was too cold for the salty moisture on his cheeks to be sweat, but Peri could not bring herself to question or care, not when his skin burned so hot against hers and his fingers dug into her shoulders so hard that his nails drew blood. There was no Sarkond or Agrond or Bregond here, no barrier between trust and betrayal; only darkness and heat and this aching soul-deep understanding they shared, the unconsenting surrender to a hunger that could not be refused. The kiss of steel on steel—

And all the while knowing that when the battlefield fell still and silent at the end, the darkness was not deep enough to hide guilt and regret.

In the morning Peri dozed in the wagon, lulled by the monotonous creak of the wheels. She felt a little stronger than the day before, perhaps, but still not back to her normal level of energy, and that worried her; tonight they *had* to get away from this caravan, whether she was ready or not. Maybe a good long nap would help.

Atheris was quiet, solicitous and seemingly worried about Peri but rarely meeting her eyes. He seemed to be dozing now, too, and no surprise; in fact, neither of them had gotten much sleep the night before. Peri came out of her doze and flushed a little at the recollection. A good thing Atheris had placed their tent away from the others.

Bright Ones, what was the *matter* with her? She'd heard stories in court about her father and her mother—vague references to her parents' legendary and sometimes scandalous passion, delivered with a chuckle and a knowing grin. Judging from the number of times she found her parents' door securely locked (Estann had chuckled and said that precaution stemmed from a poorly timed visit by the chambermaid years before), Peri imagined that that passion had in no way declined, only been tempered by a greater caution. But she very much doubted that even her fiery mother would understand, much less condone, her behavior of the last days.

Peri pushed the thought aside—she was tired, so tired of following the same track in her mind around and around in circles—and let the creak of the wagon wheels, the steady *clop-clop* of the horses' hooves lull her again.

It seemed she'd only just closed her eyes, however, before she jolted awake to Atheris's touch on her shoulder.

"Peri," he murmured, very quietly. "Wake up. We're in Rocarran."

"What!" Peri jolted upright and peered out the back of the wagon. Atheris was right; they were just passing through a broad gate in a heavy wooden stockade—in no way as dilapidated or laxly manned as the gate to Darnalek—that could only guard a holding of some significance. Everywhere she looked Peri could see priests, guards, peasants carrying their belongings and their children.

"What are we doing in Rocarran?" she demanded in a whisper. "It was supposed to be another day away."

"I know!" Atheris snapped back in a whisper. "I know! But here we are nonetheless."

"Well, what are we going to do about it?" Peri asked, clasping her hands hard to hide their shaking. "We'd better get out now, head back out the gate—"

He shook his head.

"There are priests and guards everywhere," he said. "We came with a pilgrimage, obviously to visit the temple. It will surely be noticed if we try to slip out the gate without doing so. And yet I fear there could be priests from my temple here who might recognize me." He hesitated a moment longer, then sighed and pulled his pilgrim's robe out of his pack.

"I'm not putting mine back on," Peri said firmly. "It *reeks*."

"You need not," Atheris said, shrugging, "if you are prepared to take off your sword. It would not be permitted in the temple, and without the robe you cannot conceal it."

Peri grimaced but unpacked the robe and donned it before her nose could overcome her common sense.

"If we mingle with the crowd entering the temple," Atheris said softly, "we should be able to slip back out unobtrusively without attracting attention. For now, relax and wait for the wagon to stop."

Peri sat back, but she fumed, her fingers clenching nervously. What kind of miscalculation meant a difference of a whole day's journey? And what in the world were they to do now? This was a temple, not a marketplace; there'd be no horses for sale here, and there'd be guards aplenty, too, to keep the crowds under control and to look out for the pickpockets that always seemed to attend such gatherings. So there was no way to buy horses, and precious little hope of stealing them either. There was no choice, really, but to sneak out of

Rocarran as best they could on foot. Maybe they could join some pilgrims journeying back from the temple, although to the best of her observation they hadn't passed anyone traveling in the opposite direction. No, something of considerable significance was happening here, and that meant vigilant guards at their posts on the lookout for any suspicious behavior.

The wagon slowed, stopped. Peri made sure her mask of bandages was securely in place before she and Atheris scrambled out the back of the wagon with their packs. Then, turning, she froze as she saw the Temple of Eregis at Rocarran for the first time.

The huge stone edifice was enough to take her breath away. She'd never seen anything so massive—not the royal castles of Bregond or even Agrond, not the grandest temple in Tarkesh—or so ancient in her life. The weathering of the massive stone blocks of the building had nothing to do with the strange decay Peri had seen in Darnalek; this holy place was obviously hundreds, if not thousands, of years old, with a grim and looming dignity befitting its antiquity. Gruesome statues of malformed beasts loomed over the few windows and doors; Peri's mind flitted back unwillingly to those horrible, unfortunate pilgrims she'd seen, although none of them were in evidence now—they'd likely arrived long ago and entered the temple in one of the streams of pilgrims she could see marching in every door. Where did they come out? Perhaps there was an exit at the back.

"This way," Atheris murmured, tugging her toward one of the doors. "If you stand there staring much longer, somebody will wonder."

Peri hurriedly dropped her eyes and followed Atheris, her skin crawling. Despite its size and antiquity there was nothing so strange about the building itself—in fact, the way the stone was laid somehow reminded her of some of the older temples and stone buildings in Bregond. But there was a feeling of power in that temple that both drew at Peri and repelled her. The huge cold edifice seemed to gaze down at her, and her disguise of robes and rags suddenly seemed thin and inadequate. Somehow she felt it knew who she was, waited for her to walk in its doors, waiting and licking long, sharp teeth in hungry anticipation . . .

"You are behaving," Atheris said between his teeth, "like a horse thief expecting capture. Are you deliberately *trying* to attract attention?"

"I can't go in there," Peri said, her fingers digging into his arm. "Atheris, I can't."

"We must," he said grimly. "Peri, you cannot possibly desire to enter that temple less than I do. Now follow me quietly and stop looking over your shoulder. You are a pilgrim come eagerly here, if you remember."

Peri closed her eyes and took a deep breath, forcing herself to follow Atheris more quickly.

I am Perian, she told herself resolutely. *I am warrior. I am earth, deep-rooted and strong, mother of steel—*

They fell in behind a line of worshipers waiting for entrance to the temple. Peri scanned the entrances as unobtrusively as she could. The priests at the doors were not wearing swords—apparently not every priest was trained in the Ithuara, and that substantiated Atheris's supposition that he'd been destined for training as a Bone Hunter—but the doors were also flanked by more secular-looking guards, all sturdy and armed not only with swords, but crossbows as well. Each pilgrim stopped at the door, speaking briefly to the priest, but as far as Peri could see, nobody was searched or—to her disappointment—turned away.

"Hide your healer's bag in your tunic," Atheris murmured, tucking the pouch of gold into his sleeve, "as well as anything else you cannot bear to lose."

Peri obeyed surreptitiously.

"Thieves?" she whispered.

"No." He nodded toward the temple, and looking again, she saw what he meant. There was a pile of packs, bags, pouches, and bedrolls by the door that grew as each pilgrim passed inside under the guards' stern gaze. Obviously Eregis exacted a price for His blessings.

"We can't lose our supplies!" Peri hissed. "I doubt there's a drop of clean water or a speck of good forage between here and Bregond."

"We have gold aplenty," Atheris muttered back, keeping a neutral expression on his face. "These pilgrims are not eating and drinking Eregis's blessings. There must be merchants hereabouts selling them food and drink. Nothing besides the gold and the healer's bag cannot be replaced."

Peri liked this less and less every minute, but by now they were too close to the temple doorway for her to make any further comment. She took a deep breath and reminded herself sternly that once they reached Bregond, she could survive on the plains with nothing more than a waterskin and a knife. She carefully adjusted her robe to ascertain that her sword and healer's bag made no telltale bulges, then sighed and followed Atheris forward.

The man ahead of them stepped up to the priest, laying his pack on the pile beside the door.

"Do you seek the touch of Eregis which heals all ills, or the witness of his prophet?" the priest asked gravely.

"To witness," the man murmured, bowing his head.

"Take the right-hand hallway," the priest said, and the man stepped into the temple and out of Peri's sight. Then Atheris pulled her forward, and she lowered her eyes hurriedly.

"Do you seek the touch of Eregis which heals all ills, or the witness of his prophet?" the priest asked.

"I seek to witness," Atheris said quietly. "My companion seeks the touch of Eregis."

"Take the right-hand hallway," the priest told him; to Peri's horror, the priest turned to her, laying his hand on her shoulder. "You are honored for your courage. Take the left-hand hallway to the presence of He Who Sleeps."

Peri hurried into the temple after Atheris, glad to free herself of the priest's touch. The hallway was lit at regular intervals by torches, and after a dozen paces it forked into two halls, the leftmost leading rather sharply upward. Peri saw a few sickly pilgrims hobbling up that hall.

"Now what?" she whispered, hesitating.

"This way," Atheris said, pulling her hastily into the right-hand hallway, sparing the other hall the briefest possible glance; to Peri's surprise he shivered.

"I thought I was supposed to go left. What's up there?" she whispered.

"Do you want to explore," he muttered harshly, "or do you want to get out of here?"

Peri couldn't argue with that, although as she let Atheris pull her down the hall, she murmured practically, "Well, the sick ones have to come out somewhere, too."

Atheris said nothing, only dragging her faster through the hall until they caught up with the worshipers ahead of them.

"Stay quiet," he muttered. "Sound carries well in here."

The temple had seemed huge enough on the outside, but Peri revised her estimate of its size upward as the hallway they followed continued ever deeper into the bowels of the building without turning. The unease she'd felt at the doorway intensified, her skin crawling. The place seemed to be swallowing her.

Which makes me a temple turd, I guess, when I exit, Peri thought with a sudden irreverent glee that dissolved some of her fear. *Come on, Perian. It's a building, just a big old pile of stone blocks. I'm in danger, yes, but what's new about that? The faster we go in, the sooner we come out.*

But there was more to it than that. To Peri's surprise, she could feel water deep beneath her, a great deal of it—most likely a huge subterranean reservoir—and with it, tremendous power, old and cold. She shivered again. In a land as dry as Sarkond, it certainly made sense to build their temple atop an underground spring; in a religion where priests were mages, it also made sense to build atop a magical nexus. But a spring that was *also* a nexus—Peri couldn't begin to estimate the sheer power in that water, power this temple must control. Obviously *this* source hadn't been drained dry during the war!

The worshipers ahead of them appeared to be slowing, and to Peri's surprise she thought she saw more light ahead. The hallway opened at last into a huge chamber that she could barely see over the heads of the people in front of her, but she could hear chanting from the room, the slow throb of drums, and some kind of raspy scraping instrument.

Atheris had stopped, and Peri glanced at him. His eyes were closed; he was not chanting, but his lips moved as if he mouthed the words. She wanted to shake him, to urge him to get them out of here as quickly as possible, but she wondered uneasily whether he would be so easily persuaded. Whatever was going on here was obviously as unusual as it was important; a faint suspicion began to arise in her mind that perhaps Atheris had not tried as hard to avoid the temple as he might have.

She slid away from him easily; he seemed oblivious, almost entranced. She pushed her way through the crowd, careful that nobody would feel her sword under her robe. It took some time for Peri to work through the crowd to a point where she could see the focus of their attention; when she gained a reasonably clear vantage point, however, she frowned in puzzlement.

At the center of the chamber, separated from the crowd by a low wall, was a raised stone dais. A large ornate font had been built at the head of the dais, but to Peri's amazement no water flowed there, and judging from the old, crusted stains, none had for some time. Atop the dais lay a sculpture made of what appeared to be pure gold—the image of a young man of exquisite beauty, apparently asleep, and beside him an equally gold sleeping woman, her arm draped across his chest, her head on his shoulder.

Peri shook her head. Aside from the obvious awe at the sight of so much gold in one place—much less in this impoverished country—and the marvelous lifelike quality of the statues, she could see nothing remarkable. But, then, she reminded herself, in religion it was not the object itself that held significance, but the symbolism and—

Then the golden woman stirred, and Peri froze.

"She wakes!" someone whispered. "The Whore will speak!"

For a moment her mind insisted that she was witnessing a miracle, the transmutation of lifeless metal into living flesh by some incredibly potent magic; then common sense reasserted itself and Peri breathed again. What she saw wasn't a golden statue come to life; it was only an ordinary mortal woman covered in gold pigment.

The woman stretched languidly, her hand gently stroking the chest of the golden figure beside her, leaning over to press her lips hotly to his. Peri half expected the male statue to suddenly come to life, too, but apparently that one *was* a statue, for as the woman's hand wandered slowly down the golden torso, the figure remained still under caresses which Peri was sure would have caused any living man to react in *some* visible fashion.

Undaunted, the woman sat up slowly, stretching again, showing off her sleek, gilded body to best advantage. The chanting all around Peri abruptly stopped; the sudden silence was eerie, and she had to fight to stand still, wanting very badly to duck back into the anonymity of the crowd. But everyone standing around her was utterly silent, utterly motionless, and any movement on her part would certainly draw unwanted attention, so she forced herself to stand perfectly still—

As still as the day I woke on a hunt and found a viper crawling over my leg, Peri thought grimly. *I'm certainly in no less danger now—*

Then the golden woman spoke, and absolute mind-jolting shock froze Peri, silenced her as no amount of fear could have.

"Welcome, poor fools, to the end of yesterday," the golden woman said, and Peri heard in the cadence of her words, the shape of each syllable, what she should have seen immediately in the height of the woman's cheekbones, the dark brown of her eyes, the tilt of those golden features.

Sarkond's prophet, Eregis's Whore, was a Bregond.

"You come to hear me give you promises for tomorrow," the woman intoned. "But the time for promises is over. You have waited in hope and in the slow death of hope, and the time for waiting is done. You stand at this moment on the precipice, poor fools, of death and rebirth. The time is now. The final sign has come to pass. The Harbinger has come."

A shocked murmur ran through the crowd. The sound swelled briefly, then died again.

"You have slept in the grave of your land," the woman said. "You have eaten ashes. You have drunk bitter tears. You have clothed yourselves in the shrouds of your dead. But you are waking, O Sarkond, waking with the hunger of a starving wolf ready to bare his teeth once more, ready to rend with his claws. Sharpen your claws, O Sarkond, for the time has come to hunt once more, to kill, to spill the blood of your enemy and bring new life to the land that bore you. Sarkond, I say you have slept too long. Wake! Wake your hunger, wake your land, wake your god!"

The murmur began again, swelled.

"Wake!" Eregis's Whore rolled atop her sleeping lover, kissed him feverishly.

Slowly, softly at first, then louder, the crowd took up the chant.

"Wake. Wake. Wake. Wake."

She rose to straddle the statue.

"Wake!"

Her passion seemed to infect the crowd. They were swaying now, shouting, almost wailing.

"Wake! Wake! Wake! Wake!"

Eregis's Whore threw back her head, flinging her arms wide.

"WAKE!" she screamed.

And suddenly she was no longer gold, but dripping red, coated in a crimson deluge that flowed down from the ceiling, showering woman and statue alike. Peri rocked back in utter shock, her gorge rising; her mind tried to insist that the scarlet stream was colored water, wine, paint, *anything* but—but there was no mistaking that hot coppery smell as it poured down in seemingly endless torrents. The woman seemed undismayed by the deluge; to the contrary, she smeared the pouring liquid over her face and hair and breasts, bathed in it, collected it in her cupped hands to more thoroughly anoint her sculpted lover.

The crowd seemed inflamed by the gory spectacle, swaying and chanting more strongly.

"WAKE! WAKE! WAKE!"

And suddenly Peri could not bear a single moment more, not if it cost her her life, her very *soul,* and she pushed back through the crowd, roughly this time, caution forgotten, Atheris forgotten; her mind had room only for one thought— OUT.

Then she was in the hall again, shoving heedlessly past

worshipers striving with equal fervor to push themselves into the central chamber, and for a moment she thought she was trapped. Before sheer desperation could tempt her to pull out her sword and simply hack and slash her way through the throng, however, she managed to squeeze past, and she staggered down the hallway as quickly as she could. The farther she got from the central chamber, the thinner the crowd, and at last she could move at a weak and shuddery trot, one hand steadying her against the wall as she fought down waves of helpless nausea.

She was, by her best guess, almost halfway back to the temple entrance when she remembered the priests and, more importantly, the guards at the door. There was no way she could slip past them without being observed, and no excuse she could give for her exit. No way out—

The left fork!

Hurriedly Peri forced herself onward, searching for the upward passage. Wherever that hall went, at least it wasn't to that horrible central chamber. She'd find another exit and wait as long as she dared for Atheris. If he came, fine; if he didn't, she'd have no choice but to leave for Bregond without him. Whatever evil was breeding in this diseased land and its foul temple, the farther away from it Peri could get, and the faster she could get there, the better!

There—the upward-angled hallway. Peri ducked into it, then leaned against the wall, breathing hard. There were no pilgrims here; either they'd already gone ahead, or they'd come back, attracted by the clamor in the central chamber, and taken the other fork to see what was happening. Peri was deeply grateful for the moment of solitude, no matter what its cause. It gave her a much-needed opportunity to take a few deep breaths and still her shocked trembling, fight down a panic more dangerous to her than any peril Sarkond had to offer.

Steeling herself, she made her way cautiously up the hall-way. She couldn't think beyond getting out of this insane, evil place; if she had to push her way through such diseased and malformed unfortunates as she'd seen on the road, so be it. Nothing could be more horrible than what she'd just wit-nessed.

But there was no one in the hall either to hinder her or to urge her on. The floor was smoothly worn in a sloping ramp rather than steps, and Peri found that she had to watch her footing on the slightly damp and rather slick stone as she made her way up the steepening incline. This passage wound more circuitously than the one below, as if it spiraled up through the temple; several-times-smaller passages branched off to the side, but she stayed with the main hall, thinking it most likely to lead to an exit. At last it ended at a closed door.

For a moment Peri considered simply knocking—after all, she'd been directed this way, and proceeding openly might be safer than attempting to sneak by—but immediately thought the better of it. If she presented herself for healing, she'd most likely be expected to remove her bandages and show her com-plaint, and if she exposed her face in this Sarkondish hell, she'd need considerably more than a healing spell. She pressed her ear against the door and listened intently, trying the latch after several moments passed with no sounds emerging from within.

The door opened slowly and, thankfully, without too much noise despite the damp. There was an empty room beyond, featureless except for rows of rough stone benches, now un-occupied, presumably for waiting supplicants, and a door op-posite, slightly ajar. A little more light filtered in around this door, and Peri heard the mutter of voices and sounds of move-ment. She tiptoed across the room, touching the door—

Then the smell hit her and Peri pushed her hand hard against her mouth, biting into her knuckles in her effort to stay silent. Utterly helpless to stop herself, she peered around the edge of the door, ever so carefully. Surely, she repeated to herself, nothing could be more unspeakable than what she had seen in the chamber below.

She was wrong.

Four figures in horribly spattered robes were busy at their work, tipping a large copper cauldron over sideways, spilling its crimson contents through a grate in the floor, presumably to rain down on the figures in the chamber below. The cauldron was full, steaming gently in the chill room; the nature of its contents was unmistakable.

As was the source of those contents.

Several corpses still hung, head downward, from hooks in the ceiling, thin streams or mere droplets draining from their slit throats into basins positioned beneath them. More horrible, though, were the others, the drained and discarded victims piled heedlessly in the corners like empty wineskins. Each of the corpses showed some sign of disease or malformation, and in their vacant eyes Peri saw the fate of all those other unfortunates who had come here for the "touch of Eregis."

Peri backed away from the door very slowly, biting back a scream. Every muscle was taut and shaking; her leg bumped one of the stone benches and for a moment of sheer terror the world went gray before her eyes. Then, somehow, she stumbled back out of that room, carefully closing the door behind her. Then she could stand it no longer; she collapsed, shuddering, half fainting, her hand still jammed against her mouth lest sheer horror force out a sound to betray her. She pressed her face against the cold stone of the wall and wet it with hot tears of hopeless terror.

I can't go up, can't go down, can't go back—I'm trapped, trapped in here with that obscenity—

No. Stop it.

Peri took a deep breath, choking off her sobs. She swallowed hard and reached under her robe, clenching her hand around the comforting solidity of her sword hilt. Gradually her shaking stopped.

Panic kills more warriors than the deadliest foe. The first priority is surviving the next minute. Second is surviving the next hour. Third—

Peri pushed herself to her knees, her hand still clasping her sword.

Never mind third, she thought grimly. *If I can get out of this hellhole and die in the clean open air, that's good enough for me.*

Then a hand clasped her shoulder, and Peri's heart stopped.

"Perian," Atheris whispered gently. "Come away from here."

Almost numb, Peri let him help her to her feet. She followed him back down the hall, but they did not go far; almost immediately he ducked into one of the small side passages she'd seen, listening at doors until one apparently suited him. He opened it, glanced in, and then pushed Peri inside, following her and closing the door after him.

The room was obviously somebody's quarters, judging from the pallet, chamber pot, candle, pitcher, and washbasin that were its only furnishings. A little daylight filtered in through a narrow slit in the outside wall that apparently served as ventilation as well. When Peri's eyes adjusted, she turned back to Atheris, to find him gazing at her.

"I am sorry," he said, very softly, "that you had to see that. You should have stayed with me."

"Stayed with you?" she said disbelievingly. "You think that—that obscenity was any better?" Then the meaning of his words penetrated and her jaw dropped in shock. "You mean you—you *knew*? You knew what was going on here?" The amazing gratitude Irra and Minyat had showed, and the young girl—the old woman's words—

Atheris dropped his eyes.

"I knew," he said, very softly. "But, Peri, you do not understand—"

"You're right, I don't," she said slowly. All the emotion, the horror, the outrage, drained out of her, leaving her oddly numb. She gazed at Atheris and, for the first time in days, saw a Sarkond, a stranger. "I *don't* understand. And I don't want to. Just get me out of this place, Atheris. Get me out *right now.*"

Atheris gazed at her oddly for a long moment, then nodded. "Yes," he said. "I know the way we must go."

Peri followed him quietly back out to the upper hall, but to her dismay he led her back down to the main hallway leading to the central chamber. When he turned back toward that gruesome place, Peri balked, pulling him over against the wall.

"Not in there," she whispered as loudly as she dared, given the traffic of pilgrims still passing them in the hall. "I can't go back in there."

"No," Atheris murmured. "We are taking a different path. This temple is laid out not unlike the one where I served."

He led her a little farther down the hall, then pulled her into a little nook Peri had not noticed on her first passage through; it was actually concealed quite cleverly, taking advantage of an angle in the stone of the wall and the shadows between the torches. There was barely enough light for her to see an inset stone tablet which Atheris touched in three places, but she had no difficulty in seeing the stone door which swung silently open in front of him.

Atheris all but dragged her into an almost unlit corridor, so narrow that her shoulders brushed the stone on either side of her. Peri followed eagerly; if Atheris knew the layout of this temple this well, surely he'd know the safest escape route.

This corridor twisted more circuitously than the main hall, and like the upper hall, there were numerous doors and other corridors branching off from it.

Bright Ones, I'm in the middle of a fire-ant nest, she thought. *Winding around and around deeper and deeper and just waiting to get stung.*

The silence was positively eerie—nothing but the scrape of their boots on stone, the occasional whisper of the infrequent torches, the slow drip of water—

It IS awfully damp in here. We must be getting close to the springhead. Yes, I can feel it. Bright Ones, it goes deep!

To Peri's consternation, they, too, seemed to be going deeper, lower; surely they must be well belowground by now. But likely that was necessary to avoid the central chamber and other populated areas; Peri was surprised and relieved that so far, aside from the pilgrims in the main corridor, they'd passed no one at all, so Athcris must know what he was doing. Still, it seemed as though they'd been walking far too long; surely they should have crossed even this huge temple by now.

"How much farther?" she murmured.

"Not much farther, I should think," Atheris said, very quietly, and something in his voice sent a sudden chill through her blood.

She stopped in her tracks.

"What's going on?" she asked warily, straining her eyes in the darkness, wishing she could see his expression. "What are you—"

A scraping sound behind her, stealthy, ever so faint, but to Peri's trained ears it might as well have been an explosion. She whirled, reaching instinctively for the hilt of her sword—

No, never mind that, no room, too narrow—

—and she drew both her fighting daggers instead, her mind instinctively flitting through the dagger qivashim, eliminating some because of the darkness, some because of the close quarters, some because—

Then the attack came, blindingly fast; even with Peri's razor-sharp reflexes she barely had time to counter. The very speed and skill of the strike which she deflected—*not a blade, some kind of sap*—identified her attacker as one of the Bone Hunters even before she saw the gruesome fingerbone necklace around the tall masked figure's neck. She barely registered that fact, however, and a lightning stab of fear and despair—her dagger qivashim, especially defensive, weren't nearly as well trained as her sword—but her opponent gave her no time to ponder on these things. Apparently the darkness and narrow quarters did not disadvantage Peri's attacker as much as they did Peri herself; despite the best she could do, one of her knives dropped from numb fingers as the sap struck her arm just below the elbow.

Hurriedly Peri danced back—hadn't she seen an intersection of corridors just ahead? Yes! Just a little—and then she froze, her heart skipping a beat, as a second Bone Hunter stepped silently forward in the adjoining corridor. And this one was not worried about capture—he had a short sword in one hand, and as he stepped forward he drew a throwing knife with the other.

"No," Atheris said in the darkness behind her, very quietly. "No. Not that."

Then his hand was strong and warm on her shoulder, startling Peri so that she nearly rounded on him; but between that breath and the next, all the strength flowed out of her body like water, and she slumped quietly, limply to the damp stone—

And into darkness.

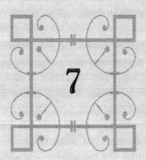

7

FOR THE NINETEENTH TIME PERI PACED OFF THE
dimensions of her cell—four paces long, three paces
wide—and for the nineteenth time she had to sit down
weakly afterward, her head spinning, on the mound of moldy-
smelling straw that was apparently meant to serve as her bed.
For the nineteenth time, while she rested she meticulously cat-
aloged her cell—pile of straw, tiny iron-barred window, small
iron-grated opening in the floor over a stinking waste pit, iron
manacles on the only stone wall, three iron-barred walls and
door with very, very sturdy lock. Nothing more.

Oh, there was Atheris, of course, in the adjoining cell, but
Peri had almost forgotten him. That was easy to do; in all the
time since she'd awakened to find a strange mage chanting
over her, he had only sat quietly in the corner of his cell, doing
nothing, saying nothing.

Which was just fine, for there was nothing in the world that
he could possibly say that Peri wanted to hear.

Peri glanced at her boot, at the empty sheath where her grace-blade had fit ever since she was old enough to wear one. The hilt had stretched her boot ever so slightly there. It had always made a rather comforting pressure against her calf, a strangely reassuring presence, reminding her that in the end, her life—or at least her death—was always her own.

But not now.

If I am captured by Sarkonds, her mind insisted, *it is my duty to die.* She'd assessed the possibilities; she could try to crush her skull against the stones of wall or floor, bite open the veins in her wrists. She could tear her clothes into strips, make a rope; if she could somehow climb up to the tiny barred window and tie it off, she could possibly hang herself.

And she could do none of these things.

She could consider the possibilities academically, speculate on the odds of success of each, but that was all. She'd tried biting her wrist; her jaws had refused to obey her even before her teeth pressed hard enough to cause pain. Peri had guessed, even before she'd tried, that the mage chanting over her had laid a geas on her. It didn't matter, not really; in all practicality, she was dead already.

Captured by Sarkonds. Nothing to a Bregond was dreaded more, not starvation or pestilence or one of the horrible grass fires that occasionally swept the plains. Death in all its forms was, to Bregonds, an unloved but at least familiar predator. It killed, painlessly or not, swiftly or not, predictably or randomly, but it didn't steal away the honor of those it took.

But a Bregond captured by her enemies could expect no honor. She could be raped, tortured, bespelled, forced by pain or humiliation or magic to betray her people, her country. And even if—when—death finally granted her release, those who loved her would continue to be tortured by imagination, by dread, by waiting and wondering. No. Better to be spared all that, to spare her loved ones that pain. Thus a quick, clean death before capture became every Bregond's right, and every Bregond's duty.

Peri had carried her grace-blade since she was five years old; the first blade work she'd ever been taught was how to use it—on herself, on a fallen companion who could not be saved—the places where edge or point might be applied to bring the quickest, most merciful ending. She'd practiced with blunted blades again and again and again until the moves were swift, unerring, instinctive. She knew that if the time came, she was prepared to give grace, either to herself or another in need.

But there was no one to give her grace and no way to give it to herself. She was captive, dishonored, at the mercy of her enemies.

And, no matter what happened, forever dead to every Bregond.

Against her will, a little despairing sound, not quite a sob, forced its way past her lips. She felt tears on her cheeks and dashed them away disgustedly. All the tears in the world couldn't help her now.

"Perian?"

Involuntarily Peri looked up. Atheris had moved at last; he was standing at the bars looking at her.

"After all that has happened," he said, very softly, "I thought nothing could make you weep."

Peri clenched her teeth.

"Enjoy it," she said shortly. "You'll never see it again." Then a thought occurred to her. "What are you doing locked up here, anyway? I figured selling me to them bought you your life at least."

Atheris was silent for a long moment.

"I did not sell you to them," he said at last, very slowly. "And I would not, not for my life, nor even my soul."

Peri gave a short bark of bitter laughter.

"If you think you can say *anything* to make me believe you didn't betray me, you're deluded," she said, shaking her head. "The only amazing thing about it is that I was actually *surprised*. Surprised that a Sarkond turned on me! Mahdha scour me with grit, it wasn't stupid enough to go saving a Sarkond's life or sleep with him; I had to go and *trust* one."

"I did betray you," Atheris said quietly. "I do not deny it. But not to anyone in this temple or this land, Perian, nor any human being. Only to—to your destiny, if you will."

"Destiny!" Peri said sarcastically. "You can take your destiny, Atheris, and you can—"

"He's right, you know."

Peri started violently at the voice. She squinted into the shadows and saw nothing, but at last a hooded, cloaked figure flanked by two guards walked down the aisle between the rows of cells, pausing in front of hers. Slender hands raised to push back the hood, and Peri swallowed hard.

Without her gold paint, the Whore of Eregis might have been any Bregondish woman who had spent too much time indoors, so that her skin had faded to a pale tan. Her long black hair hung loose, not confined in a Bregondish woman's thirty-nine braids of adulthood, giving her, to Peri, an oddly childlike appearance despite a sense of worldliness and age that hung about her, felt rather than seen. Her wide brown-black eyes, too, held a strange sort of innocence. Peri remembered the woman bathing so ecstatically in the blood of the sacrifices, and shuddered.

Not innocence, she realized. *Madness.*

"Bring me a chair," the woman murmured to one of the guards. "Then leave us."

The guards obeyed silently. Peri stayed where she was, keeping any expression of interest off her face. Lunatics could sometimes be manipulated. Even if she couldn't manage to trick the woman into letting her out of her cell, perhaps Peri could learn something useful from her.

"He's right," the woman repeated, this time in Bregondish. "He didn't sell you to us—not in any direct sense, at least. It was destiny alone that delivered you to us, Perian, daughter of High Lord Randon and High Lady Kayli of Agrond, Heir-to-be of Bregond."

Atheris started, his eyes wide, and the Whore laughed.

"Poor sheltered young heretic. You never knew? But how could our Harbinger, born of two worlds and destined to shake the very pillars of a third, be any other than Kayli's spawn?"

Peri frowned, as much at the Whore's words as at Atheris's reaction. Was it her imagination, or did the Whore's voice falter ever so slightly when speaking her mother's name?

"You knew my mother?" she asked slowly.

"For a time." The Whore's eyes narrowed slightly. "It's not a time I remember with joy."

Peri rose from her rough seat, walked as close to the Whore as the bars would permit.

"What did my mother ever do to harm you?" she said slowly.

"Why, nothing, nothing at all, young Harbinger," the Whore purred, raising one delicately arched eyebrow. "Quite the contrary. The proud Lady Kayli is the only Bregond I remember with kindness—nay, sympathy. Perhaps none but she could ever understand the horror of finding you have betrayed all you held dear—not by treason, but by loyalty. Ah, you frown, my innocent young Perian. Your mother never took you into her confidence, then. I'm not surprised. No matter. You needn't understand. You have already played your part to perfection. And—"

"Golden One." A guard stood in the shadows. "The Bonemarch summon you."

The Whore sighed.

"The Bonemarch, always the Bonemarch. Very well." She turned back to Peri, and Peri shivered again under the gaze of those terrible, innocent eyes. "I will come back soon, young Perian. We have much to discuss, you and I, and I fear our time together is short."

She turned away, but before she could go, Atheris dashed to the door to his cell, gripping the bars tightly.

"Wait!" he cried out. "Tell me one thing, only one thing. My cousin Amis—her fate—"

The Whore turned, smiling.

"Ah, your fellow heretic, the young healer. Yes, the Bone Hunters brought her here. I had no dealing with her myself." She shrugged. "It's my understanding she didn't last long under questioning. Be comforted. Her execution would have been far less pleasant. And much slower, of course. Congratulations, my handsome young heretic. Now you've led *two* women to their doom—and neither at any profit to yourself."

Then she was gone, and Peri stood where she was, gripping the bars of her prison. She had the odd and discomfiting feeling that she should have understood what had just happened, the same sort of just-missed-it feeling of catching the last two sentences of a crucially important conversation.

A hollow groan from Atheris drew her attention. The Sarkond had retreated to the farthest corner of his cell and sat there, knees folded up, his hands over his face. Peri took a deep breath, cleared her throat.

"I'm sorry about Amis," she said shortly.

After a moment Atheris raised his head.

"Why?" he asked, his voice leaden. "Why did you not tell me who you were?"

Peri laughed bitterly.

"What, you think I wanted it known that the daughter of the High Lord and Lady of Agrond was stranded and all but helpless in Sarkond? The best protection I had was that nobody *did* know. Anyway,'' she added a little self-consciously, "it didn't make any practical difference. I'm not the Heir to Agrond or, no matter what your priestess said, to Bregond either yet. I'm just a misfit second daughter, good enough to marry off to a horse-clan lord until the gods cursed me with the wrong kind of magic at the wrong time.''

"It does matter," Atheris said, very softly. "You have no idea how it matters.''

"I don't see how," Peri said, shrugging.

"No, you do not." Atheris sighed. "But I do. Peri, if I had known—''

"If you'd known, then what?'' she said sourly. "You'd have brought me to them that much sooner, or just killed me yourself?''

"No! I would—would not—'' Atheris groaned again, lowering his face back into his hands. "Eregis forgive me, I do not know what I could have done.''

Something in his tone caught Peri's attention, and she walked back to the bars dividing their cells.

"What?'' she said. "What difference does it make? Why should I be any more use alive than dead? Surely nobody thinks they can get a ransom for me. Everybody knows Bregonds better than that. Even my father and mother in Agrond wouldn't—''

Atheris shook his head.

"The prophecy," he said in a slow, dead voice. "The destiny that brought you here. It is said that the final sacrifice that will wake Eregis will be that of an enemy of royal blood.''

Peri gave a short bark of laughter and backed away, sitting back down on her pile of hay.

"You laugh," Atheris said, not raising his head. "But it is no jest, I assure you.''

"Oh, no, it's a fine joke," Peri said, shaking her head. "In fact, it's about the funniest thing I've ever heard. Do you know, six months ago I was betrothed to my best friend, my clan leader. I had a clan I belonged to, a life that suited me, and everybody pretty much accepted—no, *respected,* damn it!—that I had a true vocation for the sword. Then suddenly because I have this ridiculous, pathetic excuse for magic, suddenly I may end up the Heir to Bregond. Not because I'd have any magical talent to speak of, either, mind you—but because that's the best use for my useless, piddling hint of magic. The best use for *me*. Well, I wonder what Mother would think of this! I mean, the sacrifice that'll wake a *god,* save a country! I can hardly be more useful than *that,* can I? And better yet—I don't have to have any skill or talent at all for this!''

Atheris raised his head just enough to glance wearily at her.

''You are no more bitter than I,'' he said. ''I had no more notion than you of the path destiny laid before our feet.'' He sighed. ''I am almost relieved to see the end of that road ahead.''

Peri gritted her teeth.

''Well, I'm not ready to kick my boots off and be measured for my pyre robe yet,'' she said. ''But if you say the word 'destiny' one more time, I'll be happy to shorten your road that much more.''

Atheris chuckled mirthlessly.

''Lady Perian, if you granted me a quick death, you would be doing me a kindness,'' he said. ''But I submit that allowing me to finish out my own destiny, which is a slow public death by the cruelest tortures the Bone Hunters can devise, will far more perfectly satisfy your desire for revenge than anything you could do to me yourself.''

Peri sat quietly, staring into the darkness. There was nothing to be gained by telling Atheris what she thought—that death in one form or another, probably quite disagreeable, was no more than she'd expected if captured by the Sarkonds. If her execution was called a sacrifice to the Sarkonds' god, what did that matter? Either way, Peri would prefer to cheat the Sarkonds of their goal—by escape, if possible, and if not possible, then by a death that wouldn't serve Sarkondish purposes. She had little faith in the idea that her death would actually wake a god; but belief and magic and madness were powerful things, and here there were all three combined, and that was a dangerous mixture to her way of thinking. At the very least, she hoped she could achieve a quick and easy death and spit in her enemies' eyes one last time.

She scooted closer to the bars separating between her cell and Atheris's.

"Tell me about this prophecy," she said. "All of it this time."

Atheris shrugged tiredly.

"The prophecy says that an end will come to a time of death and hopelessness," he said. "The enemy who comes as a friend is one born of two worlds, cursed with the gift of life and gifted with the skills of death. The appearance of the Harbinger marks the time of upheaval and rebirth, when the royal blood of an enemy will wake Eregis. And Eregis will bring life out of death, and our people will rise up and live again in a land of plenty."

Peri waited, expecting more, but when she realized that Atheris was finished, she laughed again, bitterly. How could an entire nation devote its hopes so single-mindedly on a prophecy as vague and ambiguous as every other prophecy she'd ever heard?

"Did it ever occur to your Bonemarch," she said, "that maybe they were taking that prophecy perhaps just a little too literally?"

Atheris was silent. Again Peri waited, and this time a faint jolt of realization cut through her bitter lethargy.

"Of course," she said. "It occurred to you, didn't it, a long time ago. That's why you tried what you did with your cousin.

And a temple built on—Eregis was once a water god, I remember you saying that, right?''

"Before He slept," Atheris murmured, "He was the Father of Waters."

"Right," Peri said, chuckling. "Temple built over the biggest damned underground reservoir that I ever—right. Making rain, bringing life. I see where you got the idea. And your cousin, you said she was a healer?''

"A gifted and powerful one," Atheris said dully.

Peri chuckled again.

"Poor Atheris," she said. "Combining death and life. You probably got too literal, too."

Atheris raised his head at last, gazing at her somewhat narrowly.

"What do you know of it?" he snapped.

"I know that if you had *ten* healers and as many of what amount to battle mages," Peri said shortly, "you couldn't summon up enough rain to drown an ant. Healing and battle spells aren't water magic. If the two of you had raised enough raw power to crack the world in two, you still wouldn't have made one single drop of rain. You needed a water mage, like my aunt.''

"She could have made it rain?" Atheris said skeptically.

"I don't know," Peri admitted. "Maybe. Maybe not. I don't know if even *she* can make rain out of nothing. You were probably on the right track, though. Two mages combining, maybe you *could* have raised enough sheer raw magic to manipulate the weather; but then what do you do with all that energy? For that you needed the affinity of a water mage to *direct* all that power."

Atheris was silent for a long time. Peri glanced over at him; he had lowered his head again, and his shoulders shook slightly. For a moment she thought he was weeping; then a slight sound reached her ears, and to her amazement she realized he was laughing helplessly.

"What?" she said. "What's funny?"

At last Atheris raised his head and leaned it back against the wall, his eyes closed. He was still laughing silently to himself.

"Thank you, Lady Perian," he gasped. "Eregis knows I have not earned this last gift from you, but I thank you nonetheless. I can at least go to my death knowing that my dream was not a delusion, that Amis and I touched at least the hem of the truth." He was silent for a moment. "I think I can give you something similar in return."

Peri chuckled again.

"Unless you happen to have a cell door key or the like, I can't imagine—"

"Waterdance," Atheris said softly. "I know its secret."

Peri froze, silent. At last she spoke in a bare whisper.

"Tell me."

"I have been on a boat only once," Atheris said thoughtfully. "There are a few small, fouled rivers in the north country, although most have dried up now. I journeyed by river to the temple for my dedication. But as a child I would watch the boats dock, load and unload.

"The true power of the river," he said slowly, "is not disruption, but seduction. You step aboard the boat and for a time the rolling confounds your balance, but soon you adapt. Soon you do not even notice the motion.

"And then the boat docks again and you step off, and suddenly it is not the water, but the land which is in motion, which rolls dizzily beneath your feet. The river has seduced you, changed your reality. Now it is the familiar land which has become strange and unbalancing. The experienced sailor expects this and walks carefully but steadily away. But the unwary traveler who has allowed himself to be seduced finds himself feeling helpless and alien on the very solid ground on which he has tread all his life. That is the power of the river.''

Peri's eyes widened.

''Of course!'' she breathed.

How could she not have seen it sooner? Pulling her opponent with her into a new qiva, of *course* he'd be prepared for the change in balance, requiring a more extreme shift that tripped Peri up as well as she tried to simultaneously control, shift, adapt—but a more subtle shift, gradual, seductive, then an unexpected return—unexpected, at least, to Peri's opponent . . .

''So simple!'' she murmured wonderingly. ''So perfect.''

Her fingers clenched reflexively at her hip, twitching with frustration. It was so unfair, so unthinkable that she'd understand only now, now when there was no one to show, no one to share that wonderful dance of steel in which Waterdance would come to life for the first time. She'd gained her dream just in time for it to die with her.

Peri grinned sourly. A similar gift indeed. Like Peri herself, Atheris must be grinding his teeth with the frustration of seeing his goal close enough to touch at last—and knowing that he would never bridge that last tiny gap. Knowing that his dream would die with him.

But unlike Atheris, Peri was not prepared to accept the inevitability of that loss.

''You said you betrayed me only to destiny,'' she said slowly. ''What did you mean?''

''I began to suspect what you were even before we reached Darnalek,'' Atheris said, barely audibly. ''The old woman you spoke to, the healer, she knew, I think. But I did nothing. If you were indeed the Harbinger, destiny would lead you along the path chosen for you. There was nothing I needed do but wait and watch.

''In Darnalek I became almost certain. You possessed a gift

I had never seen—to generate the energy of life out of a ritual designed to prepare the skills of death. But I did not want to believe. I felt with you a—a kinship. More, perhaps." Atheris turned his head, not meeting Peri's eyes. "So I consulted the fortune-teller. What he said did not absolutely confirm my suspicions, but a part of me knew I could not refuse to see the truth much longer.

"Again I did nothing, save to keep one small secret, one small test of my suspicions. The spells I purchased to conceal us from the detection of the Bone Hunters were not permanent. They would last only four days."

"What!" A hot red rage welled up from Peri's gut; if she could have shot arrows from her eyes, Atheris would have been skewered a thousand times. "You—"

Atheris held up a hand wearily.

"If you were not the Harbinger, it would have made no difference," he said gently. "Four days was time aplenty for us to ride back to Bregond and safely beyond the Bone Hunters' reach. It was not wholly my choice—a permanent spell would have cost more than even we carried, and aroused such suspicion that the mage might well have simply brought guards down upon us immediately, rather than attempt to capture me for his own profit."

Peri clenched her hands tightly, fairly aching for the solidity of a sword hilt in her palm.

"And were you ever going to tell me about this," she whispered, "or just let us be captured by the Bone Hunters?"

Atheris closed his eyes.

"I thought there would be no need to tell you," he said. "One way or another, it would make no difference. If it was our destiny to be captured, then that would happen; if not, then not. And when you killed the Bone Hunter, I thought surely that I had been wrong, that we would escape to Bregond as planned. But when you fell ill, I realized that that, too, was only a part of your destiny, that there was no avoiding the road to Rocarran. And I was right.''

He shook his head.

''Your destiny did the rest. I betrayed you by simply allowing it.''

''Oh, I think it was a little more than that,'' Peri said scornfully. She remembered Atheris's touch on her shoulder in the corridor just as he'd touched the thugs in Darnalek, the way the strength had simply drained out of her body. ''I think you helped it along a little. If it wasn't for you, I'd have managed a clean, honorable death in combat.'' Then a new suspicion woke. ''And when I was wounded—was that your fault, too, that I stayed weak long enough to reach Rocarran? Did you just suck the life out of me then, too?''

Atheris shook his head wearily.

''No. Even had I wished to do so—which I assuredly did not—I would not have dared, lest in your weakened condition you died. But I can imagine easily enough how it was done. When the Bone Hunters found their fallen comrade, they found his weapon, still stained with your blood. I should have thought to clean or take it, but I was too shocked by your victory. Having your blood and the weapon that wounded you, the others could cast a leech spell easily enough, even without knowing your location. I tended you as best I could, but I am no healer and no life-giver. In the end it was simply your own healing magic and the potency of your will to survive that saved you.'' He closed his eyes. ''The distance to Rocarran—I did not know how far it was myself, and I did not ask the others in the caravan. I did not want to know. I left it to destiny to decide whether you would recover in time for us to escape, or—or not.''

He shook his head again.

''Yes, I prevented the battle death you sought in the corridor. If you were indeed the Harbinger, as I knew by then you must be—'' He sighed. ''I thought your life would be spared to ensure that your role in the prophecy had been fulfilled. I did not know your royal blood, you see. I did not know. And if I had known—''

He fell silent.

Peri shook her head, too.

''Mahdha scour me raw.'' She sighed. ''Well, the question is, what do we do now?''

''Do?'' Atheris shrugged. ''Sit. Wait. Die.''

Peri ground her teeth.

''Bright Ones, are you a complete idiot or just a complete coward?'' she demanded. ''Do you think there's something noble about sitting around like a cull waiting for the slaughter?''

Atheris's eyes blazed at the insult, but the anger quickly faded into weary resignation.

''No, there is nothing noble about it,'' he said shortly. ''But neither is there anything especially clever in futile struggle against destiny.''

''It's only futile,'' Peri said just as shortly, ''when you've tried and failed. And destiny is what you make it. I didn't hear anything in your prophecy that said we have to sit here passively and wait to die. If it's my destiny and there's no way to prevent it, then nothing I try is going to do any harm, right?''

Atheris shrugged.

''I suppose not,'' he said. ''No good, but most likely no harm either. Since *my* destiny appears to be death by torture, I have no compunction against attempting to avoid it. What do you propose?''

''Do you have any magic that can get us out of these cells?'' Peri asked, hoping against hope.

Atheris chuckled dryly, dashing her hopes even before he spoke.

"I am geas-bound against any attempt to escape," he said. "Do you think they would trust me, a heretic and traitor, any more than you?"

"Attempting to escape," Peri said slowly. "Just that?"

Atheris shrugged.

"As far as I can ascertain," he said. "What else might I be expected to do?"

Peri clenched her hands again.

"Can you remove the geas binding me?" she asked softly.

Atheris dropped his eyes.

"Perhaps," he said, just as softly. "But I will not. If it is your destiny to die as a sacrifice to wake Eregis . . . I owe my people that, at least. If you are meant to avoid that fate, there will be another way."

Peri ground her teeth. Bright Ones knew she wanted to escape, but there was a far more important consideration. Eregis's rising, real or imagined, could mean only one thing—a new attack against Agrond and Bregond. It meant Agrondish and Bregondish lives, more blasted earth—

"Atheris," she said slowly, "I'm going to tell you something, something you need to understand. I'm only High Lord Randon and High Lady Kayli's misfit daughter, but I'm still a child of the royal house of Agrond. By the time I rescued you, my uncle already knew I was missing. By the next morning he'd know *where* I'd gone. By noon the garrison mage would have contacted my mother in Agrond and my aunt in Bregond. Between the two houses it wouldn't take any time at all to raise at least a first-strike battalion and mount them on fast horses for the Barrier—and they've got *good* horses.

"By this minute, Atheris, I'll wager there's a good gathering of troops there and at least a couple dozen mages honing their battle magics—probably including my fire-slinging mother and my storm-herding aunt. They're not waiting for a sacrifice or a prophecy or a god. In their mind, your people came down into Bregond to capture me, and that's all the warning they'll need that Sarkond is planning something that involves Agrond and Bregond. Believe me, it won't take much to convince either country to go to war against Sarkond. I don't know whether they'll collapse the Barrier and march straight into Sarkond, or whether they'll risk sending a mage and some troops through to scry and scout, but I doubt they're going to wait too much longer before they do something drastic.''

Atheris listened silently, but his eyes widened, and Peri spoke as earnestly as she could.

"Say, just as speculation, your temple sacrificed me this very minute and your god came roaring up bright and perky from wherever He's been sleeping. Just what do you expect your god to *do*? Go walking personally down to the Barrier to stomp out our troops? Wave His hands and make all the people vanish from Agrond and Bregond so your people can walk down there and take it? Short of that, suppose He does what gods usually do—make a lot of noise and spectacle and throw out a few minor miracles to get the worshipers all fired up.

"Fine. He's done that. Your people are all raring to march right down to the Barrier and conquer two countries full of enemies. Say Eregis empowers your mages, too, because they certainly aren't going to be able to pull anything more out of those southern lands, are they? Even so, Sarkond's still got to gather an army, and from what I've seen, finding soldiers who are up to any kind of battle is going to take a miracle right there.

"But say there's enough competent fighters, too, just for the sake of argument. After all, we're talking gods and miracles here. Still, it's going to take time to gather them and arm them—we won't worry about training and drilling and strategy either, or how Sarkond's going to muster up armor and weapons. The plain fact is that by the time Sarkond could put together any kind of force—weeks at the very least, even given the best possible circumstances—Bregondish and Agrondish magics and troops will have blasted what's left of your country to ash." Peri waited a moment, and when Atheris said nothing, she pressed, "Can you look me in the eye and tell me I'm wrong?"

Atheris said nothing, but he would not meet her eyes.

"So you're hanging all your hopes on your god's direct intervention," Peri said plainly. "The same god that let your people down the last time they went to war and gambled everything on their faith. Now I'll tell you what I think. Personally I think your prophecy is so much stable muck shoveled out by your priests to keep your people going, keep their hopes up. I can't blame them for that. But never mind what I believe. Say it's a genuine prophecy. If that's true, your priests misinterpreted it once already, and look what *that* did to your country and your people. Can Sarkond afford to lose what little it's got left if that happens again?"

"What choice have we?" Atheris said flatly. "It is the only hope my people have had for decades."

"Obviously *you* think there's a choice," Peri countered, "or you'd never have taken the chance you did. Even you believe there's another way, a better way to view this prophecy. I'll tell you true, with a war and my life at stake, I've got to hope you're right."

"What do you want of me?" Atheris said wearily. "I will not kill you, Peri, and I cannot help you escape."

"For now, just think about what I've said," Peri said slowly. "Just consider it while I try to come up with an alternative, and promise me that if I *do* think of something, you'll consider it with an open mind."

Atheris was silent for a long moment.

"Yes," he said at last. "That much I can promise."

Peri scooted over to the bars, as close to Atheris as she could get, but he made no effort to move closer.

"And tell me whatever you know about this Whore of Eregis," she said.

Another long moment of silence.

"No one knows much," he said. "She came from the south around the time that Sarkond was devastated and the Barrier erected."

"She couldn't have been very old then," Peri murmured. "Hardly more than a child."

"I know only that she was revealed to the temple as a prophet," Atheris said apologetically. "And she has served Eregis ever since."

"How could a Bregondish child find her way around Sarkond, much less make it through the armies, across the border, and as far as Rocarran during the war and set herself up in the temple as a prophet?" Peri mused. "Unless she was captured and taken to Rocarran. But why would Sarkondish soldiers bother taking a Bregondish child to the temple?"

Atheris shrugged, shaking his head.

"I do not know," he said. "And why would she have even lived to be taken there? I have heard it said that even Bregondish children take their own lives if capture seems inevitable."

Peri touched the empty sheath in her boot where her graceblade had once been.

"Only two reasons," she said. "Either she was bound or geased to prevent suicide, like me, or she came to Sarkond purposefully. And I can't imagine why—"

Then she fell silent. There was a story from the war, a story of the time just following her mother and father's marriage, when—

"I know who she is," Peri said suddenly. "Her name was Seba. She was captured by Sarkonds as a child and ended up sold in Agrond as a slave. She tricked her way into my

mother's service and tried to poison her. Later, when Sarkondish raiders attacked at the border, killing almost the entire
ruling family of Bregond, Seba—supposedly the only survi-
vor—was taken back to Agrond and told my uncle that my
parents had been killed in the raid. She disappeared after that.''

Atheris stared at her, his eyes wide.

"I cannot believe any Bregond, especially a child, could so
betray her own people," he said very softly. "I cannot believe
our prophet could be such a person."

"I know," Peri said grimly. "It makes no sense. There's a
lot I've been told about the war that *doesn't* make any sense.
But grant me this much—if I'm right, then anything that
comes out of that traitor's mouth is pretty questionable prophecy, isn't it? Can you tell me you didn't see the madness in
her eyes?"

"Yes," Atheris said after a moment's pause. "I cannot dis-
pute that. But how can we know if you are right?"

"Simple enough," Peri said, shrugging. "We ask her."

In fact, by Peri's reckoning, it was no more than an hour
before the Whore returned, this time without guards. She
turned and sat down in the chair silently, taking in Peri's
change of position and smiling.

"Ah, I see you have made peace with your friend, the
treacherous Sarkondish enemy," the Whore said. "So you believe him, that he did not betray you. No, child, fate doomed
you even as it doomed me."

"If fate doomed you," Peri said deliberately, "then you
helped it along, Seba."

If Eregis's Whore was surprised by Peri's statement, she
made no sign of it, only smiling slightly.

"So you do know that much, at least," she said thoughtfully. "What else do you know?"

"I know that despite everything my mother did to help
you," Peri said flatly, "you did your best to have her killed,

and the entire royal family of Bregond with her.''

Seba laughed softly.

"Then you know nothing," she said.

"Then you deny it?" Peri challenged.

"I deny nothing." Seba gave her a dreamy smile. "Tell me, young warrior, you've lived in the horse clans, have you not?"

"I've fostered there most of my life," Peri said cautiously.

"What if your clan leader gave you an order," Seba said, "not only for the good of your clan, but for the good of all of Bregond?"

"I'd obey him," Peri said, shrugging.

"Even if he bade you do something you found horrible, even repugnant?" Seba pressed.

Peri shrugged again.

"My feelings don't matter," she said impatiently. "Mahdha knows I've been told that often enough of recent. It's what's best for Bregond that matters."

Seba chuckled.

"Then by your standards, I'm not a traitor, but a hero," she said. "For my actions were bidden by one looked upon with the greatest of respect by all of Bregond, one of its staunchest protectors, High Priestess Brisi of the Temple of Inner Flame. I was only a child then, a child abducted, sold, and raped, and then disowned by my own people for the simple crime of survival. The High Priestess and her allies were the ones who took me in, told me that Mahdha hadn't yet forgotten my name. I was given orders to perform certain acts that I was told would save my country and my people from utter destruction and restore my honor. I obeyed those orders and was named a traitor for my trouble. My crime, young Perian, was in foolishly trusting one I'd been taught to respect and obey, but my country found that as unforgivable as they'd found the fact that a mere child was too young and frightened to kill herself for their peace of mind.''

Peri flushed.

"They don't know that you weren't to blame," she said hotly. "Nobody knows."

"Oh, yes," Seba said softly. "Somebody knows. High Lady Kairi knows. Your mother knows. And yet they've kept silent, haven't they?"

Peri hesitated, remembering her mother's vagueness about the war. Yes, there *had* been some commotion about the temples, hadn't there, some hint of scandal? And her brother Estann, he hadn't gone to the temples to train.

"They kept silent," Seba said, smiling, "to shield the temples from the rage of a betrayed people, to preserve their precious Orders. They hid the truth because I made a far more politically convenient scapegoat, because the honor of one orphaned girl-child didn't matter. But it matters now, doesn't it, Perian? And *I* matter now."

"If that's the case," Peri challenged, "why didn't you stay and tell the truth, instead of disappearing?"

Seba laughed.

"The word of a child already dead to her people and deemed traitor in two countries, against the word of the two High Ladies she'd tried to kill? Assuming, of course, that I'd have been allowed to live long enough to tell at all. No, there was nothing left for me in Agrond or Bregond—no kin, no honor, no hope. But Sarkond was a country full of hopeless people, the outcast, the lost. My past association with High Priestess Brisi bought me shelter, sanctuary, from her allies here."

Peri laughed bitterly.

"It's quite a jump from escaped traitor to prophet," she said.

"No jump at all," Seba corrected. "The prophecy was

made long before you or even I drew breath. But, you see, I knew the prophecy for truth, and as the signs unfolded, I knew it was my destiny to see it fulfilled. I had the means already; I only awaited the perfect time, and of course the Harbinger, Perian, and you so kindly obliged me.''

"What do you mean, you had the means?'' Peri said slowly. Was there some army gathered that neither she nor Atheris knew about, poised to march into Bregond?

Seba smiled.

"When I reached the temple at Rocarran, I found they'd already received a most interesting prisoner,'' she said. "One taken well before the first true engagement, but forgotten in the confusion. He'd been taken in simple nightclothes, after all, and was badly injured, near death. All the healers had gone to join the army, and in his state he couldn't be questioned to learn his identity. But I knew him immediately. Ah, yes. For of all the people in Sarkond, I was probably the only one who had ever seen the face of High Lord Elaasar of Bregond.''

Peri froze, and Seba chuckled.

"Ah, yes. The greatest disgrace of the Bregondish people— the disappearance of their High Lord during the Sarkondish raid which took the lives of his lady and two of his daughters. Agrond and Bregond mourned him with all due ceremony. Your mother and her sisters mourned him. But nobody ever *really* knew, did they? And that was Bregond's shame—and your mother's even more so, for she knew the truth of why it had happened. And here he was brought, and here he lives still, disgraced even as I was, by life.''

It took Peri a long moment to force enough breath into her lungs to speak. What Seba said couldn't be true. It couldn't.

"You're lying,'' she whispered through dry lips.

Seba laughed, unoffended.

"Am I?'' she said lightly, standing. She tossed something into the cell. It sparkled on the floor. "Is this a lie? Or have all your truths suddenly become lies instead, as once they did for me?''

Peri knelt and picked up the Signet of Bregond with shaking fingers. She clutched it tightly, biting her lip so hard it bled.

''Why are you telling me this?'' she whispered.

Seba smiled.

''Because I'm going to offer you a choice, young Perian— the same choice I had. A dishonorable death, or an even more dishonorable life.''

Peri laughed bitterly.

''You expect me to believe that you'd give me a choice?'' she said. ''You have no reason to let me live, especially knowing what I know. And I'm your Harbinger, aren't I? Your sacrifice.''

''Not at all,'' Seba said smoothly. ''The prophecy requires the royal blood of an enemy, you see. And as I've just told you, *that* we already have, and a High Lord, no less!

''So you may choose. If you prefer, we'll sacrifice you. It isn't a pleasant death, I'll warn you, and such a death at our hands won't be the honorable ending you'd like. Your spirit would never fly home on Mahdha's wings, and we'd still have High Lord Elaasar, of course. But at least you'd never have to *face* your disgrace, would you?

''Or you choose to live, to carry a message back to Bregond for me,'' Seba continued. ''However unpleasant his death, I imagine your grandfather would find that ending a mercy now. You can go home, face your disgrace, become an outcast as I did. It would be amusing to see if you fare better than I have.''

Peri gazed at the signet, still almost too shaken for speech.

''You can't expect me to make a choice like that,'' she said faintly.

Seba chuckled.

''Oh, you'll choose,'' she said lightly. ''You'll choose, because you must. Think on it, young Perian—only a short time, for that's all I can give you now. Think on the value of your life." Then she was gone in a swirl of silken robes.

"Do you believe her?" Atheris asked softly. "That she has your grandfather?"

Peri turned the ring in her hands. She tried to tell herself that the signet could have been taken from High Lord Elaasar's dead body, but she knew better. If the High Lord had died by his own hand, he would have first taken measures to assure that the signet would not be recovered by the enemy—buried it or had one of his guards swallow it or some such. If he could not die then, he would have still done anything he could to keep the signet from being taken. And if her grandfather was dead, Seba had no reason to release Peri. Unless that offer was false, too. But to what purpose?

"Yes," Peri said shortly. She clenched the signet tightly in her fist. "I believe her."

"But why release you?" Atheris said slowly. "The Bonemarch would never allow it, so she must be acting without their knowledge. Even if she does not need you for the sacrifice, why let you return to Bregond to betray her plans?"

Peri shook her head.

"I don't know," she said. "I think—I think she wants me to tell them about my grandfather. I don't think there's anything in the world that would shake the people of Bregond more than knowing that their High Lord was shamefully taken captive by Sarkonds, that he'd survived all these years, only to die now to serve Sarkondish purposes. I can't even imagine what that would do to the people—or to Aunt Kairi or Mother, for that matter—if that were known. But why wait all these years to do it? There's got to be something else, something more, and for the life of me I can't figure out what."

"If she is truly mad, as you say," Atheris murmured, "then how could we possibly understand her reasoning?"

"Because she *wants* us to understand," Peri said, shaking

her head. "She wants somebody to know what she went through, why—unless that's it," she said suddenly. "Can it be as simple as that, just plain revenge for what happened to her? She was captured by Sarkonds as a child, and that made her outcast in Bregond forever. But then Brisi and her allies in the temples found a use for Seba, told her she could serve Bregond, even save it. She was just a child, frightened and desperate, and she believed in the temples, in their authority. She did what she was told, believing she was serving the greater good of Bregond and restoring her honor. And then, after it was all done, she realized she'd been betrayed again—tricked into becoming a traitor to her own country, nowhere to go, nobody to help her—"

Peri shook her head again, grimacing.

"That's got to be it," she said. "To her, I'm a younger version of herself. I've been captured by Sarkonds. I'll never be accepted in Bregond again. So Bregond's lost its Heir. I'd have to go back to Agrond instead, and when the truth about my grandfather comes out, that blow will shake Bregond even harder. And it'll hurt Mother, too—but at the same time Seba's returning me alive to her. She knows Mother will take me back—Mother accepted *her,* after all. Mother and Aunt Kairi will be shamed in Bregond's eyes because their father didn't manage to kill himself, and Mother discredited in Bregond for accepting me back—and then we'll all have to live with that knowledge, that pain, just as Seba's had to live with hers. It doesn't matter that it wasn't Mother's fault or mine. It wasn't Seba's fault either, all those years ago, but that didn't save her." Peri sighed. "Mahdha forgive me, Atheris, what am I going to do?"

Atheris did not look at her.

"Go home," he said quietly. "Go home to your family, Perian, and fulfill Seba's plan and live. I know your Bregondish custom, and perhaps I understand it. But I have tasted both life and death, Perian, and believe me when I tell you that life is better. Even with pain, even with sorrow and loss, even with shame, life is better."

Peri did not answer. Yes, she'd rather be alive than dead, even with the pain of what she knew, even as an outcast from Bregond, even with the shame that she'd been unable to take her own life. Yes, she'd pay that price to live—but, as Danber always said, "Only a fool turns over his gold without checking the horse's teeth." And she was far from certain that her life was worth the price that her mother, and all of Bregond, would pay with her.

But possibly—just possibly—there was another choice.

She turned to Atheris.

"Atheris," she said slowly, "do you believe in that prophecy about the waking of Eregis?"

Atheris lowered his head.

"I have always believed in it," he said simply. "As you said, what other hope did my people have? It was only the interpretation I ever questioned, not the message itself." He shook his head. "Even now I cannot refuse to believe. I want to doubt, but a part of me clings to that hope still."

"Then think about this," Peri said deliberately. "If these things are destined to happen, then events will shape themselves to *make* it happen, the same way that everything we did pushed me on to the temple here. Am I right?"

"Yes," Atheris said cautiously. "Yes, you fulfilled your role as Harbinger despite your best efforts." He flushed.

"Then if this is really the time that Eregis will rise," Peri said, "nothing you and I can do will stop it—in fact, anything we might try could just as easily be part of the plan. Right?"

Atheris frowned.

"I suppose so," he said.

"Then I'll make a bargain with you," Peri said grimly. "I'll need your help. Help me, and I swear to you, by what's left of my honor, that I won't stand in the way of your prophecy—and if that means my life, then I'll give it. Bargain?''

Atheris hesitated.

''I trust your honor,'' he said quietly. ''But how can I help you?''

''All I want is—'' Peri began, then fell silent as she heard the outer door open. Too late—the Whore had returned, and now all she could do was hope that Atheris had enough faith in her to follow her lead.

Seba stopped a short distance from the bars.

''You look resolved,'' she said, smiling. ''Have you decided to accept my offer?''

Peri hesitated.

''What about the Bonemarch?'' she said. ''Are they just going to let me go, just like that?''

Seba laughed.

''They can't prevent what they don't know,'' she said. ''Tonight you'll escape. It's as simple as that. There will be a search, of course, Bone Hunters dispatched to find you. But with a little care on my part, it will be some time before your absence is discovered. Few are permitted down here at all, so you shouldn't be missed too quickly.''

Peri paused thoughtfully for a moment, then nodded briefly.

''I'll go back,'' she said. ''I'll take the signet and make sure they know what really happened to my grandfather. That's what you want, isn't it? But I want something in return.''

Seba laughed.

''In return! I offer you life instead of death by torture, and that's not enough?''

''I want him,'' Peri said, pointing at Atheris. ''I still have to get back through Sarkond. I had to travel in disguise before, and his magic was all that kept the Bone Hunters from finding us more than once. Without his help I might never reach the border alive, and that won't serve your purposes, will it? And you can't exactly give me a guard escort, can you? Besides," she added practically, "my own escape will look a lot more credible to the Bonemarch if they believe I had the help of a heretic trying to escape his own punishment, won't it? Give him a priest's robe and we can actually make it through Sarkond without someone killing us."

Seba chuckled.

"And how do you think your family will react when you bring your Sarkondish lover home with you?" she said gently.

"Well, no matter." Her voice hardened, and her gaze held Peri's. "You swear on your honor you will return to your family?"

"Don't worry," Peri said grimly. "I'll return the signet to my kinfolk, and I'll make sure they know what really happened to my grandfather. I swear on my honor, on my sword, and on the blood of my family."

A faint hint of surprise, then puzzlement flitted across Seba's expression, but she nodded at last.

"Very well," she said. "Both of you will be released when darkness falls."

"What about the geas on us?" Peri asked.

Seba smiled slowly.

"Those need not be removed," she said. "Atheris's will be negated because we are releasing him, and you—well, you will have no need to take your own life, will you?"

"I gave my word," Peri said shortly. "I'll keep it. But if I come home reeking of Sarkondish magic, they won't even let me in the door long enough to deliver your message."

The faintest scowl of impatience troubled Seba's brow.

"Oh, very well," she said. "I will see that the geas is released in one day, then—time enough for you to reach the border. You'll leave here tonight, at low watch."

"One more thing," Peri said. "I need to see my grandfather." When Seba's scowl deepened, Peri said, "All I've seen is a signet. That could've come off his dead hand. I'll be returning to my family an outcast, with no honor, and they won't *want* to believe me. If you want me to convince them, I'll have to be able to tell them I saw him here alive.''

Seba was silent for a long moment, then smiled.

''I see no reason to refuse,'' she said, shrugging gracefully. ''Although I fear you'll find the old High Lord something of a disappointment.''

She disappeared into the shadows and returned shortly with two guards. The guards unlocked Peri's cell and opened the door, stepping aside to let her out. Peri half expected to be manacled or geased, but to her surprise Seba seemed content with the two guards to protect her and prevent Peri's escape.

Peri did not look back at Atheris as her captors led her out of the cells.

They emerged in a hallway Peri didn't recall from her earlier hurried flight through the temple; there was no way of knowing how far or from which direction she had been brought while she was unconscious. For all she knew, she could be hundreds of feet underground, past a dozen locked or even bespelled doors and several dozen armed guards. She was, after all, an important prisoner at a crucial time in the temple; security would be tight.

Some of her suspicions were confirmed as Seba led her through several halls and down four successive flights of stone stairs; there were guards everywhere, all armed and alert. Provisionally, however, Peri was encouraged; where there were guards and locks and keys, magical safeguards became less likely.

As they descended, the dampness of the air, the dripping of water, the fungus on stone became more apparent, and Peri felt the sense of massive subterranean waters steeped in magic closer and closer. Old, cold, trapped in chains of stone . . .

Sleeping?

Seba stopped at an iron door heavily barred and secured by no fewer than three locks. The guards unlocked two, but the third, a padlock, took a key produced from a gold loop on Seba's belt. The door opened with a loud creak of protest.

The room within was plain but clean and, despite the damp air, relatively dry; rugs and rather shabby wall hangings absorbed some of the dampness and chill, and a medium-sized fire burned in a fireplace with a narrow, carefully barred chimney. The few pieces of wooden furniture—bed, chair, table, cupboard—were rough but sturdy, and the bed was thick and piled with covers. A chamber pot in the corner stank of urine, but at least the odor seemed relatively fresh. But there was neither lamp nor candle to help light the room, nor any sign that one might be used—no books, pen, or paper, as might be expected in the cell of such a carefully tended noble prisoner.

"He's in the bed," Seba said, gesturing. "Go on, look for yourself if you like."

Peri stepped gingerly into the room.

"Grandfather?" she said softly.

No answer.

Peri walked slowly to the bed, aware to her disgust that she was tiptoeing, holding her breath. Yes, the bedding seemed mounded a bit higher than might be expected from even a most generous number of covers. Was it her imagination, or did the lump of covers move faintly and regularly, as if with the breathing of one beneath?

Peri leaned over the bed, and her breath whooshed out in a single sigh of shock.

The man who lay in the bed was not emaciated or scarred or maimed. His white hair was neatly groomed into a single braid that now lay negligently draped across the pillow. He was very pale, of course, after so many years hidden from the sun, but no more so than Seba herself, and the faintest remnant of his Bregondish coloration could still be seen. His open eyes were the rich, dark brown of most Bregonds.

Nonetheless, it took some moments for Peri to recognize in the old man who lay before her the proud High Lord of Bregond she had seen depicted in the portrait hanging in Aunt Kairi's castle or the miniature hanging in her mother's room.

His flesh was sunken on his bones, lax with age and inactivity; the pale hands that lay limply on the coverlet, one finger deeply indented where the signet had rested, were thin and flabby, not with lack of food but simply because they had not been much used. The eyes that stared upward were utterly empty. No human soul lived within that horrible still frame. The heart beat, the lungs breathed, it ate and slept and excreted, but it was not her grandfather.

Only a shell.

Peri felt a presence approach, glimpsed Seba out of the corner of her eye.

"What did you do to him?" she whispered. "Torture? Some kind of magic?"

"You needn't whisper," Seba said, chuckling. "He can't hear you, you know. At least not as far as I can tell. Torture? No. He was badly injured when he was taken, from what I've been told, and went some time without proper care, but I quickly saw that he was attended by the best healers in Sarkond and he mended quickly. He's been quite well treated, as you can see for yourself. Magic? I suppose you could say that. His mind broke years ago, striving against the geas that held him here and prevented him from taking his own life. You'll be proud to know it took him a long time to break." She glanced at Peri. "Much longer than the few other Bregonds we've managed to set a geas on in time. The geas is probably all that keeps him alive now, forcing him to eat and drink. He has no will to do it himself, of course. At least he uses the chamber pot and doesn't soil the bed."

Peri closed her eyes, fighting to stay still, silent. She wanted to scream, to vomit.

Grandfather. High Lord of Bregond. My mother's father. A leader daring enough to bring together two countries who had warred for hundreds of years, with nothing but his headstrong daughter, a controversial Agrondish Heir, and a dream.

And, oh, Grandfather, how you paid for it.

Peri turned away.

"All right," she said tonelessly. "I've seen enough."

"And you acknowledge that this is High Lord Elaasar, your maternal grandfather?" Seba asked almost kindly.

"Yes," Peri said flatly. "It's him."

Seba smiled, a secret smile.

"If it comforts you, I assure you he'll continue to be well tended until the sacrifice," she said. "It isn't a pleasant death, unfortunately, nor a quick one, but I very much doubt he has enough awareness to even feel pain now. I don't imagine he'll even scream."

Peri closed her eyes again, sickened. It was all she could do not to turn and attack, to strike, to kick, to bite, to tear away that honeyed smile.

Apparently Seba sensed that her prisoner was near the breaking point, for she said nothing more, merely led Peri back to her cell.

"Tonight at low watch these same guards will come to lead you out of the temple," Seba said when the cell door was safely locked again. "They'll return your belongings, and I've taken the liberty of supplying you horses and supplies, more than enough to reach Olhavar. It will be six hours, perhaps eight, before your escape is detected and the Bone Hunters loosed upon your trail. I suggest that you make all haste for the Barrier. Even with the best horses I can manage, you'll have a hard ride of it to make the Barrier before the Bone Hunters begin seeking you, and I assure you, their magic travels far more swiftly than their horses. And although I have every reason to want your life spared, the Bonemarch will no longer need you alive, and unfortunately it's they, not I, who control the Bone Hunters.''

Seba stepped forward, her face almost pressing the iron bars. Her eyes shone with intensity.

''So ride fast for your life, young Perian,'' she murmured. ''When nothing else in the world remains for you, not kin, not country, not rank, not honor, you'll find that although your life has no value to anyone else, it suddenly becomes quite precious to you.''

Peri crawled into the corner and sat down on the hay, not speaking. Her face felt cold and hard as stone. She would gladly die before giving Eregis's Whore the pleasure of seeing her weep.

The intensity faded from Seba's face, and for a moment she looked almost lost, bewildered. Then her eyes settled into that strange and distant innocence again.

''Rest, young ones,'' she murmured. ''Rest and grow strong for your journey.''

Then she was gone.

There was a long moment of silence; then Atheris scooted over close to the bars.

''Peri?'' he whispered. ''Was it him? Your grandfather?''

''Yes.'' Peri didn't trust herself to say anything more, didn't trust herself to look at him. The sickness and anger ran too deep in her blood right now. She was afraid that if she looked at him, she'd see not Atheris, not friend or man or lover, but Sarkond. Enemy.

Atheris slumped against the wall, leaning sideways against the bars.

''Perian, I did not know,'' he said softly. ''I swear to you, I learned only when she told you. I think that secret has been carefully kept inside this temple.''

Peri said nothing. She could barely imagine what this news would do to her mother, or to Aunt Kairi. Or to the people of Bregond's faith in the ruling house. She knew that for her own part, those empty eyes would haunt her as long as she lived.

"Is he—" Atheris said hesitantly.

"He's dead," Peri said harshly, "in every way that matters. A piece of breathing flesh, that's all."

Atheris closed his eyes.

"I grieve with you, Peri," he said softly. "But in a way—in a way it is merciful, I suppose."

"Merciful!" For a moment the swelling hatred was more than Peri could bear. She clenched her hands hard, HARD, until her nails bit deep into her palms.

"Merciful!" she spat. "What do you know about mercy, you—you—" Then her voice broke and she covered her face with her hands, and she felt tears sting in the nail gouges in her palms.

The dead were treated with care and reverence in Bregond. They were burned in a very private, intensely personal ritual of mourning, their ashes carefully scattered by their closest kin so that Mahdha would bear their spirits to all corners of the land, and from there, the world. Only when those ashes were scattered was the spirit freed from the confines of the flesh. Defilement of the dead, failure to properly observe the rituals was one of the most serious crimes in Bregond because it denied the spirits of the dead their freedom. Only those who died in battle, or those who took their own lives to avoid capture, were believed to be spirit-freed at the moment of death by the glory of their act.

Her grandfather would never fly on Mahdha's wings.

Peri turned to Atheris.

"If what you believe is true," she said fiercely, "then destiny's going to have its way no matter what we do. Right?"

Atheris did not retreat from her intensity.

"Yes," he said softly.

"Then promise me," she said, very slowly, "that you'll help me do what I have to do, and I swear I'll see to it that your blighted prophecy comes true."

"How can you do that," Atheris said suspiciously, "when you swore that you would return to Bregond and—"

"I know what I swore," Peri said grimly. "I know exactly what I swore. And I know what I'm swearing now. And I'll keep both oaths, because no traitor and self-styled prophet takes my honor away from me. It may be all I've got left, but by Mahdha's fury, it's *mine*. And you're going to help me, Atheris, because now that you can't buy atonement by torture and death, you're going to have to find your redemption somewhere else, and I'm offering you that chance."

Atheris was silent for a long moment.

"All right," he said. "I have little enough honor left to me, Peri, but beyond the survival of my people I have nothing now to claim that honor. If you can keep your oaths, my assistance is yours in whatever form you wish it." He bowed his head. "I ask you only this—tell me nothing until we are free of this place. Spare my conscience that much."

Peri chuckled mirthlessly.

"Gladly," she said. That would certainly pose no difficulty; she had only the barest skeleton of a plan herself.

Despite the fact that the advice had come from Seba, Peri wished she *could* sleep, if only to make the time pass more quickly; there was no possibility of that, however, with her mind and heart in such turmoil. At last she stood wearily and stretched, beginning her breathing patterns. If she couldn't replenish herself one way, she could another.

I am Perian. I am warrior. She felt her thoughts fall into order, calm replace turmoil. *I am earth, deep-rooted and strong, mother of steel.* Strength returned; the fatigue weighting her limbs retreated, tension transformed into focus. *I am wind, swift and light.* She faltered ever so slightly, almost lost the pattern as she was swept into that old, cold power she could feel beneath the temple. She turned her thoughts resolutely. *I am fire, steel's father, dancing, all-consuming. I am water, unbounded and ever-changing. I am warrior. I am Perian.*

She flowed smoothly out of the last of the stretches, calm and sure once more. She would do what she had to do. And when the time came, she'd know what had to be done.

JUDGING FROM WHAT LIGHT PERI COULD SEE
through the high, small window, it was almost exactly
midnight when she heard the scrape of a key in the lock
of the outer door. Atheris was on his feet before she was,
herself.

The guard said nothing, only unlocked Peri's cell, then Atheris's. He waited until they stepped out of their cells, then,
rather incongruously, locked the cells again.

"Our belongings?" Atheris said softly.

"Outside," the guard grunted.

He led them through the tangled maze of corridors and stair-
ways without another word, glancing back over his shoulder
occasionally to be certain they were following closely. Peri
tried to remember the twists and turnings as best she could,
but while she could track a lopa for hours through high grass
over hardpan in twilight back home, here, underground, with
no stars, no wind, no point of reference except that vague and

all-pervading awareness of cold, ageless, deep water beneath her, she knew she'd never be able to find her way again. She could only hope that Atheris was more oriented than she.

The guard stopped in mid-corridor, so suddenly that Peri almost collided with him; when she stopped abruptly, Atheris bumped her and swore softly. The guard turned, blocking her view with the broad expanse of his back, but Peri guessed he was pressing some hidden lever or switch in the wall, for a section of the stone slid smoothly inward, revealing a dark, narrow passageway. The guard stood aside, gesturing Atheris and Peri to enter ahead of them. Peri barely hesitated, then stepped in; no sooner had Atheris followed her than the opening behind them slid shut, the guard on the other side.

Peri steadied herself against a damp stone wall. It was roughly cut, irregular stone, not carved smooth as the more formal passageways she'd seen.

"Well," she said with a sigh, "I suppose we go from here by ourselves."

"I suppose so," Atheris said softly. "I felt my geas released a moment ago."

"I didn't feel anything," Peri said, sighing.

"She said in a day. If Seba lied, I will make sure you are released later," Atheris said impatiently. "It hardly matters just now, does it? Come, follow me. I spent time in the darkness as part of my training, and the layout of this temple almost mirrors my own."

Peri had to squeeze over against the wall to let Atheris around her. When she felt the warmth of his body brush hers, she felt a surprising, involuntary desire to cling to him. She settled for laying one hand on his shoulder when he stopped in front of her.

"You'd think they would have given us a torch at least," she grumbled. "There *is* a certain element of hurry about this."

"A torch outside the temple might be seen," Atheris said almost absently. "Secrecy is even more important than time."

Peri couldn't argue with that, and for more reasons than one; Atheris moved so swiftly through the dark passageway that she was forced to hurry and concentrate on her footing. The passage must have been short, for Atheris soon stopped very abruptly, but his murmured warning reached her in time.

"There is a wall here," he said. "I think I can open it." He was right; Peri saw moonlight almost immediately, and she could not step out into the open air fast enough. There was moonlight, there was a faint rank breeze, there was honest dusty earth beneath her feet, and for the moment she could only stand still, taking it in in sheer •gratitude. Apparently they'd exited out the back of the temple, for they were not inside the stockade. Peri could see no other openings in the back of the temple, and she could only hope that meant nobody could see them; but then, Seba had the greatest interest in utter secrecy, so if there was any unobservable exit from the temple, she'd have chosen it.

Two horses were tethered just outside the opening; there was enough moonlight that Peri could see they were heavily laden. A brief search revealed, to her surprise, her healer's kit, their weapons, even their gold; her first act was to replace her grace-blade in its sheath, then her sword and daggers. She spent another precious moment inspecting the horses, surprised by their quality. Apparently some Sarkondish raids on Bregondish herds had been more successful than others.

"All right," Peri said briefly. "Good enough." There was parchment, pen, and ink in her healer's bag; in the dim light, with Atheris reading over her shoulder, she wrote, "High Lord Elaasar died honorably by his own hand. This I swear on my honor, my sword, and the blood of my family. By my hand, Perian, daughter of High Lady Kayli and High Lord Randon of Agrond." She rolled the signet up inside the parchment and tucked the parchment into the pouch, then handed the pouch to an astonished Atheris.

"We're going back in," Peri said shortly. "If I die here, make certain this reaches any Bregond. It doesn't matter who, it doesn't matter how. It'll get where it's supposed to. That will fulfill my promise to Seba. I didn't swear I'd get there myself, only that they'd know the truth."

"But this is not the truth," Atheris said softly, tucking the pouch into his shirt nonetheless.

"It will be," Peri said simply. "Now take me back in."

"And if we are captured?" Atheris asked, his eyes on Peri's.

"*If* there's trouble," Peri said, shrugging, "you get away. I've got my sword and daggers. I can probably buy you enough time for a good head start at least. I'm the important prisoner, after all, the Harbinger, and they won't risk killing me. Anyway, the last thing in the world they'll suspect is that we'd go back into the temple, not when we've got an open escape route and fast horses."

Atheris fell silent, his eyes searching hers for another moment. Mutely he pulled the priest's robe out of his saddlebag and pulled it on, belting it with a short length of rope. Then he turned and silently stepped back into the dark passageway. Before the darkness swallowed him, Peri was relieved to see that he'd reclaimed his own blades. Thankfully he did not close the exit behind him. If by some miracle either or both of them left by this passage, it would be a hasty exit.

At the opposite end of the passage, Atheris groped around briefly in the darkness, but once more his expertise won out and the section of wall slid open. Peri was ready with her dagger, but there was no guard outside.

"No guard here," she whispered, gazing at Atheris, "but there'll be plenty more between here and my grandfather. Can you get us past them?"

Atheris shook his head.

"Invisibility may hide us," he said gently, "but it will not hide a door opening."

"Then there's two choices," Peri said flatly. "Either you do to them what you did to me and to those men in Darnalek, or—" She held up her dagger illustratively. "You choose."

Atheris closed his eyes briefly, but when he opened them he faced Peri squarely.

"I will deal with them," he said quietly.

"Good enough." Peri was, she knew, trusting Atheris far too much, especially after the earlier betrayal, but she was demanding even more trust of him; besides, she had more to lose than he, but also more to gain. "Unless you know a shorter way to the lower cells, I'll need you to get us back to our cells, and I think I remember the way from there."

"How many levels lower?" Atheris asked.

"Four."

He hesitated.

"There is a quicker way," he said. "It is risky in terms of encountering others, but should save time." He raised the hood on his robe, then pulled the rope belt from his robe and handed it to Peri. "Put your hands behind you and wrap that around your wrists once or twice. I am thankful now that Seba kept us so hidden, that very few would recognize us. My only concern now is that I might meet a priest from my own temple, come here to hear the Whore speak or to consult with the Bonemarch. And give me your sword to hide under my robe. Your daggers are not visible to a casual glance, but no prisoner would be allowed to keep such a weapon."

That hurt even though Peri saw the sense of Atheris's words, and she surrendered her sword again with the greatest reluctance.

Mahdha grant if I die, I do so with my sword in my hand, she thought grimly. It was awkward, winding the rope around her wrists behind her while she could not see; she could only hope that her sleeves concealed the ends of the rope she held in her clenched hands.

"Lead on," she said shortly.

Peri had no idea where Atheris was leading her; she knew only that it wasn't the way the guard had brought them from their cells. The first time she saw a guard in the corridor ahead of them, she tensed; she kept her head down, Atheris guiding her by his firm grip on her arm, and suddenly they were past, and her relief was so great that she nearly stumbled into Atheris. Still she held her breath each time they passed a guard or priest, grimly determined that the first sound of recognition would be the last; kill or die, she wasn't going back to that cell.

They went down a set of stairs, but then back up another; then down twice and up once. A faint suspicion began to uncoil in Peri's heart—Atheris had led her into capture before, and she had no guarantee but the word of a Sarkond that he wouldn't do it again. But then Atheris led her down another longer stairway, and now the corridors around her seemed familiar. Atheris paused briefly in a stretch of empty hall.

"The cells are ahead," he murmured. "You must have entered the block from the north, and we are entering from the south. Be sure you know exactly which cell we must go to. Any guard seeing us searching uncertainly will be suspicious."

Peri closed her eyes, concentrating. She'd turned the corner with Seba, and what had drawn her eye was the guard ahead—

"There's a guard in front of the door," she said. "It was second on the left as I came in before."

"Fifth on the right, then, from here," Atheris said softly.

"There were three locks on the door," Peri said. "Seba had the key to one. I can probably break the last lock, but I'll make noise doing it."

"The guard will be in no condition to protest," Atheris said. "You are certain, though, there are no other guards?"

Peri tried hard to remember. She'd done her best to keep count when she'd followed Seba, but there'd been so many doors, so many guards.

"Not in the hall itself," she said at last. "But there was a guard at the entrance to the cell block. He might be close enough to hear us moving in the hall."

Atheris hesitated.

"I need to be close enough to touch a guard to incapacitate him," he said slowly.

Peri slid one of her hands free of the rope, tested the draw on two of her daggers.

"I don't," she said shortly.

Atheris gazed at her for a long moment, expressionlessly.

"If you must," he said at last.

Peri replaced her hand in the loops of rope and nodded to Atheris. He took a deep breath and stepped around the corner and, to Peri's utter gratitude, walked directly up to the guard without the slightest hesitation.

The guard stepped aside almost automatically, drawing a ring of keys from his belt, but then he paused.

"The lady said—" he began.

Atheris said nothing, only laid his hand on the guard's wrist. The guard let out a little breath, almost a sigh, his eyes rolling up in their sockets, and fell back against the wall; Peri, quickly dropping the rope, barely caught him before he could fall to the floor in a clatter of keys and armor. She eased him down, taking the ring of keys; to her surprise, Atheris knelt beside the fallen guard, taking his pulse. A hectic flush had risen in Atheris's cheeks and his hands were trembling.

"What?" Peri whispered impatiently.

"If I am nervous, or careless," he whispered shakily, "it is easy to drain them too much, to—"

Peri was still.

"Kill them?" she barely whispered.

He nodded reluctantly. Now that it was obvious that the guard was still breathing, he stood again, indicating the locks.

Peri did not move.

"The pilgrims?" she asked, barely audibly.

Atheris nodded again, very slowly, not meeting her eyes.

"I did not know how sick they were," he said, his lips barely moving. "How weak. And I was very afraid. I had never tried two at once before. When I realized—I tried to save them. But healing magic, life magic . . ." He fell silent again.

Peri bit her lip hard. She didn't know which sickened her more—what he had done, or her realization that despite everything that had happened, she could not manage to hate him for it. She took a deep breath and handed Atheris the ring of keys.

"Unlock it," she said briefly. She picked up the guard's mace and tiptoed to the end of the hall, just inside the cellblock door. Flattening her back against the wall, she reached over and banged the mace against the door sharply once, then again, gratified by the almost immediate scrape of a key in the lock.

"What is it?" the Sarkondish guard murmured as he stepped through the door. "No one is supposed—"

No helm. Driven by she knew not what impulse, Peri slightly diverted the crushing force of the blow at the last second so that it only glanced off the guard's skull. The guard went down anyway without even a grunt, and she saw blood trickling down the back of his neck, but she knew without knowing how she knew that the skull was not cracked.

What do I care? she thought disgustedly. *This is a Sarkond, a guard who'd happily split me open top to bottom if it wasn't important to save me for a much nastier death! Most likely they'll just have him killed anyway for letting herself be taken by surprise. Bright Ones, what kind of a warrior am I becoming?*

She dragged the guard inside and closed the door, picking up the mace. Even at low watch, it probably wouldn't be long before someone noticed the guard's absence, but that would arouse less immediate suspicion than a guard slumped over in the hall, or even sitting on the floor, apparently asleep.

Atheris had apparently unlocked the first two locks. He stood back, glancing at Peri in surprise as she laid the second guard beside the first. Peri lifted the mace in both hands and smashed open the padlock with one sure blow. The door creaked open.

Atheris started to step inside, but Peri stopped him with an abrupt arm barring the door.

"He's my kin," she said shortly. "It's my responsibility."

"Do you require a witness?" Atheris asked softly, meeting her eyes.

Peri hesitated just a moment, then withdrew her arm, letting Atheris follow her into that horrible room. The High Lord was in the bed, exactly as she'd seen him before; this time, however, his eyes were closed.

For a moment Peri hesitated again. It seemed so simple, so merciful, to end it with one swift stroke while he slept. But . . .

No, Grandfather. You'll fly home on Mahdha's wings. I swear it.

"Help me get him up," Peri said softly.

He wasn't heavy, but neither was the High Lord emaciated and light, and Peri was glad enough for Atheris's help in getting him out of bed, especially when those empty eyes opened. Atheris cringed from the sight, but Peri forced herself to meet those eyes one last time, searching for the faintest spark of consciousness, when they'd settled him in the chair.

"High Lord, you don't know me," Peri said softly in Bregondish. "I'm your granddaughter, your daughter Kayli's child. My mother's well and happy, Grandfather, and she has another child, a son, my brother Estann. Your daughter Kairi holds Bregond. There's been peace between Agrond and Bregond since my mother's marriage, Grandfather. There's trade and prosperity. You can go with Mahdha in peace, Grandfather. You did all you set out to do, and you're remembered with love. Your name will be spoken with pride in every noble hall, at every clan fire. I swear it. I'll help you do what you must.''

She drew her grace-blade and laid the hilt in those limp, pale hands, blade inward, the clasp of her own fingers tightening the lax grip around it. She stepped around behind her grandfather and guided the point of the blade carefully into place.

"Good-bye, Grandfather," she whispered. "Fly with Mahdha.''

She'd never given grace before, but the stroke was firm and unerring. There was no twitch, no sound but the soft whisper of the final breath. Peri eased her grandfather's body back in the chair, closing his eyes. She pulled the grace-blade free and wiped it on the bedclothes, then thrust it back into its sheath.

"All right," she said tonelessly to Atheris. "Let's go.''

Atheris followed her mutely to the door and helped her drag the unconscious guards inside, then lock the two intact locks.

"Out the way we came?" he asked quietly.

Peri shook her head.

"I'm not done yet," she said flatly. "Did you think I'd keep my promise to Seba but break my oath to you?''

Atheris's brows drew down.

"Then where?''

Peri considered. She could try to find the lowest level of the temple. Closer might be better. But then escape would be far more difficult, if not impossible, and Peri's message had to reach Bregond.

"The central chamber," she said.

Atheris gazed at her doubtfully, but at last he slowly raised the hood of his robe again, handing the rope back to her. Peri resumed her "prisoner" posture and followed him.

They moved through more central corridors now, and despite the late hour, once or twice they passed robed figures in the hall—priests or acolytes, Peri could not readily determine. They did not question Atheris, although Peri received rather curious glances, and once she thought a guard eyed them just a little too sharply, but nobody stopped them. At last they emerged into a wide corridor, not the central hall they had traveled when they first entered the temple, but, in Peri's estimation, probably its counterpart on the other side of the temple. Then they turned another corner and she had no more time to muse on directions, for they faced both the heavy double door to the central chamber, and the two guards standing watch there.

Thank the Bright Ones, Atheris did not hesitate even slightly. He grasped her upper arm firmly and walked briskly toward the door, although Peri could feel his hand trembling.

The guards glanced at each other uncertainly.

"Your pardon, Holiness," one said. "No one told us the chamber would be in use tonight."

"Only a brief preparatory ritual," Atheris said, just the right hint of impatience in his voice. "Must I have the Golden One awakened to come down here and tell you personally?"

Another brief hesitation. Then the guard stepped aside, opening the double doors.

"Your pardon, Holiness," he said. "We will see you are not disturbed."

Peri expected Atheris to reach out and touch one or both of the guards, render them unconscious as he had the guard at her grandfather's cell. She mentally braced herself, ready to drop the rope and reach for the most convenient dagger in case Atheris could deal with only one at a time—

Then they were past the guards and through the doors, and Atheris was closing and barring the door behind them.

"What?" Peri demanded in a whisper. "You're just going to leave them there?" She grabbed her sword back, belting it on.

Atheris shrugged resignedly.

"If anyone checks the guard posts, they will be suspicious to find that one vacant," he said, not lowering his voice at all. "If they see the guards in their places, hopefully they will not stop to question them, but even so, it is less risk to leave them."

"Oh, yeah?" Peri said, still whispering, following Atheris as he walked around the perimeter of the room, skirting the golden sculpture of Eregis, to the door opposite. "Unconscious guards can't hear what we're doing."

Atheris smiled, barring that door, too. Lighting one torch from the central fire, he lit each of the torches in the wall sconces.

"Nor will conscious guards. You failed to observe the thickness of the doors," he said gently. "Rituals of great secrecy, permitted only to the highest orders of priests, are performed at the central altar. These chambers in each temple were built for silence. I promise you, the guards will hear nothing. And if we are quick, we should be able to leave without—"

Then he stopped.

"Tell me now," he said softly. "Tell me now what you are planning to do."

"Just what I said," Peri said grimly. "Give you what your prophecy promised."

"But—" Atheris said uncertainly.

"You can't make rain out of raw magic, especially *healing* magic," Peri said. "Rain doesn't magically appear in the sky from nowhere; it rises up into the air from rivers and lakes or it blows in from other places. Even dedicated water mages don't create it from nothing; they just move it in from some-place else.''

"Rises up into the air?'' Atheris said doubtfully.

"Never mind. Take my word for it,'' Peri said, shaking her head. "So to make rain you need a good supply of magical energy, which you had, but you needed three more things—a mage with at least some trace of water affinity, a source of water, and the skill to know what to do with those things. You only had one out of four. Now you have three.''

Peri drew a deep breath.

"I have the water affinity; you have the magical ability to use it. Under this temple is not only a power node, but a huge subterranean reservoir.'' She gestured at the font behind the altar. "At one time it must have fed the ceremonial font. Maybe the channel became blocked, I don't know. Maybe rock shifted underground and sealed it off. But it's there, all that ancient water, fairly bubbling with magic. My bet is that's what your prophecy referred to. Bring that water up—awaken it, if you like—and you have an almost limitless source of water so laden with magic that any two-copper apprentice could manipulate it. It wouldn't take much to *flood* Sarkond with rain, if that's what you want. Break that water loose and you've got everything you were promised—water, magic, life.''

"But the priests here,'' Atheris protested. "Why have they not found this reservoir, used it as you say?''

"It's hard for me to believe none of these priests has even a little water sensitivity, and it wouldn't take much to feel that water,'' Peri said, shaking her head. "But if that sensitivity wasn't trained, if they didn't know what it was they were feeling, they might feel only the power, not necessarily the water itself. Or maybe they believed they were feeling the presence of your god, and didn't have the temerity to mess with it." She shrugged. "The other possibility is that Seba just didn't *want* it found. The prophecy worked to her benefit. She's not here to save Sarkond. She's here to have her revenge on Bregond, and the prophecy—and my grandfather's capture—gave her the perfect revenge. But none of that matters now. The water's there, just waiting for you to set it free."

"But how?" Atheris asked softly.

"How did you and your cousin try to combine your power?" Peri asked. "You coupled, didn't you?"

Atheris flushed but nodded.

"But we failed," he said.

Peri nodded, too.

"Neither of you knew what you were doing," she said, sighing. "I know Bregondish mages learn that, too, joining their power as they join their bodies, but—"

"But you have not learned that either," Atheris said, very softly.

"No." Peri shook her head, meeting his gaze. "So that leaves your way. Blood."

"NO!" Atheris's eyes widened. "Peri, no. Surely there must be another way. At least we can try. Even though I failed before, still it is a chance—"

Peri closed her eyes briefly.

"All right," she said, forcing her tone to lightness. "You're the expert. If you think that's best. But one thing first."

She drew her sword, loving the heft of it, the timeless perfect balance, the slivers of torchlight that flickered off it like jewels. When had the flawlessly honed edge ever shone so beautifully? When had the hilt ever fit her hand so perfectly, with such welcome, as it did in this moment when she knew—

"Peri?" Atheris murmured.

She turned to him.

"Waterdance," she said softly. "Dance it with me this

once. Let me be a warrior just a little longer before I have to try to be a mage.''

Atheris hesitated just a moment, and Peri thought she saw a flicker of doubt, almost mistrust in his eyes. Good. That would serve her well, if only—

Then Atheris drew his sword slowly, stepping back to the proper distance.

''Very well,'' he said.

He thinks I'm going to kill him, Peri thought with grim amusement. *Good.*

No easy transition this time, no courteous testing of skill; Peri went straight into Mahdha's Fury and attacked full out, no hesitation. Atheris barely countered, astonished by the sudden ferocity of her attack, and Peri came close enough to beating her way past his guard that she saw that doubt in his eyes again—perhaps even a flash of true fear.

Good. Can't give him time to think—

Peri held forth her attack just long enough to see that uncertainty in Atheris's eyes start to shift to true suspicion, rejoicing in the sweet ring of blade on blade, the swish of steel-cut air. When had the hard, fierce beat of her heart, the sweat slickening her skin, the smooth flow of her muscles ever felt so good? When had she ever felt so strong, so free?

So alive?

Atheris tried to take the offensive and Peri beat his attempt back almost effortlessly. Her feet were married to the stone beneath them in unshakable balance. The very air rushing into her lungs was sweet and full of power. Her sword had melded seamlessly into her skin, her muscles, her nerves, her blood, become an extension of her body, her *self,* and she of it, which pleased her even more. She deflected another pitiful attack, glad to see true fear now, fear that would turn to feed anger.

Atheris pressed his attack more strongly now, a hint of desperation creeping into his qivashim. Peri flowed into Stalking Cat, knowing he would—

Yes, Leaping Flame—

The maneuver had taken her by surprise before and she faltered slightly now, ever so briefly, just enough to let Atheris press his initiative and—

She fell into Waterdance as effortlessly as sliding into her oldest boots, worn and stretched in all the right spots, so they'd molded themselves to every contour of her feet.

I am Perian. I am warrior.

And Waterdance accepted her, welcomed her, answered her, flowing like the river, rich and smooth and powerful but mutable, changeable, meeting Atheris's Charging Boar and flowing around it, buffeting Diving Hawk aside with her currents, unstirred by Mahdha's Fury.

I am earth, deep-rooted and strong, mother of steel.

And she drew him in like the arms of a lover, every move subtly guiding him deeper into her currents; flowing around his thrusts but then inexorably back onto her course.

I am wind, swift and light.

Subtlety and patience had never numbered among Peri's virtues, but it was easy now, easy as the breath that swelled her lungs, the kiss of blade on blade, touch and touch guiding rather than countering.

I am fire, steel's father, dancing, all-consuming.

Involuntarily, almost obliviously he was moving to her rhythms now, yes, like a lover, his movements answering to hers now. They moved together in the dance, ebb and flow, advance and retreat, again, almost ready—

I am—

And now he was hers, every thrust and cut of his sword guided by the lightest touch of hers, his balance answering to the rhythm of her dance. And the strength flowed through her, strong and deep and alive, alive, and she strove to prolong the moment just a little longer, just a little—

I am—

And taking one last deep breath, Peri dropped her defenses just *so*, leaving one single opening just—

And her lover entered with a single deep, strong thrust, cold and hot at the same time, sweet sharp pain that promised release but not yet, not yet—

I am—

Peri fell to her knees and one hand, her other hand clutching stubbornly at the hilt of her sword, not touching the shining blade that pierced her through. She barely heard Atheris's cry of horror, although she heard another sound now, a pounding she thought at first was her heart.

I am—

No, the pounding was at the door, the hard thud of metal against wood. Guards pounding on the door, trying to break the heavy wooden bar. No matter. Not long now.

I am—

She slumped back against the base of the altar, biting back a cry of pain as the tip of the sword transfixing her jarred and grated against the stone.

I am—

"Peri," Atheris groaned, reaching for his sword. "Oh, Eregis have mercy, Peri—"

"Don't," Peri rasped, her free hand intercepting his. "If you pull it out, I'll start bleeding heavily and die fast. Too fast."

To her surprise the pain was not so bad, fading even. She breathed shallowly, but still blood welled into her mouth. She turned her head, spat it out weakly. The pounding at the door changed tone. A ram of some sort.

"What can I do?" Atheris asked helplessly. To Peri's surprise, there were tears trickling down his cheeks.

"It's all right," she said. She had to stop and spit again before she could continue. "You did what I wanted. With the geas, I knew I couldn't"—cough, spit—"do it myself."

I am—

"Peri—"

Pounding at the door. So close. She could feel it easily now, the ancient might of it, so much power locked in its stone prison, waiting, sleeping.

"Hurry," Peri said, surprised at the clarity of her voice. She touched Atheris's hair, wrapped her fingers firmly in it. "What you need—it's yours. But you have to hurry. They're coming, and I'll fly with Mahdha soon. It's time."

Her voice was fading, and Atheris leaned close to catch her words.

"Peri—" he said again, his eyes pleading.

"No. Listen to me." She swallowed, gulped down breath, forced herself to meet his eyes. "Listen to me. It wasn't just battle heat with us. It was more."

Atheris touched her cheek very gently.

"Yes," he said quietly. "It was more."

I am water, cool and deep and flowing.

And it was there beneath her, waiting, old and cold and timeless—

"It's time," she whispered. "Take what you need."

And the grief in Atheris's eyes was close now, very close, and his lips were hot against hers, and the pounding was growing more distant, remote, like the beat of Peri's heart.

And she drew him down with her as the cold power pulled her down, pulled her in. And it was no longer beneath her now; it was around her, within her, the cold and ancient life of it, throbbing with sleeping power, pushing lazily against the stone of its prison.

Pushing harder now, stirring under the touch of power, hers, his, theirs—testing the walls of its prison for faults, seeking out that inevitable weakness that could not resist.

I am warrior.

And Peri was steel, sharp and shining, a finely balanced sword that struck *there,* right into the heart of that one weak point, so precise and perfect in their stroke, Atheris the hand and Peri the deadly sharp point, Atheris the skill and Peri the aim in a single perfect strike, a killing blow that brought life gushing forth in a violent eruption from its confinement.

And somehow, remotely in her own body, Peri felt the rumbling both below and above her as the power was freed, heard the bones of the earth groaning as they yielded before a force that could no longer be contained, the grinding of stone on stone, but even that sound seemed to grow fainter, for she could hear the sweet whisper of Mahdha calling her name, calling her home.

I am—

"Peri!"

Peri groaned in protest at returning consciousness. Then sensation returned and she cried out hoarsely as pain jarred rhythmically through her body, unbelievable hot agony ripping through her vitals. Dimly she realized Atheris had at some point pulled the sword out of her and was now carrying her, trotting along as fast as he could—but why was he stumbling in that way, crashing against one side of the corridor, making the agony flare again in her guts, then crashing against the other side so that she nearly fainted again from the pain? Why was he staggering, barely keeping his feet under him? Surely the shaking, the rumbling was only inside her—

And the screams—

"Hold on," Atheris gasped over the rumbling, over strange dull explosions. "Hold on a little longer. Do you hear me?" He leaned against the wall and shook her, or perhaps it was the wall that shook. "Do you hear me? Answer me!"

"All right," Peri said weakly, annoyed. "All right, I hear you."

Stumbling through darkness, through light, falling to his knees—*AGONY!*—and pushing himself up again, but Peri's consciousness faltered.

Then the night breeze was soft on her face, and the sound of horses whickering nearby was sweet and familiar. And heavy clouds blocked her view of the stars, but that was all right because there was still the open air and the horses, honest earth under her back, and, yes, the sweetness of the wind in her hair. She saw Atheris only dimly in the darkness, but she felt his cold tears falling on her face, and she was grateful, so grateful he'd given her this one last gift.

"Thank you," she whispered, wishing she could say more. But it was hard to breathe, so hard.

"Oh no, Peri," Atheris said, right in her face, his breath fanning her cheeks. "You have not yet given me all that I need."

Then his lips met hers and she tasted her own blood, and fierce hot pain exploded in her vitals as Atheris took what he wanted from her—

And gave her darkness at last.

9

COLD. SO COLD.

So very, very cold.

Peri opened her eyes and saw only darkness, heard a strange roaring hiss around her, and for a moment sheer terror gripped her soul. Had she somehow failed to restore her honor? Had her death on Sarkondish soil, in a Sarkondish temple, denied her the freedom of flight in Mahdha's embrace? Had she—

She sucked in a deep breath and pain made her expel it again immediately in a groan.

Pain. Cold. Darkness. I'm not dead. Nothing hurts this badly but life.

"Awake at last," Atheris murmured, bending over her. She could barely see him, but she heard the relief in his voice. "I would say 'Thank Eregis,' but I fear He had nothing to do with it."

"It's so dark," Peri whispered.

"We are under an overhang," he said. "And I made a lean-to against it with a blanket for shelter. I dared not move you far."

Peri shivered, then could not stop shivering.

"So cold," she said, her teeth chattering uncontrollably. "I'm so cold."

Atheris chuckled, and then the warmth of his body against her side was the sweetest, most luxurious sensation she'd ever felt.

"You are cold," he said, "because your hair, your clothes, our blankets, everything we own is soaked through. And that, my Bregondish warrior lady, is why there is no fire, because there is no dry tinder to be had."

No dry—for a moment Peri had the absurd notion that Atheris's tears had somehow drenched everything they owned. Then her mind finally fumbled the pieces together—cold, wet, that sound around her.

"Rain?" she whispered disbelievingly. "Is it rain?"

Atheris chuckled again, and a flash of lightning, followed by a resounding clap of thunder, answered her before he could.

"My lady, it is rain the likes of which my land has not seen in decades," he said. "You and I can count ourselves fortunate if we are not flooded out of our poor hiding place within the hour. But I dared not move you far before, and now the storm has grown so strong that I think it would be more dangerous to go than to stay."

Peri took a deep breath, which aborted in a fit of coughing. A dull pain seemed to echo off the walls inside her chest, but she knew, and wondered at the knowing, that it was only the ache and sensitivity of newly healed flesh.

"I'm alive," she murmured. "I can't possibly be alive. I *can't*." The realization came with a confusing mélange of emotions—wonder, relief, apprehension, dread. She *couldn't* be alive. Atheris's stroke had been true. She'd felt Mahdha's breath all around her. She *had* died. How could she be alive again? *Had* Atheris's magic included necromancy, pulled her back from her flight into her dead flesh? What kind of monstrous thing did that make her?

Atheris leaned over her, and a flash of lightning lit the sky—even through the blanket there was enough light to show her the reassurance in his eyes.

"You gave me the use of your water sensitivity," he said. "At the moment when life was leaving you there was nothing to prevent me from touching your healing magic as well. There was power aplenty around us, more than enough for even so great a healing, and you had the skill I needed to guide it." Another flash of lightning showed Peri his smile. "Besides, as you know, I have some acquaintance with death. I denied her successfully once before. Tonight I dared do so again."

He chuckled.

"That effrontery will cost me, no doubt, someday when I meet Lady Death again and can no longer refuse her embrace."

"Lady Death?" Peri asked dubiously.

Atheris's fingers touched her cheek.

"Perian, after dancing the Ithuara with you, there is no doubt in my mind that death is a woman." His lips brushed hers ever so lightly. "And a lady of quality."

Peri raised her hand, surprised to find herself tired, but not as weak as she would have expected. The front of her tunic was torn open—by Atheris, no doubt—but she felt no embarrassment, only wonder and consternation as her fingertips found the scar just under her sternum.

"You have another on your back," Atheris said, touching her hand. "And I have no doubt it will give you pain in bad weather such as this." He chuckled again. "Unfortunately you were attended by a healer of considerable power but no experience or skill of his own whatsoever."

Peri felt no answering levity. Her fingertips traced the scar again. There was a faint coldness within her, a memory of darkness.

It is a test that leaves its mark upon the spirit even more than the body.

"The temple?" she asked slowly, trying to distract herself. "We did it, didn't we? Raised Eregis?"

"Yes." The humor was gone from Atheris's voice, and Peri felt him tremble against her. He was silent for a long moment.

"We raised the greatest power I have ever touched," he said at last. "We brought it bursting up out of the earth. And once it was freed—the rain, it almost came of itself. The force of the explosion, the shaking of the earth—the temple was falling down around me as I carried you out. Some surely escaped, but many must have died." He fell silent.

Peri remembered the slaughterhouse above the central chamber and shivered. Yes, many had died.

"One final sacrifice," she said.

Atheris shivered, too.

"As soon as you are strong enough," he said slowly, "we should go. There were many people running around outside the temple—guards, worshipers, priests. It was very chaotic and many will simply flee, surely. But I think when the storm dies some will be back—to look for survivors trapped in the rubble, perhaps, or even to loot the wreckage for the temple's treasures. There will be guards, priests—perhaps even Bone Hunters. We must be gone before then."

Peri sat up, grimacing at the dull pain.

"I can ride," she said.

Atheris laid his hand on her shoulder, pushing her back gently; she resisted stubbornly.

"You cannot," he said. "You need rest."

Peri chuckled bitterly.

"I'm a Bregond," she said. "I can ride blind, deaf, sound

asleep, half-dead, through fire or earthquakes or windstorms. Trust me, if you can lead, I can stay in the saddle.''

Atheris pushed her back again more strongly, and this time Peri lay back irritably.

''When we are both struck by lightning,'' he said patiently, ''there will be nobody left to drag us back from the edge of death. The storm is moving north—slowly, but it is moving. As soon as it is safe, we will go, even through hard rain, I promise. But in the meantime there is nothing to do but rest.''

Peri could not argue with that, but now that she was awake it seemed impossible to sleep again.

''Did you check the packs?'' she said. ''Is everything there? Our supplies, gold, weapons—''

Atheris hesitated for a long moment.

''Our packs are intact,'' he said slowly. ''Even your healer's bag and our gold.''

''But?'' Peri pressed.

''But—'' He hesitated a moment longer, then sighed. ''Your sword. You dropped it in the temple.''

Peri bolted upright, ignoring the pain this time.

''My sword,'' she whispered. *Oh, Mahdha, no, not that, not the one thing I've held on to, not when I've lost everything else.*

''Peri, we have gold enough,'' Atheris said hurriedly. ''We will buy another, the best steel that can be bought.''

''My sword,'' she said through clenched teeth, ''*was* the best steel that can be bought. My foster brother, my best friend and instructor and clan leader, had it made for me when I learned the Ithuara. I'd rather leave my right leg behind.'' When Atheris said nothing, she added acidly, ''You've got your prophecy, you've got your rain. If I get myself killed now, it hardly matters, right?''

Peri felt Atheris recoil slightly at her words. Then, unexpectedly, his lips crushed down on hers in the darkness and lightning flashed through her; weariness, pain forgotten, she pulled him to her, her fingers digging hard into his shoulders. There was a brief fumbling struggle with wet clothes; then Atheris's skin was wonderfully hot against hers, and it was as if the warmth of life itself entered her body again. She clung to him with all her strength as if he was her only anchor to this world, but by the time the wave of pleasure crested and broke, Peri knew without doubt that she was alive again.

"All right," she gasped against Atheris's cheek, still holding him close as their hearts slowed. "All right. You win. It matters."

Atheris chuckled in her ear, then drew back slightly, enough that Peri caught a glimpse of his smile when the lightning flashed— outside, this time.

"More than battle heat, remember?" he said gently.

Peri flushed.

"Yes," she said, so softly that she could barely hear herself over the rain. "More than battle heat."

Atheris gazed at her a moment longer, then pulled a tunic out of the pack and handed it to her.

"We will find your sword if we can," he said. He grinned. "A fine strong blade is worth some risk to keep."

Peri chuckled wryly.

"You can take that to the market and buy—"

"—two skins of brandy and a hot bath, if I had my way," Atheris said, chuckling, too. "Come. Best go now if we are going. Anyone near the ruins now will be more concerned with themselves than us, and when the storm lessens, we should start south."

Peri and Atheris's robes, on which they had been lying, were damp from the wet ground but better protection from the rain than the soggy blankets. Atheris insisted that Peri rest while he loaded the horses, but she balked at riding while he led. In any event, as he had said, the storm was still violent enough that riding was a risk she preferred not to take.

Peri was amazed and appalled to see what she and Atheris had wrought upon the temple. The slight rise on which it had been built was now a noticeable concavity in the earth, and the once majestic structure was now little more than a huge, jumbled heap of stone blocks and broken columns. Even the gate and outer wall were a complete shambles. Peri's heart sank. There was no chance at all that she and Atheris could make their way back to what had been the central chamber.

Then she saw the still forms scattered here and there in the ruins and she swallowed hard, struck silent by the sight. Many had lost much more than a sword. Eregis had had his final sacrifice, indeed, and it had been a great and bloody one. Peri closed her eyes.

A few tears won't grieve this one away, she thought numbly. *How do I weigh the lives we saved against the lives we ended here by our deeds?* She thought of the guards she'd "mercifully" left alive, locked in her grandfather's cell, and swallowed hard against the lump rising in her throat.

Atheris said nothing, but he led the horses closer without hesitation, not wincing from the sight. He walked up to the nearest body and bent down, touching the throat. He shook his head briefly and stood again, but Peri had known even before he stooped that no life remained in that pale form. There was no life here; hours had passed since the temple fell, and those who had survived had already walked or staggered away, alone or with the help of their fellows. She could feel that clearly even—

No!

Peri grabbed Atheris's arm, shouting over the noise of rain and thunder.

"Over there!" she said, pointing. "I think there's someone still alive."

Atheris glanced at her strangely, but obligingly pulled the

horses in the direction she had indicated. Peri had to steady herself against the nearest horse as she followed. She couldn't blame Atheris for his skepticism. She'd never been enough of a healer to sense anything at such a distance, much less through a downpour like this.

Then through the darkness Peri caught a glimpse of gold partially under a fallen column, and for a moment her breath caught as she remembered the golden statue of Eregis in the center of the temple. Had the statue been thrown clear of the ruins somehow, or had, incredibly, the god indeed risen and walked? Given the sheer power she and Atheris had raised, Peri was not prepared to discount the latter possibility entirely.

A second glance, however, told her that what she'd seen was only the edge of a gold-trimmed robe, and for a moment she let out her breath in a sigh of relief; then she froze again as she recognized the robe and remembered when she'd last seen it. Atheris stopped, too, apparently sharing her recognition; then he moved forward more slowly, and Peri made no effort to hasten him.

Seba lay unmoving, the fallen column covering most of her left side, and even the driving rain did not entirely wash away the blood that trickled from her mouth and nose, but her eyes were open and she gazed at Atheris and Peri calmly, unsurprised.

"Well, Lady Perian, so you came back, just as I did," Seba murmured, blood and rain bubbling on her lips. "At least you had the sense to stay away while the stones were still falling. I congratulate you."

Silently Peri knelt in the mud, holding out the edge of her robe to keep the rain from Seba's face.

"Ah, thank you." Seba sighed. "You're a charitable child."

Peri laughed bitterly.

"You think I'm charitable after I ruined all your plans?"

"Ruined?" Seba chuckled weakly. "Oh, no, my Harbinger, you're all that I hoped, and more. But you didn't come back for me, I know." Her free arm fumbled under her robe, and her eyes sparkled. "Was it for your grandfather? Or for this?"

She pulled back the edge of her robe, and a shock ran through Peri as she saw the hilt of her sword.

"Why?" Peri asked, gazing into Seba's eyes. "Why did you find it for me?"

Seba smiled, coughing briefly as new blood stained her lips.

"You give me too much credit," she rasped. "I saw it on the ground and picked it up, and then the column fell." She touched the column and her smile widened. "You see how Eregis repaid me for my service? Much the same as my own people. And now I'll oblige them all by dying at last." She coughed again, grimacing with pain. "Although not quite fast enough to suit me."

She glanced back at Peri.

"I don't suppose you would do me the honor?"

Peri carefully eased the sword out from under Seba's robe and her free leg; then her eyes widened as she glimpsed a familiar bulge on the outside of Seba's calf. She raised the edge of the robe slightly, shivering at the amount of blood muddying the ground, and slowly drew Seba's grace-blade from its sheath. She turned and silently placed the hilt of the grace-blade in Seba's free hand.

Seba glanced at the knife, then at Peri, and laughed, and went on laughing, even when wet, choking coughs punctuated the laughter.

Peri rose slowly and took the reins of her horse, turning away, and Atheris followed her just as silently. Seba's laughter, too, followed her through the rain until at last it stopped, and Peri did not turn to see what had stopped it.

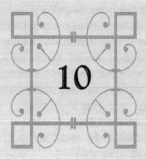

10

"**P**ERIAN!**"

Startled, Peri dropped the pen, her hand reflexively reaching for her sword hilt. Then she recognized the voice and turned to meet Danber's wide eyes, laying her hand on Atheris's arm when he would have drawn his own blade.

"It's all right," she murmured. "He's a friend."

Danber stepped forward slightly, his eyes still on Peri's.

"Am I, Perian?" he asked softly. "You stand alive in my tent with a Sarkond at your side. Is it a friend I see before me, or a traitor whom honor will not permit me to see or hear?"

"Atheris isn't an enemy," Peri said slowly. "He saved my life, got me out of Sarkond. And his magic got me into this tent to deliver a message." She drew a deep breath. "Judge me however you like. I didn't die when custom demanded it. Bregond needed my life more than my death."

Danber's eyes hardened, and Peri felt her heart breaking,

but she stood firm, drawing the signet ring from her pocket and laying it on the table.

"If you won't hear me, read what I wrote," she said deliberately. "But give this to my aunt Kairi and make sure my mother knows, too, that High Lord Elaasar died honorably by his own hand and flies with Mahdha."

She glanced at Atheris, then back at Danber.

"And tell Uncle Terralt that he can withdraw the troops and mages I saw camped at the border. There's no danger of an attack from Sarkond. The people of Sarkond—what's left of them—will have enough to keep them busy with their own country for a long, long time to come."

Danber's eyes searched hers.

"Is that true, Perian?" he asked softly.

Peri met his gaze squarely.

"Five days ago it wasn't true," she said. "Now it is. I swear on my sword, and on the blood of my family, and what's left of my honor."

Danber closed his eyes briefly as if pained, and when he opened them, he did not look directly at Peri, but slightly off to one side.

"I don't know what to tell you, Perian," he said. "I don't know if Mahdha remembers your name. Bregond doesn't forgive easily."

"It doesn't matter." Peri wanted to tell him she *had* died, that she'd heard Mahdha whispering her name in welcome, but . . . no. "I'm leaving anyway."

"Perhaps—that would be best," Danber said slowly. "It might be wisest to return to your parents and—"

"No." Peri glanced at Atheris. "I'm not going back to Agrond either."

This time Danber met her eyes involuntarily.

"But, Perian—" Then he stopped, looking at Atheris, too.

"Back to Sarkond?" he asked softly.

Peri laughed a little bitterly.

"Bright Ones, no!" she said. "South. After that, who knows."

"Perian—" Danber hesitated, but did not avert his eyes again. "No matter what might be said of you here, there's still Agrond, your kin, waiting to welcome you."

Peri touched Atheris's hand, felt him clasp her fingers.

"They won't welcome *him*," she said. Then she shook her head. "Anyway, I can't go back to my family. Mother—it'd tear her up just like it's tearing you up now. I won't do that to her. And Mother and Father still have to *deal* with Bregond, and harboring me would only shake a peace that took generations to build. Besides—" She took a deep breath. "There are things about my grandfather's death that everybody will sleep easier not knowing, and Mother would never let it rest until she'd heard it all. Just tell her what I told you. It's true, and it's all she—or anyone else—ever needs to know."

Danber searched her eyes again, then nodded slowly.

"I will deliver your message," he said.

"Anyway," Peri said, more lightly, "it gets me out of living with Aunt Kairi. Now she'll have to find another Heir."

Danber barely smiled, but the smile didn't reach his eyes.

"She already has," he said.

Peri sighed with relief.

"Oh, good," she said. "Who's the unlucky one? Aunt Fidaya's son?"

"No." Danber sighed. "Kalendra."

"*Kalendra?*" Peri chuckled again. "How in the world did Aunt Kairi settle on *her,* especially since she's barely even related by Mother's marriage?"

"Easily enough." Danber shrugged. "High Lady Kairi married Terralt."

That shocked Peri to silence. If someone had told her that

every watering hole in Bregond had filled with wine, she couldn't have been more astonished.

"Your uncle seemed well pleased to take the seat as High Lord," Danber said, smiling again at Peri's reaction. "And High Lady Kairi finds it helpful to share those responsibilities. She says it will enable her to take her power to those sections of the land desperate for rain, and High Lord Terralt is well suited to serve as envoy to Agrond."

Then he grimaced slightly.

"But it's a political marriage and there's no knowing whether they will be able to produce an Heir. So they agreed that Kalendra and I would be best suited to take the seats if they bear no children of their own."

Peri chuckled.

"Better you than me," she said. "For your sake, I wish my aunt and uncle happiness and fertility. But even though it lets me off from being Heir, it doesn't change my decision."

Danber nodded, glancing briefly at Atheris.

"Yes," he said. "I understand."

Then he hesitated.

"Perhaps Bregond will never know it owes you a debt," he said softly. "But I know. If there's anything you need—money, supplies?"

Peri thought of the Bregondish gold in her saddlebags, then the supplies Seba had given her—much of it ruined in the torrential rain.

"I have some money, but I'll take what I can get," she said, grinning ruefully. "Especially if—I don't suppose you found Tajin?" she added wistfully, holding her breath.

This time Danber gave her the old familiar smile.

"What do you think brought me here to the border—and kept me here, even after I mourned you?" he asked gently. "I'll have him saddled and loaded. And one for your—your friend."

He pulled his purse off his belt and handed it to Peri rather apologetically.

"Kalendra has more," he said. "Shall I call her? Perhaps you'd like to speak to her."

Peri shook her head quickly.

"She won't understand. She'll make a fuss, and I don't want that." She hesitated. "Give her a chance, Danber. She's stronger than she looks."

Then she chuckled.

"Just make her ride outside the carriage."

Danber nodded, smiling slightly.

"She's a kind and tolerant lady," he said. "She deserves a husband who could properly appreciate her. But we will manage."

"Well, then—" Awkwardly, Peri held out her hand. Danber ignored it and pulled her close, holding her tightly.

"Good-bye, Danber," Peri whispered, burying her face in his hair. "You'll always be more than a brother to me."

"And you," Danber murmured, "will always be more than a sister. Perian—if Mahdha has forgotten your name, then I will remind her, again and again, until she remembers."

Abruptly he released her, turning away. As he reached for the tent flap Peri cleared her throat, and he paused.

"Danber," she said softly. "I found Waterdance."

Danber glanced over his shoulder, and this time the smile reached his eyes.

"I knew you would," he said. "Someday, when Mahdha blows you home again, perhaps you'll teach me."

Then he was gone. Peri reached again for Atheris's hand, and the clasp of his fingers was as solid and strong as steel.

On the plains of Bregond, Peri pulled Tajin to a stop. A fierce hot wind combed dry fingers through her braids, sucked the sweat off the back of her neck. The setting sun poured blood and gold over sharp-edged grass that scratched against Peri's boots. Atheris reined in beside her.

"Shall we stop here for the night?" he asked, smiling. His gray eyes sparkled suggestively, and Peri felt her heart beat faster, joyfully.

"Just a little farther," she said. "There's a water hole to the southwest. The border's not far now." Reaching down, she carefully pulled loose a handful of grass tops. To the casual observer they looked dead, but peeling off the dry outer husk, she reached the moist green core. It was tough and sour and good between Peri's teeth.

"Just think," Atheris said softly. "You may have saved all this."

"No." Peri shook her head. "I think—maybe Seba did."

"Seba?" Atheris turned to her. "How so?"

"I've been thinking," Peri said slowly. "Seba had to know the ruling houses would have an army at the border. She *had* to know Sarkond had no chance against united Agrondish and Bregondish troops and magic. Even mad she had to know. And she sent me south to tell about Grandfather, yes, but to warn them, too—to make sure the army was ready. I don't think she was saving Sarkond, Atheris. I think she was delivering it up to Bregond for the slaughter. Our one remaining enemy, finally vanquished at last. I wonder now whether it was revenge at all so much as"—she remembered the grace-blade still sheathed on Seba's leg after twenty years of exile—"love and honor. The honor of one orphaned girl-child. She was right. In the end it did matter."

Atheris shivered.

"She said you played your part to perfection," he said softly. "Yes, a bitter and merciless love."

"Not merciless," Peri corrected. "She could have sent anyone to make sure I made it out of Sarkond. But she let you go. I don't know, maybe it was one last joke on Bregond—

me and my Sarkondish lover. But I don't think so. She knew how it felt to be exiled and alone.''

Atheris gazed at her steadily, and in those gray eyes he said something without words, and Peri let her own eyes answer.

''Southwest, then, a little farther,'' he said, smiling. He turned to gaze at the darkening horizon. ''And after the border? Straight south? East? West?''

Tajin danced impatiently. Peri threw the dry grass husks into the air and watched Mahdha bear them away.

''I don't know,'' she said, returning Atheris's smile. ''Wherever the wind takes us.''